The HEATHEN

The HEATHEN

Narcyza Żmichowska

TRANSLATED BY URSULA PHILLIPS

NIU PRESS / *DeKalb, IL*

© 2012 by Northern Illinois University Press

Published by the Northern Illinois University Press, DeKalb, Illinois   60115

Manufactured in the United States using acid-free paper.

All Rights Reserved

Design by Shaun Allshouse

Library of Congress Cataloging-in-Publication Data

Zmichowska, Narcyza, 1819–1876.

  [Poganka. English]

  The heathen / Narcyza Zmichowska ; translated by Ursula Phillips.

    p. cm.

  Includes bibliographical references.

  ISBN 978-0-87580-684-6 (pbk : acid-free paper) — ISBN 978-1-60909-0692 (e-book)

  1. Women—Poland—Fiction. I. Phillips, Ursula. II. Title.

  PG7158.Z58P613 2012

  891.8'536—dc23

                    2012034095

Contents

Acknowledgments

I am pleased that Narcyza Żmichowska's *The Heathen*, a remarkable text of Polish Romanticism by a woman, is now available to the English-speaking and wider international audience. I am indebted to Alex Schwartz and Mark Heineke of the Northern Illinois University Press for agreeing to publish it. I would also like to express my gratitude to David Goldfarb for his support for this and other translation projects, as well as to the M.B. Grabowski Fund and the late Ryszard Gabrielczyk for the grant given to support work on the translation.

The preparation of this edition was enhanced by the advice received from Grażyna Borkowska, who recently completed a new annotated Polish edition, who reviewed my introduction and also identified the eighteenth-century Latin volume about the kings and queens of Poland mentioned in the text. I am likewise grateful to Dorota Hołowiak for her assistance regarding obscure vocabulary and other linguistic difficulties; to Theodore Zeldin and Olive Duncan who read through earlier versions in their entirety and provided useful feedback; and to other colleagues who also gave advice on specific points including Antonia Lloyd-Jones, Knut Andreas Grimstad, Urszula Chowaniec and Klara Naszkowska.

Introduction

Ursula Phillips

Narcyza Żmichowska (1819–1876) was born in Warsaw in the Congress Kingdom of Poland on 4 March 1819. The Congress Kingdom was a political entity created within the Russian partition following the Congress of Vienna in 1815 and based on the territory of the former Napoleonic Duchy of Warsaw. Throughout Żmichowska's lifetime Poland remained partitioned between the empires of Russia, Prussia and Austria (1795–1918). She was a Russian subject. She was born in the same year as Queen Victoria and British novelist George Eliot (1819–1880) and the same year in which a very different Polish writer Klementyna Tańska (1798–1845), whom Żmichowska would later take to task in a vigorous polemic (1876), made her debut with the influential but conservative guide to female education, *Keepsake Left by a Good Mother* (*Pamiątka po Dobrej Matce*).

Żmichowska is remembered mainly as a teacher and governess, and in some quarters as an early emancipationist and feminist. She is also the author of several novels, of which *The Heathen* (*Poganka,* 1846) was the first. She began her literary career as a poet. One of her best-known early poems, published in the Warsaw journal *Primrose* (*Pierwiosnek*)—which had already published poetry and short stories by several women including Żmichowska's untitled debut poem in 1839—was *The Poet's Happiness* (*Szczęście poety,* 1841). *The Poet's Happiness* has been compared by, among others, critic and biographer Marian Stępień (1968) to Romantic poet Adam Mickiewicz's *Ode to Youth* (*Oda do młodości,* 1822) as a similar programmatic declaration of youthful intent; indeed, it is a kind of female answer to Mickiewicz. A collection of her poems entitled *Gabryella's Free Moments* (*Wolne chwile Gabryelli*) appeared in 1845 in Poznań. She also wrote short prose pieces, most of which appeared in journals in the early to mid-1840s.

Many of her longer prose texts are hybrid constructions, consisting of several levels of narration and even commentary, composed of letters, novels and other shorter prose pieces all contained within a higher structure, as Ewa Owczarz (1993) and Grażyna Borkowska (2001) have discussed. Her two earlier novels—*The Heathen* and *A Book of Memories* (*Książka pamiątek*, 1847–1849)—form part of one such structure, while a third novel *White Rose* (*Biała Róża*, 1858) forms part of the structure of texts published in 1861 under the collective title *Several Writings of an Anonymous Female Author Published by a Completely Unknown Editor* (*Niektóre pisma bezimiennej autorki przez zupełnie nieznanego wydawcę ogłoszone*). The strategies adopted here by Żmichowska's narrator, concealed behind several different personae (the "anonymous" authoress, the "unknown" editor, various other authors of letters or persons discussed in them), address the prejudices and criticisms a female author typically had to face in the mid-nineteenth century in order to be published and fairly appraised—a situation similar to that experienced by contemporary women across Europe. In this context, it is interesting that Żmichowska chose a female and not a male pseudonym, but a pseudonym nevertheless, even though it was generally known who Gabryella was. The name may be a reference to the French poet Gabrielle Soumet (1814–1886), as Borkowska (2001) suggests drawing on the memoir of Łucja Rautenstrauchowa (1798–1886), another Polish visitor resident in Paris at the same time as Żmichowka (1838–1839)—hence a hidden reference perhaps to Żmichowska's self-identification with Soumet's "Sapphic" leanings—but it could simply reflect a desire to distance her public persona as a writer from her private self, which she felt was threatened with exposure through published writings.

  Żmichowska's final novel, which remained unfinished (though she left an outline of its planned structure) is an autobiographical text—not autobiography as such, but a fictional text whose explicit purpose was to reflect "the life of a female type living between the second and seventh decades of our century"; the completed part of the novel, however, stretched back in time to cover the histories of female family members living in earlier centuries; its unstable generic status is reflected in the title itself: *Is this a Novel?* (*Czy to powieść?* 1876). All of her novels attracted limited critical interest during her lifetime. Three (*The Heathen, White Rose* and *Is this a Novel?*) were republished in 1929–1930, *The Heathen* by publisher Ossolineum in the *National Library* (*Biblioteka Narodowa*) series. These editions of Żmichowska's novels were edited and introduced by critic Tadeusz Boy-Żeleński (1874–1941), who was the son of Żmichowska's former pupil, close friend and correspondent Wanda Grabowska-Żeleńska (1841–1904); Boy also published Narcyza's letters to Wanda (1930, republished 2007). These publications inspired a more positive reception by leading critics in the 1930s. Since the publication of Grażyna Borkowska's study *Alienated Women* (*Cudzoziemki*, 1996; English translation 2001) and research inspired by feminism and gender studies, interest in Żmichowska's work has grown among recent scholars.

Mention should also be made of Żmichowska's correspondence, now available in five volumes. One point especially deserves emphasis: despite the vast knowledge and worldly wisdom contained in these letters written throughout Żmichowska's life, mainly to close female correspondents, they reflect her sense of her own marginalization, lack of recognition as a writer by conventional criticism, search for a suitable language in which to express her everyday concerns, life-long struggle against poverty and lack of a space (a room of her own?) to fully develop her career. They reveal something of her depression and sense of resignation and waste, though this rarely slips into bitterness, rather a feeling of being out of her time. Her almost compulsive letter-writing might even be said to be the place where she wrote out what could not otherwise be expressed or would not be accepted by conventional, critically acclaimed forms of "literature"—in this sense it was her alternative to "art." This is not the place, however, for a general analysis of Żmichowska's entire work. While I shall offer a few suggestions towards interpreting the novel translated here, first, I would like to briefly discuss her biography and ideas as important context and background to these suggestions.

Żmichowska's family had once been modest landowners, originally from the Grand Duchy of Posen/Poznań—in the Prussian partition—but at the time of her birth her father, Jan Żmichowski, held an administrative post in a salt-mine. She was the youngest of nine children. Her mother, Wiktoria Żmichowska (née Kiedrzyńska) died a few days after the birth. Subsequently rejected by her father, Narcyza was raised by various aunts and older siblings. Close relationships with her brothers and sisters and later with their offspring, were to prove the emotional backbone of her life. She never married. Her relationships with two of her three brothers: Erazm (1809?–1868) and Janusz (1814–1843) were extraordinarily intense. Janusz was a budding writer and literary critic who encouraged her early career and whose untimely death came at a crucial moment in her own life. Erazm fled Poland after the November Uprising (1830–1831) against the Tsarist authorities. Of democratic and socialistic persuasion, he was a member of the Polish Democratic Society and other patriotic leftwing organizations. Permanently resident in France, he was an important guide to Narcyza's intellectual development, advising her on what to read of contemporary European literature and thought, sending her books, and influencing the ideological bias of her own sympathies. Something of the unusual intimacy of these relationships (which may be compared perhaps to George Eliot's closeness to her brother Isaac), as well as Żmichowska's conviction that a well-disposed brother is an important factor in a woman's cognitive development and emotional security, is clearly reflected in two of her novels: *White Rose* and *Is this a Novel?*

For a woman from a poor background, Żmichowska received a good formal education. Education—both her own phenomenal self-education and her dedication to the teaching of the young, especially girls and young women—was to become the chief preoccupation of her life. She was unable to earn a living from literary activities. As a small child, she was raised by her uncle Józef Żmichowski and aunt Tekla Żmichowska (née Raczyńska, who was also the sister of Narcyza's maternal grandmother, Maria Raczyńska) and then by her maternal uncle and aunt, Józef Kiedrzyński and his wife Maria. Her very early, happy experience of living with her aunt Tekla on a small country estate at Siodło in Mazovia, near Minsk Mazowiecki, is reflected in her story *The Spinning Women* (*Prządki,* 1844). Aged six, she moved to Kuflew, to the home of Józef Kiedrzyński, where her older sister Wanda and brother Janusz were also living, to begin her education. At seven, she was taken by her aunt Maria Kiedrzyńska to Puławy, the Czartoryski estate on the Vistula, where she is said to have so impressed Izabela Czartoryska (1749–1835) with her precocious intelligence and vast knowledge of Polish history that Izabela invited the child to dine with her.

From 1826 Żmichowska attended Zuzanna Wilczyńska's boarding school for girls in Warsaw, and in 1832 entered the recently established Institute for Governesses, from which she graduated in 1833 at the age of fourteen. It was at the Institute that she first encountered Klementyna Tańska, now under her married name: Hoffmanowa, who was one of the teachers there—Hoffmanowa made a bad impression on the new pupil, who found her to be snobbish and patronizing towards girls from poorer backgrounds, especially those who were not beautiful, and her views on women to be traditionalist and confining.

After leaving the Institute, Żmichowska did not work for three years and lived on the estate of her aunt Maria Kiędrzyńska at Mężenin near Łomża in the Podlaskie voivodeship of present-day north-eastern Poland. Despite the dearth of intellectual stimulation from the provincial society around her, this was a period when Żmichowska read widely—her diary kept at the time records that she read, for example, Germaine de Staël's *Corinne, or Italy* (in French, it was not published in Polish until 1857—translated by Łucja Rautenstrauchowa) as well as Victor Hugo, George Sand, Lamartine, Michel Masson (*Un Coeur de jeune fille*), the historians Claude Carloman de Ruhlière, Louis Philippe de Ségur and Pierre François Tissot, and Goethe's *The Sorrows of Young Werther* (also probably in French, in which she was fluent). Her first assignment as a governess was with the family of Konstanty Zamoyski, with whom she travelled to Paris in July 1838. Although her relationship with Zamoyski was strained, mainly because of differences in their political views and her close contacts with democrat brother Erazm, the time spent in Paris was a crucial formative period for her and had a fundamental influence on her views on religion, politics, education and the women's question. At this time she was particularly attracted to contemporary utopian thought, including that of Pierre Leroux, but was also reading, among others, Lamennais, Fichte, A. W. Schlegel, Kant, Schelling. She was a regular reader, one of the first female readers, at the Bibliothèque Nationale. She left her post as governess in January 1839, but then spent several months with her brother in Rheims, leaving France only in the late summer of 1839.

For the next several years she was a private teacher to various Polish landed families in both the Russian and Prussian partitions, including a two-year spell (1843–1844) with the Turno family in the Grand Duchy of Posen/Poznań (Prussia). From 1844 she was based mainly in Warsaw, but made several trips across the Prussian and Austrian borders, meeting with underground liberationist conspirators and serving as a courier. It was during this period that she was most deeply involved with progressive circles in both Warsaw and Poznań (in person and through correspondence), in particular with the group of intellectuals associated with *The Scientific Review* (*Przegląd Naukowy*, Warsaw 1842–1848). This was the immediate context for the writing of *The Heathen* and the high point of the activity of the sisterhood of women closely linked to Żmichowska known as the Enthusiasts. Following the uprisings in 1846 and 1848, she was arrested (October 1849), interrogated and imprisoned; she spent four years in prison in Lublin, two years in jail and two years under house arrest. She returned to Warsaw in 1855 and remained there until the 1863 January Uprising. Having revised her earlier attitude to armed insurrection, she refused to support it despite her close contacts with several revolutionary leaders and sympathy with their ultimate aims; the severe repression that followed in the Russian partition after the defeat of the uprising, could be seen as retrospective justification of her pacifist position.

Following her return to Warsaw, Żmichowska's career as a teacher expanded. She wrote several textbooks for use in schools or by private tutors, including one on geography. Perhaps the happiest period of her life was the time she spent (1858–1862) as resident teacher at the school of Julia Baranowska (née Bąkowska, c. 1827–1904) on Miodowa Street. Baranowska's memoir is an interesting testament to Żmichowska's ideas on education generally and girls' in particular: for example, Baranowska records curriculum plans that Żmichowska developed already in the early 1840s, when she was considered for the post of headmistress of a new girls' school in Poznań supported by the philosopher Karol Libelt (1807–1875), indicating how she envisaged developing girls' skills so they might contribute usefully to society as well as support themselves. She suggested a separate programme of study for particularly academic girls—realizing that this was not what many girls were capable of, or wanted yet at the same time keen to provide the opportunities for those that did. The Poznań plan came to nothing, as Żmichowska was not appointed—she was already considered by many contemporaries as too radical and feminist to be accepted by pupils' parents; her time in France had resulted in perceptions of her as a Saint-Simonist or even an atheist, while her public support for the divorce of her friend, journalist Zofia Węgierska (1822–1869), attracted much vociferous opprobrium.

On Miodowa Street she encountered, among others, the four Grabowska sisters, of whom Wanda was to become a lifelong friend and correspondent, as well as Maria Ilnicka (1825–1897), future editor of the journal *Ivy* (*Bluszcz,* founded 1865). Here Żmichowska cultivated a second but entirely separate group of women followers, as she had done with the Enthusiasts in the 1840s, but this time consisting mostly of younger women of the next generation. The few records that remain indicate that she was a highly skilled teacher and regarded with affection and respect by her pupils. During 1861–1862, Żmichowska delivered a series of lectures to this group on women's education. These were published (in *Ivy*), by Wanda Grabowska only forty years later, when the debate on female education had advanced considerably. Based on Żmichowska's notes, which she left to

Grabowska, they were entitled *Pedagogical Talks* (*Pogadanki pedagogiczne,* 1902). Here, she expounds on the need for girls to be educated to the same level as boys (she makes no distinction at all in the academic programme, and pours scorn on contemporary textbooks designed specifically for women—on mathematics or science, for example: why should they be different?) and also emphasizes the need for physical exercise and healthy physical development, usually neglected in girls' education. She saw this programme as beneficial for the nation: society could only benefit from having well-educated women responsible for the upbringing of the nation's children. On the other hand, she also had an individualistic agenda: she mentions the negative impact of the Napoleonic Code on women's property rights in the Congress Kingdom; she realizes the urgent need for women to gain skills to be able to earn a living—economic independence being the key to self-determination. Many of these points are repeated in her later critique of the educational works of Tańska-Hoffmanowa, *Introductory Word to the Didactic Works of Mrs Hoffman* (*Słowo przedwstępne do dzieł dydaktycznych Pani Hofmanowej,* 1876), where she argues that Hoffmanowa's patriarchal standpoint is not only discriminatory against women but also redundant, ideologically and practically—younger generations having moved on. However, the *Talks* (1861–1862) are much more than an educational programme; they contain an entire philosophy, inspired by an inclusive—and radical for its time—approach to Christianity, based on the spiritual and social equality of women, and on the notion of existential unity, the idea that the human person is an indivisible whole—that body, soul and mind are not separable. Influenced by thinkers as disparate as the French utopians, and Herbert Spencer and Charles Darwin (both of whom she read), she saw the human being as an indivisible organism, where the health or sickness of one part affected the whole, an understanding she also extended to society. In order to fully appreciate it, Żmichowska's "feminism" needs to be understood in this context. I shall return to Żmichowska's religious views below.

Baranowska records that on Christmas Eve 1861, the year which also saw publication of Żmichowska's collected literary works, *Pisma Gabryelli*, the pupils expressed their appreciation and gratitude to Żmichowska by presenting her with a parchment containing their signatures as well as a silver cross (which she subsequently sent to Erazm in France). Her words of acceptance suggest the character of the relationship between the women: "I don't deserve such recognition from you, my sisters, nor do I rate my talent so high, but I accept it as gift from your hearts." On this occasion, Maria Ilnicka also read out a laudatory poem written by herself, although the relationship between Żmichowska and Ilnicka, in her public role as editor of *Ivy*, later became problematic as Żmichowska attracted criticism from Catholic clerics for her religious non-conformism. Ilnicka's obituary of Żmichowska (1877), published in *Ivy*, concentrated on her as a literary writer and avoided discussion of her religious views or educational programme where her feminism was more obvious.

In 1862 Żmichowska received recognition as a teacher also from the authorities when she was appointed teacher of geography at the Aleksandrysko-Maryjski Institute in Warsaw, a new Tsarist establishment for girls. She did not survive long in this post, however, as her teaching was deemed too political; Ignacy Baranowski (1923), in particular, records the misgivings she had about accepting the appointment in the first place, but also notes the general recognition of her ability to understand young people and the psychology of learning. She indeed took a keen interest in child psychology and pedagogical theory and was familiar with Polish antecedents and contemporaries such as Jędrzej Śniadecki (1768–1838), Ewaryst Estkowski (1820–1856), Karol Libelt (1807–1875), Julia Molińska-Woykowska (1816–1851) and Bronisław Trentowski (1808–1869), but also other European thinkers such as Johann Heinrich Pestalozzi (1746–1827) and Friedrich Froebel (1782–1852). She discusses practical educational matters in her correspondence with Julia Baranowska, Izabela Zbiegniewska and Matylda Natansonowa-Godebska, curator of a Jewish school in Warsaw. In 1867, she visited the Paris Exhibition in order to observe developments in primary education (she was especially impressed by the American models, the practical educational aids such as reading schemes) and attended two pedagogical conferences at the Sorbonne. In later life she also took an interest in educational establishments ("ochrony") caring for the children of working parents, not only in Warsaw; in this capacity too she corresponded with other pedagogues, such as Lucjan Tatomir in Lwów/L'viv.

Following her decision not to participate in the 1863 uprising, according to the chronology established by Baranowska's memoir and Żmichowska's letters, Żmichowska went to Mienia, the estate where her eldest brother Hiacynt Żmichowski (1801–1871) was employed as land manager. From 1863 to 1867 she was private tutor to Ludwik Lewiński, the son of her niece Wiktoria (at Olszowa and then Pszczonów) and then from 1867–1874 to the children of another niece, Paulina Grodzieńska, at Dębowa Góra. She returned to Warsaw only in 1874, living in poverty in a tiny rented room and in poor health; between then and her death (on Christmas Eve 1876) she was engaged mainly in editing the collected works of Tańska-Hoffmanowa, and writing her last novel *Is this a Novel?*

Żmichowska's approach to religion is hard to recognize as that of someone who was reared in a more or less exclusively Roman Catholic environment. Clearly, she was influenced by her brother Erazm, by the time she spent in France, by her reading of Lamennais and Lamartine as well as Leroux and other utopians, George Sand, contemporary German philosophy (including Hegel, and possibly also Feuerbach—whose *The Essence of Christianity* appeared in 1841) and theology (she was acquainted with the biblical criticism of David Friedrich Strauss and Christian Bauer, and later with the writings of Ernest Renan). She was adamant that she was not a Hegelian, despite her close association with Edward Dembowski (see below). She was accused of this and of anti-Catholic sentiment by her contemporary Eleonora Ziemięcka (1815–1869), anti-Hegelian philosopher and conservative editor of *The Pilgrim* (*Pielgrzym,* 1842–1846), where Żmichowska published some of her prose pieces in the early 1840s. Why did she do this? It would appear from a letter to Erazm that she was impressed by the very fact that the editor was a woman. However, the two women were to exchange polemical letters on the subject of religion, inspired by a triptych of short pieces that Żmichowska published in *The Pilgrim* in 1841–1842 under the collective title *Excerpts from a Woman's Journey* (*Wyjątki z podróży kobiety*): *Gibraltar* (1841), *The Storm* (*Burza,* 1842) and *The Ruins of Luxor* (*Zwaliska Luksora,* 1842).

The work reveals many references to utopian and pantheistic thought—including the element of reincarnation, metempsychosis or palingenesis—although Żmichowska also noted in a later letter to Wanda Grabowska (October 1867) that the major inspiration for the triptych was Jean Paul Richter's novel *Titan* (1800–1803). Without informing the author, Ziemięcka "corrected" the third part (*The Ruins of Luxor*) to make it conform to the Catholic doctrinal position, emphasizing the importance of piety and atonement. In their correspondence, Ziemięcka defends traditional Catholicism, whereas Żmichowska, still claiming to be a Christian, emerges as an ecumenical figure seeking relationship with God on direct and individual terms and a religious perspective securely based in the material and social world. Ziemięcka was also a disappointment to Żmichowska with regard to women's education: her *Thoughts on the Upbringing of Women* (*Myśli o wychowaniu kobiet,* 1843) express a patriarchal position just as deeply embedded in conservative essentialist views on marriage, motherhood and women's role in society as that of Tańska.

During her years of imprisonment and house arrest in Lublin, Żmichowska read the Bible from cover to cover, and around 1855, converted at least for a while to the mystical sect of Andrzej Towiański (1798/99?–1878), famously promoted from 1841 in Paris by the Romantic poet Adam Mickiewicz (1798–1855) and considered by conventional pious Catholics as nothing short of blasphemous. It should be noted that this sect, however bizarre its spirituality and practices, and whether or not its leader was divinely inspired or simply a charlatan, gave considerable prominence to women—Mickiewicz even spoke of the need for female priests. This may have been one reason why it appealed to Żmichowska. Bibianna Moraczewska (1811–1887), in her diary, takes a more cynical view claiming that Żmichowska was persuaded to convert by fellow Towianist Władysław Dzwonkowski (1818–1880) with whom Żmichowska was allegedly in love: to Moraczewska's rationalistic outlook, the sect was appalling and the women's disagreement over it marked the end of their friendship. It was probably Dzwonkowski nevertheless who gave Żmichowska access to Towiański himself, to whom she wrote a confessional letter full of humility—a document that seems otherwise very out of character. Her interest in the sect was short lived, but it is significant that she would continue to defend the Towianists against the many criticisms levelled against them—defending their right to believe what they did, their pacifism, and what she saw as their spiritual energy when compared with the uninspired Catholicism she saw all around her; these views she expressed especially in letters of the 1860s and early 1870s to Wanda Grabowska and Izabela Zbiegniewska.

Although 1855 is usually regarded as the date of this "conversion," as established by Stanisław Pigoń (1935), it is interesting to speculate as to whether she may have encountered Towianism earlier—even as early as 1841, on her return from Paris perhaps when she spent time in the Grand Duchy of Posen/Poznań. The critic Maurycy Mann (writing in 1916) finds Towianist influences in her early work, including in *The Heathen*. While this connection is difficult to prove, it may nevertheless be significant that at this very time Żmichowska shared many female acquaintances in the Duchy with a certain local landowner, Konstancja Łubieńska (1798–1867). Łubieńska had once been the lover of Mickiewicz, still kept up a regular correspondence with him, and herself converted to the sect at about this time. It is possible that this mystical perspective, which has elements in common with certain trends in contemporary utopian philosophy—for example the belief in reincarnation—also fed into Żmichowska's religious views already in the early 1840s, i.e. in the years immediately preceding the writing of *The Heathen*.

One thing we can say for sure, however, on the basis of her correspondence in the 1860s, is that she was seeking throughout her life a liberal and inclusive form of religion. Her most stunning revelation comes in a letter to Zbiegniewska of 27 September 1870, where she talks of her preference for American Quakerism or Unitarianism. The Protestant sympathies expressed here, her ecumenism and pacifism as well as their connection with a specifically female perspective are so ahead of their time and so unusual in the context of nineteenth-century Polish culture, it is worth quoting part of the letter:

> "Here I have the Moravians or Herrnhütters to choose from. I would vote, however, for some shade of American Quakerism. [...] This is where there is the most spiritual truth. Read the works of Channing [she means here the Unitarian William Ellery Channing— U.P.], and imagine what effect it would have on the future, if several thousand women shrouded in mourning, despairing of their losses, impoverished by plunder, were suddenly to run away and shelter under the care of a religious belief which restrains its followers— in the name of Christ, with the weight of several centuries' experience—from war, killing and murder."

As I have discussed elsewhere (2008b), it is hard to know whether her radical spirituality stemmed from some hidden element in her personality, from her hyperconsciousness of herself as a woman—or whether it was the other way round: did her radical religiosity determine her feminism, her demand for inclusivity? Below, I discuss aspects of Żmichowska's sexual identity and her possible/probable preference for women specifically in relation to *The Heathen*, for which there is no "factual" evidence as such, but which can nevertheless be potentially asserted on the strength of such statements as the above. Given that religious (existential) allegiance and sexual preferences are two of the most fundamental markers of identity, and also deeply interconnected, it would seem that such fundamental awareness of self as "different" indicates something rather more than purely denominational preferences.

The Heathen (*Poganka*) is a frame story or *Rahmenerzählung* where a main story (Benjamin's account of his love for a fatal older woman named Aspasia) is surrounded and contextualized by a group of frame characters, who comment upon it. The work first appeared in 1846 in Warsaw in the progressive journal *The Scientific Review* (*Przegląd Naukowy*) in serial parts (numbers 18–19, 23–24, 26, 32, 36) *without* the frame; that is, the original publication included only Benjamin's account of his love for Aspasia. It was republished in 1861 with the frame, which was entitled *Introductory Scene* (*Wstępny obrazek*), in volume two of the collected edition of Żmichowska's works. Described as "introductory," the scene surrounds Benjamin's story however at both ends, returning in the second part of chapter six. Even though the frame scene, which I re-title in the current translation as "By the Fireside," did not appear in the original 1846 edition, there is evidence to suggest that it was written at roughly the same time: in at least three places in Benjamin's story he turns to address one of the frame characters by name (Albert twice and Anna). It is probable that Żmichowska suppressed the frame in order to protect the friends represented by the characters, many of whom were involved in underground patriotic conspiracies, from the attention of the authorities.

In later letters to her friend Izabela Zbiegniewska, Żmichowska retrospectively unveils the identity of the "fireside" companions and their respective pseudonyms. According to a letter to Zbiegniewska of 20 March 1871, she identifies Teofil the Kid (Teofil Dzieciak) as Hipolit Skimborowicz (1815–1880), critic and joint editor of *The Scientific Review,* and Emilia (or Emilka) as is his wife, Anna Skimborowicz (c.1808–1875); Tekla is Wincenta Zabłocka (dates unknown); Felicja is Bibianna Moraczewska (1881–1887), sister of historian and critic Jędrzej Moraczewski (1802–1855), and herself a writer; Seweryna is Tekła Dobrzyńska (c.1815–c.1876); Jadwiga is Kazimiera Ziemięcka (1820–1874), also close friends of Żmichowska. According to this same letter, Anna is Stefania Dzwonkowska (d.o.b unknown, died before March 1871), sister of Władysław Dzwonkowski, although Tadeusz Boy-Żeleński in his 1930 introduction (2nd edition 1950) claims it is Faustyna Morzycka, known to her friends as Fochna (dates unknown); while Augusta the Phanariot (Fanariotka) is Zofia Węgierska (1822–1869), another close friend who moved to Paris and became a journalist, and who was much admired by the poet Juliusz Słowacki (1809–1849).

Also according to the same letter, Albert the Philosopher (Albert Filozof) is the philosopher and literary historian Jan Majorkiewicz

(1820–1847), author of the work *History, Literature and Criticism* (*Historia, literatura i krytyka,* 1847); and Henryk the Zealot (Henryk Zapaleniec) is philosopher, critic of Hegel, and joint editor (with Skimborowicz) of *The Scientific Review,* Edward Dembowski (1822–1846). Dembowski espoused a patriotic but extremely radical politics of action as well as revolutionary social views, and was deeply involved in the Kraków revolt against the Austrians in 1846; author of *An Outline of Polish Literature* (*Piśmiennictwo polskie w zarysie,* 1845), he was also a gifted critic of contemporary German philosophy, as Andrzej Walicki has shown (1982). Leon the Methodist (Leon Metodista) meanwhile is a combination of three "committee members" of 1848 (a direct retrospective reference to the involvement of the group in the revolutionary events), one most likely being Żmichowska's close associate Henryk Krajewski (1824–1897). Some uncertainty surrounds the identity of Edmund the Mystic (Edmund Mistyk). Żmichowska suggests it is the poet Teofil Lenartowicz (1822–1893), but Tadeusz Boy-Żeleński, in his edition, insists it is rather a combined portrait of Karol Baliński (1817–1864) "along with other poets," taking his information from the memoir of Skimborowicz who interpreted "Mystic" as referring to an adherent of Towianism, although Lenartowicz as well as Baliński was involved with this same spiritual movement. Not all these figures were literary, especially the women: but all were well-educated and socially engaged. The women were involved in various educational enterprises, such as the schools founded by Kazimiera Ziemięcka (not to be confused with Eleonora Ziemięcka), visited prisons and did charitable works; they came from a variety of social backgrounds. One of the most active in the underground conspiracy was Anna Skimborowicz. Żmichowska herself played a role as a courier, as noted above. But this was by no means the only element that bound the female friends together.

The only frame character not mentioned here by Żmichowska is Benjamin. In another letter to Zbiegniewska of 18 August 1871, she states that Benjamin is the only one who belongs "purely" to the novel, and is not based on any living person—which adds weight, in fact, to the argument that Benjamin may well have been herself, even though she also gives the overall narrator her own pseudonym, Gabriella (which varied in her published works: Gabryella or Gabriella). She also states that the frame of *The Heathen* is an exception in that this is the only occasion when she took characters directly from life (it was not, she claims, her usual practice) and mentions the frame's removal from the 1846 edition: "it was originally not to be published at all and only after many years, with the explicit agreement of the majority, did it squeeze onto the pages of the collected edition [1861]." This confirms that the frame was indeed written at the same time as the novel.

One interpretation of the main, central tale is to regard it as an allegory or parable, whereby transgression—Benjamin's failure to follow a particular paradigm of moral behaviour—is deservedly punished. This seems to be the consistent view of a major critic of Żmichowska, Maria Woźniakiewicz-Dziadosz, in her book of 1978 and subsequent articles. According to this reading, Benjamin deserts his class and national loyalties, for which his father and several brothers sacrifice their lives, in favour of the cosmopolitan values and lifestyle of a rich, aristocratic older woman, with whom he pursues a passionate love affair—outside conventional marriage—travelling with her abroad. Despite the enormous energy he derives from his passion while the affair lasts, and his fantastic successes in academe, commerce and politics, he is left morally and emotionally bankrupt when Aspasia rejects him and he murders his rival in a fit of jealousy. Returning home to his family, about whom he had almost forgotten (he had failed to take seriously letters that reached him earlier), a broken man and a criminal fugitive, he realizes the extent of the changed situation in his home country and the enormous suffering of his close relatives.

This background is not necessarily clear to a non-Polish audience, and is not elaborated upon more explicitly in the text itself, probably because of the political censorship then pertaining within the Russian Empire; but to Żmichowska's contemporaries, references to these personal sacrifices would have been obvious, as would the connotations associated with "mother" ("matka"), which could be read as the mother country and its culture and values, as well as the biological mother. (The word in Polish for "homeland" is "ojczyzna," "fatherland"—not "motherland"; "Polska," however, the name of the country, is a feminine noun). Hence Benjamin's contrition and remorse before his own mother might also be seen as recognition of his guilt in ignoring wider political issues linked to the suppression of Polish national identity, or in failing to participate in the armed struggle to regain national self-determination, while his preference for cosmopolitan culture could be seen as lack of sympathy for the national culture. Moreover, a parallel would seem to be being drawn between patriotic and Christian values: loving relationships extolling traditional Catholic marriage and conventional gender roles are the ideological domain of the patriotic "mother"—whereas the cosmopolitan world of Aspasia, and also of the artist Cyprian, creator of the fatal picture, is represented as "heathen," i.e. without God and transgressive. Given that Żmichowska was herself involved in the mid-1840s in underground activities (although later, at the time she was republishing *The Heathen* in the full version with the frame, she rejected armed insurrection), and that some of her closest associates, notably Edward Dembowski (Henryk the Zealot in the frame), were patriotic revolutionaries, it seems right to suggest that Żmichowska does indeed make allusions to this contemporary background. However, it is quite another matter to claim that Benjamin's story somehow proves the correctness of political self-sacrifice, that Żmichowska punishes her hero for his transgression against family and nation. Moreover Benjamin's contrition is only a temporary state: when he sees Cyprian's painting again, after the death of his biological mother, he tries to reignite the romantic-erotic love represented by it. It is possible that his particular transgression—if indeed it should be regarded as such—comes from quite a different source.

It is a striking fact that the most inspired parts of the text are those where Benjamin recalls his love for Aspasia, as Sławomir Walczewska points out in her analysis (1999), or when Cyprian anticipates it in his picture. Given the intensity of these passages, it is very difficult to accept that Żmichowska condemns this love. Love, debated, condemned or approved, in various philosophical, religious, social and individual guises is, after all, the topic of the *Symposium*-like frame discussion between the young friends—and in keeping with the tradition of the frame story or *Rahmenerzählung*, the frame provides clues to the possible meaning of the central story. *The Heathen* is a novel about love, all forms of love, including the individual, romantic and erotic—and, as far as the main protagonist is concerned: about the loss of love. It bears the stigmata of personal rejection, of suffering cruelly inflicted.

Walczewska is not the first to suggest a biographical interpretation, or to imply that the relationship between Benjamin and Aspasia is a fictional portrayal of a real-life same-sex relationship. We should beware of taking too literally a biographical approach—the novel is a work of art, the product of creative imagination, yet critical thinking on the relationship between autobiography and fictional writing has now gone full circle: from the death of the author to the reinstatement of the autobiographical perspective. There is now a general recognition, in the wake of research and theory especially on women's writing, proved by such compendiums as that of Smith and Watson (1998), that all fiction is to some extent autobiographical and that all autobiography is in part fiction. The earlier critic Maurycy Mann (1916) makes a similar assertion to Walczewska, as indeed does Tadeusz Boy-Żeleński. In his introduction to *The Heathen*, Boy points to Żmichowska's friend Paulina Zbyszewska (1822–date of death unknown) as the model for Aspasia while hinting at a similar attachment between Żmichowska and Zbyszewska as between Żmichowska and his mother. Is this just pure conjecture? Mieczysława Romankówna (1955), one the most active twentieth-century critics of Żmichowska and compiler of several volumes of her correspondence, denies that Żmichowska's falling out with Zbyszewska had anything to do with a romantic or erotic attachment, and claims it was linked rather to Zbyszewska's less than committed attitude towards the patriotic cause.

Female friendships among literary women in the nineteenth-century were often intense, as commentators such as Lillian Faderman (1998) or Sharon Marcus (2007) have shown—women's correspondence sometimes using vocabulary which today feels highly suggestive. This does not necessarily imply homoerotic attraction, although it may well do. Persuasive pointers nevertheless support Mann's and Boy's intuitions and

Walczewska's interpretation. Two distinct problems are at stake for *The Heathen*: does Żmichowska portray a same-sex relationship concealed behind a heterosexual one? And was Zbyszewska the model for Aspasia?

There is at least one piece of material evidence to suggest that a feeling of exceptional intensity existed between Żmichowska and Paulina Zbyszewska in the early 1840s, at least on Żmichowska's side, that Żmichowska spent some weeks at Zbyszewska's estate (Kurów) near Lublin, but was forced to leave abruptly due to some indiscretion on her part. In a letter to another close friend, Bibianna Moraczewska, of August 1846, Żmichowska confides the incident in cryptic terms but implies that she was the one responsible for the breaking-off of the friendship because she overstepped some critical boundary: "I sinned heavily" ("zgrzeszyłam ciężko"), and believes she must accept the punishment for having "loved like that" ("but to love like that isn't seemly, hence after the evil comes the punishment"—"ale tak się kochać nie godziło, więc po złym kara"). Żmichowska was distraught for some time after this incident. The rejection by Zbyszewska came hot on the heels of the death of her brother Janusz, to whom Żmichowska had also been intensely attached. In another letter, this time to Augusta Grotthusowa, she suggests that had it not been for the loss of her brother, she would not have allowed herself to be so "swept away" by Paulina. These incidents of 1842–1843 immediately precede the writing of *The Heathen*.

It is probable that Paulina Zbyszewska was indeed a model—one at least among several—for Aspasia. She was a rich, intelligent, musical and attractive aristocratic woman with cosmopolitan tastes and a fine palace. According to contemporaries, she had a self-assured but somewhat unpredictable personality. The poet Jadwiga Łuszczewska (better known by her pseudonym Deotyma) found her imperious: "as knowing as Minerva, as threateningly beautiful as Juno." There is no doubt that Zbyszewska was of a superior social class to Żmichowska, an important factor in Benjamin's initial wariness of Aspasia's true motives and a cause of their ultimate incompatibility. It is possible that Zbyszewska amused herself with her socially inferior friend without realizing the strength of the latter's feelings, much as Aspasia makes fun of Benjamin's innocence, sincerity and thwarted desire for exclusivity in love, in a destructive power-game of her own. Meanwhile, there are elements in the novel's text that suggest identification, if only partial, between Żmichowska and Benjamin. For a start, she herself was the "Beniaminek" of her own family: the youngest of nine children (of three boys and six girls: Benjamin has four brothers and four sisters). Here, however, we must note at least one fundamental difference: Żmichowska's mother died a few days after her confinement (although this parallels, of course, the death of the biblical Benjamin's mother Rachel), and Żmichowska was then more or less rejected by her father, left to the care of aunts and older siblings—she was, however, the cosseted spoiled baby or "Beniaminek" of all these substitute parents. Also, is the raw shock of the death of Cyprian in the novel possibly inspired by the loss of Janusz?

But above and beyond such attempts at precise identification—which we can never establish for sure anyway—the novel sometimes seems to represent the male protagonist as female, or associate him with attributes more conventionally associated with women; or, it even occasionally reverses gender identity. This makes it at least possible to regard Benjamin's story as one of two women—because of these moments when gender suddenly becomes ambiguous. One such moment is Cyprian's description of Benjamin's "Greek" beauty and his identification of him with Alcibiades, especially in the scene when Cyprian admires Benjamin's sleeping body lying half-uncovered on his bed (somehow it feels like a woman's body?).

Another is the moment when Benjamin first meets the woman in the forest; her voice seems to be that of a young man—the gender of the mysterious figure is initially not clear at all. Another is Aspasia's discovery of the unconscious Benjamin floating in the river: the image of him almost drowning in his clothes, entangled in his flowing locks and the undergrowth by the bank, immediately recalls Shakespeare's Ophelia (gender roles are reversed: it is the male protagonist who "drowns")—and also links him by association to his fey sister Ludwinka, first portrayed contemplating her own image in a "glassy stream" among the flowers. Rescued from the river and regaining consciousness, he dissolves into floods of bitter tears "like a woman." On the night of his homecoming, his mother makes him kneel before her together with his little niece: the identification made by the mother seems to imply much more than their identical golden locks. Felicja, in the second part of the frame, suggests he would make a "beautiful caryatid."

Żmichowska's portrayal of gender ambiguity, as well as hidden same-sex love, was certainly not lost on one of Boy's contemporary reviewers. The interwar feminist writer and critic Irena Krzywicka (1899–1994) notes both these aspects of Żmichowska's fiction in her review of Boy's 1929–1930 editions of *The Heathen, White Rose* and *Is this a Novel?* Also anticipating present-day commentators, playwright Tadeusz Różewicz (b. 1921), who alludes to *The Heathen* in his play *Marriage Blanc* (*Białe małżeństwo,* 1975) and names two of the personae dramatis Paulina and Bibianna (not names of characters in Żmichowska's novel but names of her friends), reads *The Heathen* as a "lesbian" text. In a short article published in 1977, Różewicz explains why he felt he could not proceed with his project to dramatize the novel itself—his "internal censor" warned him that even contemporary (i.e. mid- to late-twentieth-century) society was not yet ready to accept "lesbian love" on stage. Izabela Filipiak (b. 1961), a contemporary lesbian writer, remarks in her recent book (2006) on Maria Komornicka (1876–1949), another Polish woman author with a complex sexual identity, that she identifies with Żmichowska as a writer, and also devotes space to her as a rare advocate of female friendship who gave women succour and space to be themselves, rather than expecting them to find their true calling in relationship with a man.

Apart from the national-patriotic (specifically Polish) or autobiographical (lesbian) interpretations, there are at least three other ways of approaching the novel. One understands the novel in the context of contemporary European literature, especially French and German literary texts. Another regards the work as a philosophical novel about love, written—significantly or not— in the wake of the publication of Søren Kierkegaard's *Fear and Trembling* (1843) and concurrently with his *Works of Love* (1847), not just romantic or erotic love between individuals, but the Christian *agape* and its wider social implications and responsibilities. And it is likely, given the various views expressed in the frame regarding erotic love, that Żmichowska was also familiar with Stendhal's famous work *De l'Amour* (1822). The inclusion of Alcibiades (Henryk the Zealot) as a participant in the frame discussion (irrespective of what he actually says) cannot but be a reference to Plato's *Symposium,* while the word "uczta" (literally: "banquet" or "feast," and the word regularly used to refer to the *Symposium* in Polish) occurs frequently in Benjamin's own story. Yet another approach relates to the growing contemporary demands for female emancipation, to Żmichowska's attitude towards women's rights and self-development, and to her ideal models of "femality"—to use Żmichowska's contemporary Margaret Fuller's term from *Woman in the Nineteenth Century* (1845) as more neutral than the ideologically loaded "femininity." All these approaches shed light on the origins and personality of Aspasia, suggesting that the novel's eponymous Heathen, is just as much a product of culture and imagination as a real-life model.

Narcyza Żmichowska is often claimed by feminists and researchers of women's literary history to be the first significant "emancipationist" figure in the Polish context. While a case can be made to justify this claim, it is important to be clear what we mean by it, because the term "emancipation" may be misleading in the context. To speak of "emancipation" or "rights" in the context of Polish history of the first half of the nineteenth century, one has to acknowledge that men also had no political rights, and that Poles were divided between three absolutist Empires. Proto-feminist movements in the Polish lands should not be thought of, without qualification, in terms of west European or North American suffragette movements demanding women's political rights. When the term is used by Polish women in the period we are discussing here (1840s), it refers to women's educational rights, their right to undertake employment, be fairly remunerated and gain a degree of financial independence, their right to divorce and their role within the family. The group of young men and women associated with *The Scientific Review,* including the editors Hipolit Skimborowicz

(Teofil the Kid) and Edward Dembowski (Henryk the Zealot), were sympathetic to this programme for women's rights; in his retrospective article about the Enthusiasts (1880), Skimborowicz speaks of both male and female Enthusiasts—although the Enthusiasts were usually referred to subsequently as exclusively female, and indeed in her own retrospective commentary (for example, in her introduction to the works of Tańska-Hoffmanowa) Żmichowska herself gives the impression it was exclusively female. The following quotation from the latter text (1876) describes her interpretation of the women's aims—this was clearly not a self-conscious political movement, it makes no mention of "emancipation," yet it can be interpreted, in my opinion, as a feminist or proto-feminist programme:

> "the women [...] did not themselves think up any title for themselves, precisely because they were not characterized by any separate distinction, by any special feature. With regard to their position as women they without doubt had certain ideals and needs in common, but it never occurred to any of them to tie themselves to the shared dogma of some creed. They were united by sincere friendship, where the basis was equally honest and where circumstances favoured it, but they were often united by quite contradictory understandings, by opposite principles: Orthodox and Protestant, even the values of high society and the harsh asceticism of committed partisans."

It has proven impossible to establish beyond doubt a consistent listing of precisely who these women were and what specifically bound them together. Different commentators give different names, some of which overlap—and no other list maps exactly onto the women identified by Żmichowska in letters to Zbiegniewska or in the frame of *The Heathen.* There are various theories. Skimborowicz's article in *Ivy* (1880), as mentioned, includes male as well as female Enthusiasts but otherwise closely follows *The Heathen.* Literary historian and critic Piotr Chmielowski treats the female Enthusiasts as writers, including a chapter on them in his book *Polish Women Authors of the Nineteenth Century* (1885), even though most of the candidates he includes—with the exception of Żmichowska herself and the lesser figures of Moraczewska and Węgierska—were not literary figures. Historian Anna Minkowska (1923), who includes additional names, sees the women only as patriotic underground conspirators, as does Romankówna (1957), including some different names again and omitting others. Grażyna Borkowska (2001), however, offers a solution closer in spirit to Żmichowska's own words, regarding them as a loosely associated proto-feminist sorority:

> "The Enthusiasts were a loosely connected, informal group, linked by ties of friendship and sympathy, 'built onto' existing social and family structures. The Enthusiasts did not adhere to any defined ideology. Their activity was directed simultaneously in two directions, usually separated in feminist programmes by the level of the women's experience: active participation in public life, and personal realization, understood in its broadest sense."

My only addition to this conclusion would be to consider the etymology and history of the term "enthusiasm" and trace its application in the literary texts that we know Żmichowska was reading. In particular, it is a word liberally used by Germaine de Staël in *Corinne, ou l'Italie* (1807) and even more so in another work by De Staël, *On Germany* (*De l'Allemagne*, 1810). My suggestion (2008b) is that the inspired utopian love of one's neighbour represented in these works, among others, was a major aspect of Żmichowska's understanding of the idea of "enthusiasm," a word which rarely occurred in Polish (unlike in English or French) before her specific usage, as dictionaries of the Polish language testify. It was "enthusiasm," not "emancipation," that drew the women together.

Also, Żmichowska was critical of more radical "emancipated" contemporary figures, in particular Julia Woykowska (1816–1851), educationalist, journalist and writer of children's books (based in Poznań), whom she regarded as having gone too far in living with her partner outside of conventional marriage and advocating so-called "free love." A similar reticence marked her views on George

Sand (1804–1876), despite her great admiration for her as a writer, as well as on the Swedish feminist Frederika Bremer (1801–1865), as is evident from her letters to Grabowska and from Julia Baranowska's memoir. On the other hand, she was an outspoken supporter of Zofia Węgierska (Augusta in *The Heathen*) in her bid to divorce her first husband.

So what kind of "feminism" was it? How does Żmichowska endorse a feminist programme? It is significant that she does not include among the frame characters of *The Heathen* the women who did indeed write articles—under pseudonyms—on women's "emancipation" in the 1840s for *The Scientific Review*: "Delfina" (Teresa Kossowska née Karska) and "Bronisława" (Julia Janiszewska). I believe she was seeking above all to free women from cultural stereotyping: to help them get away from the values and roles awaiting them in patriarchal, male-dominated power structures and cultural models. She wanted women to be free to choose their own models according to their own desires—but in order to do this, of course, they had to have access to education, and to financial independence.

This is the style of feminism also apparent in *The Heathen:* here we see how the frame interacts with the main story, how models of femininity (or *femality*) in the frame scene are contrasted—to their positive advantage—with the cultural stereotypes of femininity presented in Benjamin's tale, i.e. Aspasia and Mother. In the frame characters (Emilia, Felicja, Seweryna, Tekla, Augusta, Jadwiga, Anna), the virtues of real-life, educated, articulate and socially active young women are extolled. All are individuals and none stereotypical models, though all are marked by a certain idealization. These are the women Żmichowska admires: not either of the two extremes introduced by Benjamin. In other words, the women in the frame, including the narrator Gabriella, do not endorse Mother in some kind of moral victory over Aspasia, where the model of femininity embodied in Aspasia is condemned as the opposite to Mother, although it is also clear that Aspasia is not—in Żmichowska's view—a positive model of female emancipation. The function of the frame characters is therefore this: by their own real existence, experience and example, they cause both stereotypes of femininity in the main story to be questioned, to be shown to be fantasy figures, but also ideological poles of a binary opposition, both of which are devalued.

The critique of Mother, as an ideological symbol or matrix of cultural identity, should not be taken as a critique of motherhood per se on the part of Gabriella-Żmichowska. Nor indeed, should she be understood as anti-patriotic. On the contrary, Żmichowska separates the concepts, unlinking patriotic sentiment from any necessary connection with a submissive and patriarchal model of femininity and motherhood. "Motherhood" itself should be understood as a wider concept than purely biological maternity— and moreover as a quality of potentially all women, whether or not they have biological children—hence the positive portrayal of Anna, the childless "mother" of the frame. Such "motherhood" of everyone in her social sphere—friends, pupils, not just family members—was a quality perceived by several contemporaries in Żmichowska herself. Cecylia Walewska, a critic of the next generation, made this aspect the crux of her portrait of Żmichowska, albeit giving it a more sentimental, idealistic gloss than Żmichowska warrants. Mother, as presented in the central story of *The Heathen* is clearly therefore problematic. It cannot be denied that she possesses desirable qualities. Benjamin emphasizes the positive aspects of his relationship with his mother. He remembers her great love for him as a child and her good moral influence—it was she who made him sensitive to the suffering of others; later she forgives him unconditionally. At the same time, she is the matriarch, the patriarchal woman: when her husband makes the ultimate sacrifice, she takes over the man's role as head and moral authority of the whole family. The critique in the frame, however, suggests that this idealized model of patriotic motherhood should not be taken at face value but should be problematized: Żmichowska unhitches the concept of nurturing "motherhood," necessary for the development of any happy, healthy child—and as a broader humanitarian concept—from any necessary mapping onto ideological motherhood linked to the nation. This flies in the face, of course, of the ideology promoted by her contemporaries

Klementyna Tańska-Hoffmanowa and Eleonora Ziemięcka. These writers sanctioned a stereotypical ideal of submissive femininity (limited educational aspirations, no social role outside the family, total obedience to husband, the culture of making oneself "liked" and "attractive," and so on) inspired by, among others, the French writer on female conduct Stéphanie de Genlis (1746–1839), and which had taken deep root in European societies in the first decades of the nineteenth century: it was nothing particularly Polish. However, both these writers made "Polishness" the cornerstone of their ideal of femininity, imbuing it above all with a sentimental, superficial yet extremely rigid Catholic didacticism. It was against this style of "Polishness," this style of religiosity and this style of "femininity," that Żmichowska rebelled.

A few significant moments in the frame itself give an idea of Żmichowska's own ideals. In her portrait of Felicja, narrator Gabriella emphasizes how Felicja is the "type of woman most able to make a reality of women's dreams of independence." Having described her self-confidence, single-mindedness, intelligence and intolerance of human weakness, Gabriella makes the following denial of "suffering," i.e. martyrdom—one of the key virtues of the contemporary patriotic ethos, a perspective that sets this positive model of self-assured "femality" apart from contemporary cultural stereotypes of submissive femininity, and from the specifically Polish stereotype of the self-sacrificing Polish Mother:

"She alone could stand so firm that pain never toppled her, so high that ridicule never reached her, and so beautifully and securely that others wanted to stand together with her. All those virtues that could develop freely only in normal conditions of human existence were the virtues of Felicja; for indeed, she lacked the abnormal virtues, the trifling virtues of suffering. But what use are those nowadays: the virtues of suffering—humility, contrition, pity that knows no bounds, resignation that is never exhausted? Fine for ascetics, hermits of Thebaid, martyrs of the Coliseum. But what we need now are the virtues of strength, the virtues of triumph; we need absolutely the virtue of happiness, so that others will believe in us and become virtuous like us."

"Normal" and "abnormal" refer here to the "abnormal" state of Polish national existence, political life and society, as well as to the model of personal self-sacrifice promoted by Mickiewicz, among others, where the narrator appears to see Polish conditions as "abnormal" compared to other, "normal" societies. Żmichowska was not an admirer of suffering; she did not believe that it brought any constructive social or political benefits (hence her ambiguous portrait of Henryk-Alcibiades-Dembowski in the frame) and certainly did not believe in any beneficial moral effects for the individual. On the contrary, she believed suffering to be the cause of depression and moral degradation, the sympathetic portraits of the unfulfilled women in the frame being cases in point (Anna is *not* a mother, Jadwiga is *not* a poet, Augusta is *not* an artist). In the fragmentary novel sequence entitled *Several Writings of an Anonymous Female Author* (1861), one of the characters claims that suffering is the cause of sin: it is not the result of or reward for sin, and furthermore that Christ relieved suffering on earth and did not come to mete it out. In the model of Christian love, or *agape,* which emerges as possibly the strongest model of love presented in the frame debate, no positive gloss is put on suffering at all, suffering is not seen to be personally or socially useful—on the contrary, *agape* stands for a model of social engagement that promotes humanitarian care and personal happiness.

"Normal" and "abnormal" may also have another reference here: some of these women, although presented by narrator Gabriella in a very positive light, met with disapproval from contemporary conservative society. Kazimiera Ziemięcka (Jadwiga in the frame) was considered to be out of her mind when she set up a school for peasant children on her own estate. Meanwhile, Zofia Węgierska's divorce (Augusta in the frame) attracted much opprobrium. In letters to her brother Erazm in Paris, as well as publicly, Żmichowska vigorously defended Zofia's right to divorce a man whom she had been forced to marry by her parents and whom she did not love, in favour of her lover and chosen partner Feliks Węgierski. The portrait of Augusta makes reference to this unjust, according to Gabriella, condemnation of her entire person as immoral. But again, Żmichowska puts her own Christian interpretation on this:

writing to Erazm, she states that true Christian marriage should not be contracted without genuine love, hence forced marriage without love was un-Christian and divorce should be permissible. If Felicja is portrayed as "what we need now," then Emilia (or Emilka: Anna Skimborowicz) is portrayed by Gabriella as a woman of the future. She mentions in passing Emilka's first husband, "who poisoned the days of her first youth"—Skimborowicz was her second husband. The narrator envisions a time when women will be able to be themselves, as they want to be (implication: not how men, religion, cultural stereotypes wish them to be). However, this is a dream whose realization is postponed to the future: only Emilka, in tune with and at ease with her natural inclinations, gives an inkling of what this may be like: "she was angel and saint— two beings who came together to create the kind of woman who will be able to live safely, blessedly, happily, only in three hundred years time—at the very earliest, reckoning by the most flattering accounts of the human race." Żmichowska returns to this idea in her next novel *A Book of Memories* (1847–1848) in relation to one of her protagonists, Helusia, designated as the "woman of the future" who will live according to her own nature and desires, and is more specific about the date: the end of the twentieth century (sic!).

The participation of these "modern" or "futuristic" women in the "symposium" about love considerably broadens conceptions of "love" beyond the choice of the only two options portrayed by Benjamin's story: on the one hand, love of Mother and her traditional Catholic piety, designated "good" or "holy"; or, individualistic romantic and erotic love outside Christian marriage with a cosmopolitan (even "foreign," Benjamin calls her at one point) "heathen" woman, who is designated "evil." Each of these two contrasting ideals represented within Benjamin's story is satirized in turn in the songs of Aspasia's little "devils," Cain and Abel, at her banquet. First, the older boy Cain sings of his erotic passion, of tormenting physical desire and frustration born of idleness, ennui and spleen—invoking images of the desired woman, her physical attributes, clothes and jewellery, in fetishist terms that map closely onto Benjamin's description of Aspasia's costume. Cain's fantasy is then interpreted in brutally cynical terms by his brother Abel, who then sings his own song parodying praise for the exact opposite—the self-sacrificing angel, man's complement, "priestess of the domestic hearth," who always looks up to her man and provides him with unbending moral support whatever he does, in turn sarcastically debunked by Cain. The interpretation of the songs, of course, depends on other factors: they are retold within the context of Aspasia's cynical approach to love, announced at the banquet, with Benjamin's disapproving reception. On the other hand, if we read them in the context of the frame, they indeed seem to be highly charged contradictions of *both* extremes of femininity present in Benjamin's story.

The title of the novel, however, refers not to Benjamin but to Aspasia. We may speculate as to why: perhaps Żmichowska was exorcizing her own demons, her own ghosts? As already mentioned, one possible source of the figure of Aspasia is Żmichowska's friend Paulina Zbyszewska. Whether or not this is true, there are other possible inspirations noted by critics. The theme of a young man emotionally and morally harmed by doomed romantic involvement with an older woman, as in Benjamin Constant's *Adolphe,* for example, was a trope of contemporary literature. Also, there are pointers within in the text itself that suggest Żmichowska may have been referring to specific texts. She mentions in letters written from Paris in 1838–1839 to Feliks Michałowski her reading of George Sand's *Lélia.* Is then the question that Benjamin—still unsure whether she comes from heaven or hell—asks of Aspasia, when she rescues him from the river and he surrenders to his love for her ("Who are you, Aspasia?") a direct reference to the opening words of *Lélia* ("Qui es-tu?")? Tadeusz Boy-Żeleński, on the other hand, sees the inspiration of Balzac, as do Maurycy Mann (1916), Wanda Morzkowska-Tyszkowa (1934) and Alicja Gollnikowa (1995), specifically the short story *La Salamandre* and novel *Le Peau de chagrin.*

Aspasia has many of the characteristics of the contemporary *femme fatale*, a figure found in Romantic fiction produced by women as much as by men, as Adriana Craciun discusses in her book on the topic (2003). Here, an interesting comparison may also be made between the "fatal" figures discussed by Mario Praz in *The Romantic Agony* (albeit from texts only by male authors) and the list of writers we know Żmichowska had read (from contemporary or later correspondence, or from her Diary, 1835–1837) by the late 1830s or early 1840s: Chateaubriand, Eugène Sue, Frédéric Soulié, Jules Janin, Bernadin de Saint-Pierre, Balzac, Victor Hugo, Alfred de Musset. Praz does not mention George Sand or Germaine de Staël—both of whom are mentioned in contemporary correspondence by Żmichowska (she not only read De Staël's *Corinne, ou l'Italie* in 1835, she also discussed it in a letter of June 1845 to Bibianna Moraczewska). A writer who is mentioned by Praz and not by Żmichowska, however, but in whom several critics also suggest possible inspiration for *The Heathen* is Théophile Gautier and his *Mademoiselle de Maupin* (1835); the fact that she does not specifically mention this novel in letters, does not mean she did not read it. One critic who sees Gautier as pivotal for the novel is Tadeusz Sinko, writing in 1933, especially in the conception of Cyprian, creator of the painting, Cyprian's idealized eroticism and his preference for art for art's sake over Christian art. An unusual name in Polish (Teofil) is given to one of the frame characters. Another element suggesting the possible inspiration of this work is the ambiguous sexuality of Gautier's heroine, her movement between two sexual identities and Gautier's introduction into the novel of the idea of a "third sex": Rosalind does not identify herself with any known sexual self-definition, but rather desires to be open to any possibility, a theme that might conceivably have appealed to Żmichowska.

Sinko also points to other significant potential sources. In addition to the French, he also mentions German sources, literary and aesthetic. Sinko connects Aspasia and her castle, for example, with the Venusberg of the Tannhäuser legend, then undergoing something of a revival: Richard Wagner's opera, based on his own libretto written 1842–1843, was first performed in 1845 at the time Żmichowska was writing *The Heathen*. The "Venerian Mountains" also appear as a meeting-place of witches in Polish witchcraft and folkloric literature, as Wanda Wyporska discusses (2002), thus associating the "mountain of love" with the witches' Sabbath—an overtone tangible in Benjamin's description of Aspasia's banquet.

Sinko discusses in addition the possible inspiration of Wieland's *Geschichte des Agathon* (1766–1767), Heinse's *Ardinghello* (1789), Hölderlin's *Hyperion* (1799) and Friedrich Schlegel's *Lucinde* (1799). *Agathon* contains an Aspasia-figure as did other west European works of the period, including Walter Savage Landor's *Pericles and Aspasia* (1836), though it is unlikely that Żmichowska would have known this work. Most importantly, Sinko sees the prototype of Aspasia not in classical Greek antecedents (Aspasia of Miletus, for instance) but in eighteenth-century artistic and literary examples of so-called "aesthetic immoralism": he sees her not so much as an attempt at authentic portrayal of an actual Greek figure but of contemporary "aesthetic" neo-Hellenist and hedonistic ideals, where beauty and pleasure merge and are pervaded by sexual amorality.

This would indeed seem to embody the attitude of Cyprian: his picture of the love between Aspasia and Alcibiades is not a portrayal of a classical scene as such, nor is his long speech to Benjamin glorifying alleged Ancient Greek ideals of love, beauty and heroism— these are contemporary, or late eighteenth-century aesthetic ideals, designated "pagan," where "pagan" does not refer primarily to a pagan (i.e. classical) past but to contemporary aestheticism and even atheism. Hence my preference, following the earlier decision of David Welsh (1973), to refer to the eponymous protagonist as The Heathen, and not The Pagan: Aspasia is a contemporary atheistic figure, driven above all by pleasure-seeking individualism and her own will to power. The artist Cyprian combines a similar worldview with another contemporary ideal: that of the Romantic artist, where art itself—art for art's sake—is seen as the highest value, to which he is prepared to sacrifice both his brother Benjamin's future happiness as well as his own life, and where the artist, divinely or otherwise inspired, is somehow granted an exceptional status, freeing him (or her) from the moral standards and responsibilities incumbent upon ordinary (i.e. less talented) mortals. There is no evidence to suggest that Żmichowska subscribed to this idealization of artistic genius. On the contrary, in her next novel, *A Book of Memories*, through the figure of the gifted violinist Romuald, she demonstrates its destructive effects on other human beings.

Mention should be made in this context of the contemporary Polish poet and artist Cyprian Kamil Norwid (1821–1883). Cyprian is not a common name, so the choice for Żmichowska's artist suggests possible hidden allusions. Cyprian Norwid did not espouse the same views on art as his namesake in *The Heathen:* on the contrary, he took an anti-Romantic, utilitarian, ethical view that the artist should be an excellent craftsman dedicated to humanitarian and social ends; he did not support the idea of art for art's sake. This view of art was very close to Żmichowska's own. Norwid also suffered a similar sense of class inferiority. Like her, he was fêted for a brief time by the Warsaw salons, but was severely misunderstood, being unconventional and far ahead of his time—and was only rediscovered by poets of the next generation. The fictional Cyprian spends time living in Rome and studying art, as did the real-life Cyprian Norwid. Although the views on art of the two Cyprians differ, they thus have other elements in common. An additional reference is also potentially significant. Zygmunt Wasilewski, writing in 1935, saw Norwid's attachment to the pianist Maria Kalergis (1822–1874), a rich, beautiful and unattainable aristocratic woman, as the model for Żmichowska's Aspasia and Alcibiades; it is possible that this was indeed the case, alongside Zbyszewska and other additional, strictly literary inspirations.

It is therefore important to remember that Aspasia is a contemporary and not a classical figure. She possesses certain characteristics of the Ancient Greek hetaera or courtesan, but any association between Aspasia of the novel and Aspasia of Miletus, for example, needs qualification. Historically, according to Plutarch, Aspasia of Miletus was the lover of Pericles of Athens, not of Alcibiades, as in Cyprian's picture. It is possible, of course, that Żmichowska found her inspiration precisely in the *Symposium* and in Alcibiades's unpredictable personality and views on love expressed there. On the other hand, she states in a later letter to Wanda Grabowska (9 October 1867) that the inspiration for Alcibiades in *The Heathen* came from her reading of Thucydides's *History of the Peloponnesian War.* We should note also that the personality of Alcibiades in the picture is dictated by Cyprian; it does not reflect Benjamin's own personality, even though the incorporation of his own physical image into the picture predetermines Benjamin's actual behaviour towards Aspasia—and here we should be careful again, since the woman in the picture (Cyprian's fantasy of ideal love, whom he names Aspasia) is not necessarily the same woman whom Benjamin meets in the forest, follows to her castle, falls in love with, and actually names Aspasia. Like with Sand's Lélia, we never know precisely who she is; she does not exist "objectively," i.e. in the words of the narrator—we, the readers, encounter her only through the words first of Cyprian, then of Benjamin. Meanwhile, in the frame, Żmichowska uses the name Alcibiades to describe Henryk the Zealot, based, as we saw, on Edward Dembowski. However much driven by self-sacrificing patriotic ideals, Henryk is shown in his own words to be a hothead; the narrator Gabriella does not endorse him unreservedly—several times she mentions his tendency to tell lies, prompting the possible question: does the cause justify any kind of behaviour? Dembowski died in the Kraków uprising against the Austrians in 1846 at the age of twenty-four, in an act of rash bravado which brought no relief or practical long-term benefits to Polish society.

Aspasia's atheism, or godlessness, the clearest mark of her "heathenism," is most evident in the scene where she describes how she understands love, namely as "mystery and destruction." After calling for a glass lyre (which would be impossible to play anyway) she smashes it to bits on the floor and declares: "I love like God loves. Isn't God's love the highest exclusivity, the most total destruction, the most inaccessible mystery? [...] God loves eternally because He possesses eternally; He possesses eternally because He destroys eternally." She displays a god-like desire for power, yet recognizes no actual God or god, thus again confirming her identity as a contemporary and not a classical, historical figure. Later, she declares: "How I love the stars [...] they tell me that I am young, that I am the mistress of my fate, that no other laws weigh upon me, only the laws of my own will and of time." But this is later, when she is already draining Benjamin of his strength, emotional and moral. He describes how, once he had surrendered to his love for her, she seems to take over and direct his life. With time, this destroys his own desire to live: he once loved flowers, but as soon as he brings her flowers and she enjoys them, he somehow no longer loves them; it is the same with the stars—she, as it were, takes over his enthralment with the stars, leaving him no longer enthralled. And here, we encounter another important aspect of Aspasia's personality: her life-sucking vampirism.

Several critics, including Alicja Gollnikowa (1995) and Barbara Zwolińska (2002), have noted Aspasia's vampiric qualities. Indeed, the imagery associated with her in Benjamin's first description has such connotations: her soulless "stony" eyes, "corpse-like" pallor, sensual lips full of blood, pearly white teeth. The strongest indication of Aspasia's vampiric personality, however, is the folk tale about the princess and the fisherman, which occurs in Benjamin's narrative as part of the fifth chapter. Its positioning at this stage in his retelling of his own story is important, of course. It occurs immediately after his description of Aspasia rescuing him from the river, at the very moment when he makes his choice to surrender to his love, even though he still has severe doubts about who she is and whether she embodies good or evil (it is in this moment too, that he poses the *Lélia* question: Who are you? And to which she answers only with riddles and further questions). The folk tale, one that his sister Terenia related to him as a child, is therefore an expression of Benjamin's fears—but also his way of illustrating to the group of friends in the frame, what happened to him, what he allowed Aspasia to do to him. Maria Woźniakiewicz-Dziadosz (1978), who takes a structuralist approach to the novel, sees the tale as the structural centre of the work, a parable around which the rest is constructed: the folk tale within Benjamin's story, within the frame. While the tale does not occur in the centre of the novel in terms of number of pages, but rather towards the end, this structure nevertheless supports Woźniakiewicz-Dziadosz's interpretation, if we choose to regard the novel as a parable about selfish erotic love versus selfless patriotism, where apostasy is duly punished. Although I am not persuaded by this particular interpretation, the structure of the novel understood in this way does support another hypothesis: quite independently of the Polish national issue, irrespective of any judgement on the narrator's part either way of the morality of Benjamin's behaviour, this structure (with the vampiric story of the princess and the fisherman at the centre) does suggest that the crucial point is to illustrate what can happen psychologically, psychically, morally, to individuals when emotions and sexual feelings are misplaced—not only Benjamin, but Żmichowska herself, invested too much in someone who did not share her high standards of "love."

The frame "symposium," or debate about love, remains however unresolved and inconclusive as a commentary on the central story—although, given all the evidence discussed above, it would seem to tend towards an *agape* with a strong social, humanitarian emphasis, but an *agape* that is not an opposition to *eros*. On the contrary, as an ideology of anti-suffering, anti-martyrdom, it appears to argue for happy, fulfilled relationships between individuals, suggesting even that such relationships are a precondition for positive social engagement and activism. But here I am straying into the dangerous waters of my own interpretation, and it would be against the dialogic or polyphonic spirit of Żmichowska's text to try to impose one way of understanding it.

For this translation I have used the second, revised version of Tadeusz Boy-Żeleński's edition (1950) but I have also taken into consideration the occasional adjustments made by Grażyna Borkowska in her new Polish edition, as yet unpublished. I have preserved Polish names throughout, except in the case of Benjamin himself, believing that the biblical and other references (e.g. the reference to Benjamin Franklin) might otherwise be lost to English-speaking readers. However, in order to preserve the special connotations of the form "Beniaminek," which has a wider application than merely the diminutive or affectionate form of the name "Beniamin," signifying the spoiled baby of a family who never quite grows up, I have used "Beniaminek" in places where it appears in the original Polish text. As to other diminutive or affectionate forms, several of which occur in relation to each of the names of Benjamin's brothers and sisters, I have chosen one form to accompany each adult form of name, hence: Teresa alternates with the diminutive form Terenia, Bronisława with Bronisia, Adam with Adaś. In some cases, I have preferred only the affectionate form, as this is the most frequently used, e.g. Julcia, Ludwinka; in others, for the same reason, I have preferred the standard form: Karol, Józef, Cyprian. In the frame scene, only one such alternative use appears: Emilka, as the affectionate form of Emilia. I have re-titled this first part of the novel as "By the Fireside" (in preference to the original "Introductory Scene"). While this may be controversial, it is justified by Żmichowska's own use of the phrase in titles of other works evoking similar fireside discussions.

Bibliography

Baranowski, Ignacy. 1923. *Pamiętniki*. Poznań: Poznańskie Towarzystwo Przyjaciół Nauk.

Borkowska, Grażyna. 2001. *Alienated Women: A Study on Polish Women's Fiction 1845–1918,* translated by Ursula Phillips. Budapest: Central European University Press.

————. 2010. "Conversation as Female Experience: The Case of Narcyza Żmichowska." In *Mapping Experience in Polish and Russian Women's Writing,* edited by Marja Rytkönen [et al.], 32–49. Newcastle upon Tyne: Cambridge Scholars Publishing.

Chmielowski, Piotr. 1885. *Autorki polskie wieku XIX. Studium literacko-obyczajowe. Seria I.* Warsaw: Wydawnictwo Spółki Nakładowej Warszawskiej.

————. 1893. "Żmichowska i Ziemięcka." *Ateneum* 4: 132–144.

Craciun, Adriana. 2003. *Fatal Women of Romanticism.* Cambridge: Cambridge University Press.

Faderman, Lillian. 1998. *Surpassing the Love of Men: Love Between Women from the Renaissance to the Present.* 2d ed. New York: Harper Collins.

Filipiak, Izabela. 2006. *Obszary odmienności. Rzecz o Marii Komornickiej.* Gdańsk: słowo/obraz terytoria.

Filipowicz, Halina. 2005. "The Wound of History: Gender Studies and Polish Particularism." In *Poles Apart: Women in Modern Polish Culture,* edited by Helena Goscilo and Beth Holmgren. *Indiana Slavic Studies* 15: 139–157.

Fuller, Margaret. 1994. *Woman in the Nineteenth Century and Other Writings,* edited by Donna Dickenson. Oxford: Oxford University Press.

Gollnikowa, Alicja. 1995. "Czy powinniśmy sie bać *Poganki?*" *Zeszyty naukowe Wyższej Szkoły Pedagogicznej w Bydgoszczy. Studia Filologiczne* 38. *Filologia polska* 16: 77–99.

Ilnicka, Maria. 1877. "Narcyza Żmichowska." *Bluszcz* 4–6, 11–12, 15–16.

Jakóbcówna, Milica, and Aleksandra Zamorska. 1963. *Próba nowego odczytania 'Poganki' N. Żmichowskiej.* Acta Universitatis Wratislaviensis 13. Prace literackie 5. Wrocław: Wydawnictwo Uniwersytetu Wrocławskiego.

Krzywicka, Irena. 2008. "Rozmowa kobiet o Narcyzie Żmichowskiej." In *Kontrola współczesności. Wybór międzywojennej publicystyki społecznej i literackiej z lat 1924–1939*, compiled and introduced by Agata Zawiszewska, 174–179. Warsaw: Wydawnictwo Feminoteki.

Kurkowska, Mirella. 1994. " Narcyza Żmichowska w środowisku warszawskim lat czterdziestych XIX." In *Kobieta i świat polityki. Polska na tle porównawczym w XIX i w początkach XX wieku*, edited by Anna Żarnowska and Andrzej Szwarc, 235–244. Warsaw: Instytut Historyczny Uniwersytetu Warszawskiego, "DiG."

Łuszczewska, Jadwiga [pseud. Deotyma]. 1968. *Pamiętnik 1834–1897*, edited and introduced by Juliusz W. Gomulicki. Warsaw: Czytelnik.

Mann, Maurycy. 1916. *Poganka Narcyzy Żmichowskiej. Geneza, źródła, artyzm i idea utworu*. Warsaw: Towarzystwo Naukowe Warszawskie.

Marcus, Sharon. 2007. *Between Women: Friendship, Desire and Marriage in Victorian England*. Princeton and Oxford: Princeton University Press.

Minkowska, Anna. 1923. *Organizacja spiskowa 1848 roku w Królestwie Polskim*. Rozprawy Historyczne Towarzystwa Naukowego Warszawskiego 3(1).Warsaw: Towarzystwo Naukowe Warszawskie.

Moraczewska, Bibianna. 1911. *Dziennik Bibianny Moraczewskiej*. Wydany z oryginału przez wnuczkę dr. Dobrzyńską-Rybicką. Poznań: Fr. Chocieszyński. [Supplemented by] Jadwiga Rudnicka. 1961. "Z papierów Bibianny Moraczewskiej." *Pamiętnik Literacki* 52(2): 187–197.

Morzkowska-Tyszkowa, Wanda. 1934. "Żmichowska wobec romantyzmu francuskiego." Lwów: Ossolineum.

Olszaniecka, Maria. 1951. "O 'Pogance' Narcyzy Żmichowskiej." *Pamiętnik Literacki* 42(1): 77–101.

Owczarz, Ewa. 1993. *Między retoryką a dowolnością. Wśród romantycznych struktur powieściowych w okresie międzypowstaniowym*. Toruń: Uniwersytet Mikołaja Kopernika.

Phillips, Ursula. 2005. *"Femme Fatale* and Mother-Martyr: Femininity and Patriotism in Żmichowka's *The Heathen.*" In *Gender and Sexuality in Ethical Context: Ten Essays on Polish Prose*, edited by Knut Andreas Grimstad and Ursula Phillips, 19–51. Bergen: Department of Russian Studies, University of Bergen.

———. 2008a. "Authorship and Masquerade in Narcyza Żmichowska's *White Rose* Texts." In *Masquerade and Femininity: Essays on Russian and Polish Women Writers*, edited by Urszula Chowaniec, Ursula Phillips and Marja Rytkönen, 72–92. Newcastle upon Tyne: Cambridge Scholars Publishing.

———. 2008b. *Narcyza Żmichowska. Feminizm i religia*. Przełożyła Katarzyna Bojarska. Warsaw: Instytut Badań Literackich Polskiej Akademii Nauk; Fundacja Akademia Humanistyczna.

Pigoń, Stanisław. 1935. "Towianizm Narcyzy Żmichowskiej." *Ruch Literacki* 9–10: 233–240.

Praz, Mario. 1970. *The Romantic Agony,* translated by Angus Davidson. 2d ed. Oxford: Oxford University Press.

Romankówna, Mieczysława. 1955. "Zagadka 'Poganki.'" *Życie literackie* 36: 9.

———. 1957. "Sprawa Entuzjastek." *Pamiętnik Literacki* 48(2): 516–537.

Różewicz, Tadeusz. 1977. "Miłość lesbijska w romantycznym przebraniu." In *Przygotowanie do wieczoru autorskiego,* 128–129. 2d ed. Warsaw: Państwowy Instytut Wydawniczy.

Sinko, Tadeusz. 1933. "Dookoła 'Poganki' Żmichowskiej." *Przegląd współczesny* 132–133: 80–90, 233–239.

Skimborowicz, Hipolit [pseud. Sfinks].1880."Gabryella i Entuzjastki." *Bluszcz* 10–16, 18–19. 21, 27, 30.

Śliwińska, Wiktoria. 1994. "Kobiety w konspiracjach patriotycznych lat czterdziestych XIX wieku (Ewa Felińska, Eleonora Wolańska i inne)." In *Kobieta i świat polityki. Polska na tle porównawczym w XIX i w początkach XX wieku,* edited by Anna Żarnowska and Andrzej Szwarc, 45–57. Warsaw: Instytut Historyczny Uniwersytetu Warszawskiego, "DiG."

Smith, Sidonie, and Julia Walker, eds. 1998. *Women, Autobiography, Theory: A Reader.* Madison: University of Wisconsin Press.

Stępień, Marian. 1968. *Narcyza Żmichowska.* Warsaw: Państwowy Instytut Wydawniczy.

Walczewska, Sławomira. 1999. *Damy, ryczerzy, feministki. Kobiecy dyskurs emancypacyjny w Polsce.* Kraków: eFKa.

Walewska, Cecylia. 1919. *Narcyza Żmichowska (Gabryella), poetka uczuć rodzinnych—wychowawczyni narodu.* Warsaw: Księgarnia Polska.

Walicki, Andrzej. 1982. *Philosophy and Romantic Nationalism: The Case of Poland.* Oxford: Clarendon Press.

Wasilewski, Zygmunt. 1935. *Aspazja i Alcybiades.* Warsaw: [s.n.]

Welsh, David. 1973. "Ayesha, Aspasia and Isabella." In *American Contributions to the Seventh International Congress of Slavists, Warsaw, August 21–27, 1973.* Volume 2: Literature and Folklore, edited by Victor Terras, 559–565. The Hague: Mouton.

Winklowa, Barbara. 2004. *Narcyza Żmichowska i Wanda Grabowska.* Kraków: Wydawnictwo Literackie.

Woźniakiewicz-Dziadosz, Maria. 1978. *Między buntem i rezygnacją. O powieściach Narcyzy Żmichowskiej.* Warsaw: Państwowy Instytut Wydawniczy.

———. 1997. "'Pisma Gabrielli'—romantyczna formuła dyskursu powieściowego." *Pamiętnik Literacki* 88(4): 37–52.

Wyporska, Wanda. 2002. "Early Modern Exclusion—The Branding of the Witch in Polish Demonological Literature 1511–1775." In *Studies in Language, Literature, and Cultural Mythology in Poland: Investigating "The Other,"* edited by Elwira M. Grossman, 153–165. Lewiston [et al.]: Edwin Mellor Press.

Zwolińska, Barbara. 2002. *Wampiryzm w literaturze romantycznej i postromantycznej na przykładzie* Opowieści niesamowitych *E.A. Poego,*

Poganki *N. Żmichowskiej oraz powieści Stefana Grabińskiego*. Gdańsk: Wydawnictwo Uniwersytetu Gdańskiego.

———. 2007. *O kwestiach kobiecych w korespondencji Narcyzy Żmichowskiej*. Gdańsk: Wydawnictwo Uniwersytetu Gdańskiego.

———. 2010. *Podróże Narcyzy Żmichowskiej*. Gdańsk: Wydawnictwo Uniwersytetu Gdańskiego.

———. 2010. *W poszukiwaniach tożsamości. O bohaterkach powieści Narcyzy Żmichowskiej*. Gdańsk: Wydawnictwo Uniwersytetu Gdańskiego.

Żmichowska, Narcyza. 1846. *Poganka. Przegląd Naukowy* 18–19, 23–24, 26, 32, 36.

———. 1861. *Pisma Gabryelli*. 4 vols. Warsaw: J. Jaworski.

———. 1876. "Słowo przedwstępne do dzieł dydaktycznych pani Hofmanowej." In *Dzieła Klementyny z Tańskich Hofmanowej*, edited by Narcyza Żmichowska, 12 vols, 8: 207–297. Warsaw: Spółka Wydawnicza Księgarzy.

———. 1885–1886. *Pisma Narcyzy Żmichowskiej (Gabryelli)*, edited by Piotr Chmielowski. 5 vols. Warsaw: M. Glücksberg.

———. 1929. *Biała Róża*, edited by Tadeusz Boy-Żeleński. Warsaw: Dom Książki Polskiej.

———. 1929. *Czy to powieść?* edited by Tadeusz Boy-Żeleński. Warsaw: Dom Książki Polskiej.

———. 1950. *Poganka*, edited by Tadeusz Boy-Żeleński. 2d ed. Wrocław: Ossolineum.

———. 1957–1967. *Listy*, edited by Stanisław Pigoń and Mieczysława Romankówna. 3 vols. Wrocław: Ossolineum.

———. 2007. *Narcyssa i Wanda. [Listy N. Żmichowskiej do Wandy Grabowskiej (Żeleńskiej)]*, edited by Barbara Winklowa and Helena Żytkowicz. *Listy* 5. Warsaw: Instytut Badań Literackich Polskiej Akademia Nauk; Fundacja Akademia Humanistyczna. [Contains Tadeusz Boy-Żeleński's introduction to the 1930 edition].

———. 2009. *Rozmowy z Julią*, edited by Barbara Winklowa. *Listy* 4. Warsaw: Instytut Badań Literackich Polskiej Akademia Nauk; Fundacja Akademia Humanistyczna.

Żmichowska, Narcyza, and Julia Baranowska. 2006. *Ścieżki przez życia. Wspomnienia*, edited by Mieczysława Romankówna. 2d ed. Wrocław: Ossolineum.

The HEATHEN

By the Fireside

HOW BEAUTIFUL THAT FIRESIDE in Emilka's house where we, our company of good friends, used to gather years ago almost every day, throughout the long autumn and winter evenings. Low-set, inlaid with black marble, it had a small bronze fender to prevent the burning wood from slipping out, and two iron stands where the logs were stacked—alder logs, so brittle they scarcely left any char or ash, so clean, bright, flaming red that even though sadness weighed on the heart, trouble on the conscience, our thoughts would shine in their blazing light and point the way to salvation. Now you have to imagine that precious hearth set in a spacious high-ceilinged room, that immaculate fire illuminating four spotless white walls, two gothic windows with shutters closed on the garden side, snow-white folds of muslin curtains, gilded frames of landscape paintings, furniture upholstered in crimson damask, a grand piano lurking in the shadow—and from eight o'clock, a little to one side, a small table laid with a tea-service, glasses, dainty cups and a gleaming samovar hissing or growling when the water boiled inside, depending on how much coal was added. The gloomier the weather outside, the more we relished the fire in the hearth and the tranquillity of the room, the music of the samovar—Ah! for how well we all got on in those days! How sincerely we loved, trustingly respected, entertained such high hopes of one another!... And today? Fate has scattered us across the wide earth. Indifference, forgetting, a bitter grudge or bitter regret haunts one or another of us. If someone were to kindle again the welcoming fire, were we all to gather round it once more—would the injury then be forgotten? Would longing be thrust from every heart? Would hands be drawn together in friendship, brows transfigured by cheerful thoughts? No, my advice is never attempt to relive your past. May he who loved once not encounter again those whom he loved! May she who laid in earth her nearest and dearest, not look today for their resurrection! Those who lost loved ones, may they never recover them, for it is terrible to observe after two, three, ten years how different they have become from what they were, how different we are ourselves. To be disappointed by them or by ourselves, to have our memories dashed or hear in their presence a clock strike the sad hour of infirmity!... May God spare us this—all those who sat then by the fireside and conversed so happily, freely, amicably. And there was quite a crowd of us, and sometimes someone from our wider circle of acquaintances also came to greet us. My memory has preserved each one of them and preserved them just as I knew them in those bygone days; not how they are now, nor how I think they should be. First Emilka, our hostess, widow of a husband who had poisoned the days of her first youth[1]: was she angel or saint? I hesitate in my choice of words for there is a great difference between an angel and a saint, though in Emilka there was much likeness to both. An angel, a messenger, is a pure calm spirit who drives straight towards the good in line with God's bidding. But a saint is a daughter of this earth who, in toil and in pain, through struggle and triumph, earns her place in heaven.

And so Emilka's thoughts were the thoughts of an angel, her heart the heart of a saint—like an angel calm and assured, she never had doubts; no impulse, no need of body or mind stood between herself and the truths of the Christian religion. But the battle unwaged in her mind shifted to her heart and her heart suffered terribly.

The crimes of those close to her, the imperfections of those whom she loved, the disasters that befell her brothers and sisters, were like the intense suffering of an open wound. Emilia's lips uttered no resentment, complaint, condemnation; her soul knew instead the horror of futile effort, the trials of exhaustion. She survived it all, however, always clement as the sun that shines alike on the evil and the good, patient as the craftsman who begins his same work afresh day after day, yet always easily deceived—like a child who has not yet learned to lie; for she was angel and saint—two beings who came together to create the kind of woman who will be able to live safely, blessedly, happily, only in three hundred years time—at the very earliest, reckoning by the most flattering accounts of the human race. Young minds and trusting hearts, be on your guard! Emilka will clothe the whole world for you in her own dresses, go with you in search of fine images too far-fetched to be true, pamper you in exchange for any well-meant promise, never scold, never spurn you, though you may deserve it a hundred times over, though it may be the most necessary thing for your health! Am I not right? But then the life of an angel flows on in such a bright stream of light that entirely "black devils" never cross its path. And that is no doubt why Emilka is so very rigid in her own convictions, since she has not yet had to forgive any black devils, while other shades of ash-grey, livid blue or mucky brown never detract from her whiteness and are even enriched by it. Emilka never doubts anyone. I used to laugh at her sometimes, saying that if it depended on her, even Judas would be forgiven one day, and I must confess she never gave me an honest reply to that joke.

Beside Emilka I liked to place Felicja,[2] as someone totally different. For me Felicja was the ideal of the present moment. Felicja possessed the necessary strength to face the moral challenges of the age, a passionate desire for every kind of good, violent hatred of evil, opinions based on reason not mercy, a greater love for her own thought than for people, and yet she extended a brotherly hand to those who were of like mind, ready to lay down her life for them. Whereas Emilia never knew human failings and imperfections, Felicja never understood them. Emilia would excuse her neighbour's sin as misfortune or misplaced virtue; Felicja as a total fall. For Felicja there was no sacrament of atonement, no exonerating tears; if she did not scornfully rebuke, then she passed by unmoved, wrapping her skirts tight around her to prevent them brushing against the filthy excrement. When I chided her for such a ruthless sense of justice, she explained it as lack of time. According to Felicja it was easier to raise the new than restore the ruined; destruction was the most logical consequence of all forms of imprecision, and she surrendered to it without regret for her severed relationships, for the forgotten names of companions left standing along the way. Felicja never wished to be late, even if rewarded for it with unforgettable artistic impressions! Her activity was astounding—from the simplest almsgiving to the noblest work for the enlightenment of her fellow creatures, from housework to philosophy, needlework to poetry, gossip to serious study. She found days enough for everything, and everything was done well, beautifully, nobly, courageously. True, the Lord God had made the path easy for her, had surrounded her since childhood with a decent family, given her a loving mother, educated brothers, an independent position in the world, high intellectual ability and an upright nature.

Caressed and cosseted, intelligent, pretty, white as a lily, bright as a little star, she soared so effortlessly to the heights of human achievement, secured her personality so comfortably in its lack of egoism and joy in obligation, that she was unable to find a scale against which to measure the transgressions of her neighbours. Her whole life was pure and moved from lesser to ever greater beauty, developing like a musical composition according to the rules of rhythm and harmony, unfolding in ever bolder, richer, more graceful cadences. Felicja never had cause to doubt herself even for a moment. With her penetrating eye directed constantly into the depths of her own soul, she saw such sanctity, such truth in its secret recesses that, for her, truth and personal feelings became merged into one so that in the end, like every being destined for higher things, she began to believe in herself. And she did not lack for fellow believers, I myself was one of their number. Felicja, full of charm and fascination, brave, witty, surrounded by the friendship of devoted hearts—by the envy of the petty-minded but the respect of people in general—was for me the type of woman most able to make a reality of women's dreams of independence. She alone could stand so firm that pain never toppled her, so high that ridicule never reached her, and so beautifully and securely that others wanted to stand together with her. All those virtues that could develop freely only in normal conditions of human existence were the virtues of Felicja; for indeed, she lacked the abnormal virtues, the trifling virtues of suffering. But what use are those nowadays: the virtues of suffering—humility, contrition, pity that knows no bounds, resignation that is never exhausted? Fine for ascetics, hermits of

Thebaid, martyrs of the Coliseum. But what we need now are the virtues of strength, the virtues of triumph; we need absolutely the virtue of happiness, so that others will believe in us and become virtuous like us. Oh! For this is mainly about the others. Nowadays it seems God no longer admits individual souls into His kingdom. The selfish salvation of fasting and mortification, sustained prayers and confined lives, is not the salvation of the present hour. Suffer! But so your brothers may live more happily in this world. Pray! But so your enemies may be more enlightened in spirit. For one day God will count the sufferings and accept your prayers. And if he doesn't, so be it.

My conviction in this respect was so strong that I preferred all the faults of Seweryna[3]—faults that had taken root in her soul as a result of the long train of unhappy experiences that had befallen her—to those thousands of passive virtues that enrich an individual personality yet never radiate through to the exterior. Her faults, at least when taken alongside her most noble character and fine inclinations, seemed to cry out demanding the right to happiness, the right to that thing which makes it easier for the kind to be kind, and the willing to be active.

Seweryna's youth was spent among wicked and careless people; she witnessed with her own eyes the sordidness of the "noble" way of life, the meanness of fashionable salons. Nourished on sneering and hatred, she digested sneering and hatred and regurgitated them as outrage, oversensitivity, mistrust and contempt. Her countenance was severe, her tone harsh and cutting—but her heart? Never was there a more sincere, more intensely loving heart amongst all God's chosen. Ready at any moment to forget herself, at any moment to work for others without hope of return, for even when they loved her, Seweryna did not trust them, even when they extended a hand in friendship, Seweryna—isolated in the agony of her suspicion— did not grasp it. For Felicja the performance of any obligation was always the greatest joy; for Seweryna—distrustful of herself and others—it was a real torment. She never shrank however from the demands of her conscience; when she recognized something as necessary or just, she carried out her duty with determination, but through bearing her own agony and the slander of others. Felicja

perhaps did more good; Seweryna never failed to make a greater
personal sacrifice even in doing wrong. Were I free to imagine
some form of human rebirth for these two women in keeping
with their present work, then in future Felicja would be an artist,
Seweryna a priest. Felicja would reveal to people the beauty of
moral excellence. Seweryna would bring them comfort. The
bounds of our earthly life as yet know no way of accommodating
the misfortunes of Seweryna. Fruitless misfortunes that have made
her less good, and wicked people around her a little worse. But I
see that I am rather too careless with such words as "happiness"
and "unhappiness," "joy" and "suffering," and that some readers
might suppose that what I call "happiness" and "joy" are merely
life's great pleasures and what I call "misfortune" and "suffering"
no more than some unpleasantness. And thus that personal wealth,
home comforts, little luxuries, a big win on the lottery, a lucky
hand of cards, a horse, country residence, fashionable dress,
pretty ribbon, gold crucifix, when taken together might constitute
happiness; while conversely, poverty, the daily grind, last year's
hat, shabby clothes, a lost pair of gloves, a tight bodice, a cramped
rented room, would constitute unhappiness. Oh, my God! Let us
at least agree on the meaning of such expressions, or if we cannot
agree, then for the duration of your reading of this book you will
have to accept my definition. Happiness and unhappiness do not
depend on any external circumstances. Happiness is not even being
loved by the person we love most, unhappiness not even the death
of our dearest friends—by happiness I simply mean anything which
has a salutary effect, which cultivates and ennobles our spirit; and
by unhappiness I mean those things which degrade, humiliate and
oppress us.

So it is that there are different kinds of happiness and different
kinds of unhappiness. And so it is that I have more often seen
unhappiness in the midst of pleasure, just as I have seen it amid
much unpleasantness. Which brings the greater benefit is hard to
judge: and therein lies the whole mystery of the human personality.
I called Felicja happy because she grew up surrounded by goodness,
and the good Seweryna unhappy because the whole of her goodness
could not unfold amidst evil, and sometimes even took on the

appearance of evil. Tekla,[4] however, I never called unhappy though her life-story was sadder by far.

Tekla had withstood heavy losses but her pain did not poison her relations with people; true, it was fate that made her suffer rather than people. Always calm and serious, it was if the vicissitudes of her own experience made it easier for her to be kind to everyone. What had she to be angry or fret about when those who had been the objects of her earthly egoism—and whom she might have cherished with all the weakness of her womanly sensitivity, fussing over minor troubles—had lain in their graves for many years? Orphan and childless widow, she remained coiled up within herself like a tiny ball, a half-opened leaf, rather too religious, rather too noble: coiled up within herself, not *for* herself. On the contrary, her seductive courtesy, full of quiet dignity, embraced all hearts and—what might seem even stranger—especially those hearts beating more passionately and violently in younger breasts. For I should also say, that of all the women I knew then Tekla alone knew how to be genuinely indulgent. Emilka's clemency was more a kind of eternal justification. When I had done wrong myself and did not want my wrongdoing to appear so absolutely black to my own conscience, I would simply go to Emilka and accuse myself before her; and she would immediately prove to me how I had desired to act for the best, how I could still change things, how I was always honest, until I believed her word for word. And it even transpired that I felt stronger in my renewal and self-improvement than if I had confessed before a priest in a spirit of humble penitence. But Tekla was another matter. Tekla had an unswerving opinion and a clear, unflinching idea of what was good and evil, and yet it was always compatible with cold common sense. Tekla judged every event according to society's official prescriptions, every motive according to a strict code of morality, yet the greatest debtors had access to her and she never turned her back on those who had strayed. For me she represented a kind of principle of unsavoury reality manifested through the mercy of a Christian heart and bolstered by the example of Christian deeds. Very often we quarrelled abominably. Her ideas were locked in certain set patterns which were so opposed to my own disposition that I was

unable in the course of a conversation to agree with two words
of what she said. But whenever I felt the symptoms of aimless
daydreaming coming over me or my thoughts fleeing into the land
of fantasy, whenever I needed fortitude, discipline, reconciliation
with the world or cold water thrown over my head, I would stand
before her and say: "Scold me, Tekla." And once Tekla had scolded
me, I picked no further quarrel with her.

Alongside these four women with fixed and well-defined
characters, imagine three others who lived not as the Lord had
created them. Jadwiga was not a poet. Augusta was not an artist.
Anna was not a mother. I am convinced that before they entered
the world their pre-baptismal names in heaven were: poet, artist,
mother. But those names could not be realized on earth since
Jadwiga lacked talent, Augusta diligence and Anna a child.

Jadwiga[5] even threw herself into a walk of life quite contrary
to poetry: the pantry and the loom described the innermost circle
of her life. She said herself she was a practical woman, and so
she was—almost. The internal history of Jadwiga's soul unfolded
meanwhile in disjointed bursts of wild longing, ecstatic joy, utter
despondency and adoring worship. The contradiction between
the contours of her inner world and the backdrop of her daily life
produced a curious blend: something akin to the sultry clouds of an
Italian sky, beneath which an artist might depict the northern snows
and an orange-tree in bloom; a Samogitian in his sheepskin and
Neapolitan women kneeling by a wayside shrine. To all outward
appearances Jadwiga's life flowed on quietly, monotonously,
absorbed in household chores; only someone who examined it at
close quarters saw the full extent of its tragic drama—though it
never took the form of events—or heard its lyric poetry, though
its words were never uttered. Jadwiga possessed strings stretching
from heart to brain for every beautiful thing and every impression;
and these strings would resound with wondrous shades of emotion
and imagination at the slightest touch, but resounded for her alone,
locked in deep recluse. Sometimes a woman's beauty would absorb
her as keenly as a spell-bound lover; for hours on end Jadwiga
would imbibe the pleasant tones of her voice, gaze into her black
or blue eyes, tidy the twists of her fair or dark braids. One winter

season she was madly fond of dancing. Then it was flowers, then music. Her fancies matched the passions of other women in strength and changeability, except Jadwiga gained ever new powers and ideas from these fancies, whereas passion drained other women of life and truth. In those whom she loved, Jadwiga always loved best the first moment of her own attraction to them, her own sympathy, but at the same time—so as to justify her own notions—she had to create perfection in them. Yet she was separated from many by insurmountable disgust. She had no feeling for mediocrity. In the world of her own day she encountered terrible disappointments, yet she could solve riddles of the past with such speed and accuracy, it was as if the history of distant ages was contained in her own memory; while zeal and self-sacrifice bound her so closely to the future that her hopes appeared at times as the gift of prophecy. Restless, inspired, oscillating between enthusiasm and weariness, weariness and doubt, then restored to life by a single moment of ecstasy, a single ray of beauty, always running—through haste and through exhaustion—towards the very pinnacle of goodness, in happiness and despair always bearing the unseen, mysterious God of her ideal in her breast: was not Jadwiga a real poet? Oh, I can assure you that she was! But not everyone guessed it for she was a woman of few words and stony exterior. Only occasionally, very occasionally, did her soul flash through her eyes in a glance of fire.

Augusta[6] was manifestly everything that Jadwiga could be only in secret, in the hidden substance of her life. God had endowed Augusta with such a huge share of talent and eccentricity and clothed her in grace so beguiling that we all spoiled her a little. Jadwiga especially, venerator of every form of beauty, set Augusta as a gem in her heart—a diamond purer than the most crystal-clear water. It was hard to imagine a more attractive creature—her every movement a wood-carver's living model, every twist of her slender figure the envy of oriental *bayadères*. And how she sang! A veritable nightingale such as was harkened to on the banks of the Pilica,[7] though the nightingale rarely made itself heard—we'd be jostled instead by the wing of a young eagle and scratched by its claws. Her sarcasm was always ready to pounce, sarcasm followed by endearment—disagreeable perhaps, but it never made us angry. Augusta's volatile temper, equally vehement in its every permutation, led me to suppose some foreign ancestry. According to her parents she was a genuine Pole, a noblewoman even—I believe—from Great Poland,[8] but her spirit was surely conceived in some French or Italian mind. Anyone who had not met her could never have imagined how such diverse elements could be so mingled in the creation of one woman. The extraordinary delicacy with which her senses grasped the play of the sun's rays, evaluated sounds, savoured to the full every work of nature or work of art. Childish moodiness, but masculine tenacity in getting anything she desired. Incredible elasticity—if I may put it like that—of mind and opinion, yet at the same time relentless drive to consume any object that might feed her impressions. Bohemian wantonness yet imperious demands, exuberant tenderness yet merciless curiosity, spectacular downfalls revealing the most commonplace weakness, yet moments of unexpected enthusiasm and purest exaltation of spirit. And apart from all that, there was her double gift—for painting with her brush and painting in words, in colour and in song: that was Augusta. She also painted her own life, painted it in ravishing images, love, friendship, devotion; but I suspected she painted those images only so she could enjoy looking at them. Respectable people, harsh and narrow people who lived strictly according to the letter of the law, accused her of grave faults. They said she was a licentious and frivolous woman, had a deceitful and mendacious heart; but what do they know, such people? They never ask themselves how much truth there might be in a single moment of ecstasy, how much virtue in a single mistake. It is not for me to justify and I am not going to explain, but I see things as they are, and I know that I loved Augusta sincerely, and I know she never lied to anyone because she never lied to herself, and complete untruth, grievous untruth, begins first and foremost with oneself. It was dangerous admittedly to believe her every word; yet whoever did believe had only themselves to blame: for did they ever consider the circumstances in which her words were spoken? For the value of her words changed with circumstances. Despite the uncertainty of the morrow, despite the passing whims of the present day, what especially attracted strong noble hearts to Augusta was

their intuition of her weakness, of her—if I may put it like this—
her woman's infirmity. In her arrogance, in all her transgressions,
in every command of this proud woman, it was not hard to discern
the would-be slave, submissive, stripped of her individuality.

For let us suppose that such a woman were to eventually fall in
love and that her love were to be returned: I guarantee that the man
of her choice would be one of extraordinary abilities before whom
she would fall on her knees, and in whom she would place more
faith than in herself or in the truths of religion. This man might beat
her, abuse her, keep her in eternal subjection, but woe betide him
if he becomes intoxicated with the siren's charms or sets his heart
on such an artist as the exclusive desire and only aim of his life.
The artist will gnaw her way into his heart. In her foreign, southern,
oriental feeling there was no balance or self-possession; with her,
it was always a perpetual battle for the crown or the shackles—if
there were no battle, there would be no feeling either.

Anna[9] was more beautiful than Augusta, a little older, yet a man
standing beside her, even a passionate young man, was far more
likely to forget he was beside a woman with whom he was free to
fall in love—in his dreams and desires, in holiness and sin. Though
it does not follow that some man or other did not lose his head
or offer up to her the burning prayers of his young heart, rather
that—insofar as his prayers went unanswered—he slowly began
to entertain another sort of relation and—insofar as he felt himself
worthy—became at least her bosom friend and kind-hearted
brother. In fact, I sometimes wondered myself, though in vain,
what man Anna could have loved with that ordinary, submissive,
very womanly love of hers? Her soul was always replete and
sufficient unto itself, her character stable and forceful without
any effort on her part, without her doing battle with others or
with herself. Her days were busy and active, occupied with useful
work. Her personality was so beautifully and perfectly developed
that love—according to her own conviction—had nothing more
to offer, since love—as is my conviction too—is given to human
beings only as an extra, an addendum to their existing feelings,
for the higher perfection of their powers and inclinations. If any
conclusive evidence could be found to support my opinion of

Anna, then it would be that special maternal feeling aroused in
her breast—although she had no child of her own, as I said. No
private passion had initiated her in the symptoms of this instinct,
just as no symptom was hidden from the marvellous omniscience
and intuition of her heart. All children interested her as whole-
heartedly, as sincerely as those good mothers who observe in their
own offspring a likeness or difference to themselves, or the hope
or horror of their future. But please don't imagine that her maternal
instinct only made itself felt in relation to those little creatures.
Anna was always a mother in every feeling: friendship, good
acquaintance, even toward her own parents. Anyone who entered
the circle of her life could not fail to experience her solicitude and
care: relatives, members of her household, neighbours, peasants
in the village where she lived, found her standing beside them
immediately and without fail in time of distress, trouble, sickness,
and when they saw her there beside them they at once grew more
patient, calm and well again, for Anna could deal with anything,
always knew where to find help or medicine. And yet this same
Anna, constantly preoccupied with others, might have thought only
of herself with far greater reason than a hundred other women, and
nobody would have been surprised by it and many would have
forgiven her. Our subject might have justified even a touch of self-
love. Her build was as willowy, as ethereal as a young poplar, her
features sharply delineated like in the finest sketches by Retzsch,[10]
the same who translated the poetry of Schiller and Goethe with his
pencil: eyes radiant like magic garnets, legs made to lie on Persian
carpets, hands to bear gold rings, bodily curves to flaunt soft satin...
And all this would be bustling around you, and so proficiently and
deftly you somehow got used to it and always missed the moment
to pass any quarrelsome remark, because it never really occurred to
you. True, Anna also could assume an imperious authority. Rarely
did anyone break loose from the grip of obedience. I never tried,
sometimes I even kissed her hand. Oh! I would kiss it with such
pleasure... for what a hand it was!

The silhouettes outlined here rather clumsily, in order to
acquaint my readers with the female half of our gathering, will
have to suffice. In the interests of accuracy, I ought to insert my

own portrait as well, but this unfortunate vanity of mine! ... And after the above portraits it's too burdensome a duty.

I would do better to say: skim through this book and you will get the broad drifts. I am a little of everything I have written in my book, though I am much more the things I have not written at all.

Of the male friends, who almost every evening made up our fireside company, I remember best: Albert the Philosopher, Henryk the Zealot, Leon the Methodist, Edmund the Mystic, Teofil the Kid and Benjamin, who had two nicknames: on festive days he was called Humboldt[11] and on ordinary days Baldie, because he had no hair.

Albert "The Philosopher,"[12] as his title indicated, loved wisdom. He loved it sincerely, honestly, but only the wisdom in books. He had not yet learned anything of life as it was lived, though he strove towards it with great energy. His mental abilities—extraordinarily sound in working out ideas and implications—stood out against his naive inability to perceive the real world and his constant struggle to make his every action comply with his every notion.

Erudition and practicality were both deeply rooted in Albert's soul yet were like two parallel lines, never able to come together at any point of mutual recognition. When we discussed history, Albert, like an expert historian, was able to assess different political factions, their deeds and principles, but it seemed to me that if he'd withdrawn some plan and implemented another himself, he would have bestowed upon it so many different angles, trimmings and conditions that he would never have finished it because of the unfinished nature of his own outlook—or at least the course of events would have been completely different from his original design. In our conversations with Albert about feelings, he would often recite aphorisms about love. He would quote a few given words, developing them logically and subtly adding his own shades of meaning so that it was a pleasure to listen to him: but could he have loved into advanced old age, and not known for sure whether love was what he said it was? Or perhaps he was unable to reciprocate love at all, yet was convinced in all conscience that he was genuinely, passionately, poetically, in love—because of such and such a circumstance of which he had some *a priori* notion, or such and such an affair which he might have equated with the effects of love, in accord with his principles of reasoned argumentation? Albert read and wrote far too much, a rare misfortune among us. His Germanic diligence channelled his powers in two separate directions, began to threaten them with exhaustion, like a young sapling is threatened with drying up if it wastes its luxuriant juices on nourishing the superfluous branches at its foot. It seems our climate is not conducive to erudition—an empress demanding exclusive loyalty and total subjection; our heads are too light sometimes from a surfeit of poetry, our hearts too heavy from a surfeit of feeling.

There are many who would make erudition the instrument of their desires and inventions. They deceive themselves, just as Albert was deceived. Between erudition and our native propensities there remains an imperceptible unspoken gulf, a struggle to which either intellect or youthful high-mindedness or the young person himself must fall victim. But this is only my own intuition. The one certainty in Albert's life was his unblemished morality, his upright character, so full of dignity he won the universal respect of his peers. He who was young, he who was poor and silent became for them a source of moral strength and authority.

Oh! This is because our youth—though spoiled, idle, untaught—possesses at least the instinct of always respecting people who are truly moral, especially when they write and read books. Literature has not yet lost its spell among us—she has become a deity that demands sacrifices from life, happiness, thought, but has not yet reduced herself to the level of a foster-mother hiring herself out merely for the sake of vanity, luxuries, gold.

Henryk the Zealot[13] acquired his nickname because he lived impetuously, greedily, violently, as though the final hour were destined to strike earliest for the one who was youngest among us.[14] An alchemist—out of mere curiosity or a wish to unnerve peaceful lovers of whist or tranquil fathers of families—might take three people with tempestuous and contradictory tendencies, plus another four who were sublimely virtuous and then mix them together, pound them with mortar and pestle, pour on water from the Vistula, boil them beside a volcano, strain them by moonlight, add a little sulphur and saltpetre, yet would produce but a tiny drop of the essence of such a man as Henryk. The amount that boy devoured of knowledge, feeling and adventure even before his coming of age would have supplied an elderly Frenchman with eight volumes of memoirs, each volume in octavo and no spaces between the lines. Despite his extraordinarily slight frame and sheltered upbringing, his iron constitution never collapsed from any excess of sweat and effort, egoism and dedication. Ah! I regret now having chosen that word: egoism. Henryk and egoism? Henryk, who so squandered health, fortune, happiness; who would never have hesitated to sacrifice his good name for the sake of friendship or a noble end, to call him an egoist! Nowadays, when any reader understands an egoist to be a person who gathers everything unto himself—especially money—and who gives nothing of himself—especially money—shame! What a hideous abuse of the word! Henryk was not an egoist. It was just that his personality was so clearly conspicuous in whatever he did, so interested in what he desired, so involved in the things to which he had dedicated himself, that he was ready to die for them. And it may even seem to some, myself included, that he did die for them, because it afforded him so much pleasure. The other thing he shared with egoists was the tenacity with which he pursued all his designs. Sometimes these were matters of no direct concern to himself and always ones from which he could gain no exclusive personal advantage. Whether it involved bringing about the marriage of two friends, procuring a suitable position for someone, carrying a book from one library to another—once he told himself the project would be good and useful, he immediately set about putting it into effect. And then he would become entirely indifferent to secondary issues. He would stamp on any obstacle he encountered with cruel indifference and approach his intended goal with perfect peace of mind and cheerfulness of face, even though he had pushed someone aside or strangled them along the way. It was terrifying to observe this child with the bright blue eyes, blind inexperience and burning thirst. It felt as though his soul had been catapulted into space by some powerful divine thrust and then forced to describe its fatal orbit without rest or deviation. Henryk never shrank from any means that facilitated his ends. He chose cunning Machiavellian stratagems with relish, though his nature

seemed more inclined to acts of violence. This was precisely the
most peculiar eccentricity of his eccentric and peculiar personality,
but perhaps it was also a remnant of student humour that saw only
wit in crafty ruses, only mischievous pranks in malicious trickery.
Be that as it may, Henryk rejoiced far more when he hoodwinked
an evil man than when he convinced a good one. His Sundays, his
days of recreation, were the days when he wrong-footed others,
days of mystification, subterfuge and deception; then he would leap
about like an excitable child, singing to himself, rubbing his hands
and smoothing his hair. The many different elements of his moral
being rushed to his aid at such moments.

A modern Alcibiades, he could impersonate any role with
astonishing precision, since every part he played drew on one
aspect or other of his real character. This dangerous talent cultivated
one hideous shortcoming. Henryk was a merciless liar, whether he
needed to be or not. When it came to a point of fact, matter of
detail, external circumstance—an insignificant triviality or subject
of utmost concern—he never told the truth. And yet he alone among
liars never aroused disgust—sooner hatred or a desire for revenge.
In the wake of lying usually come disgust and contempt, since
lying presupposes cowardice and dirty tricks. From the highest to
the lowest, a liar is someone who is afraid; a liar is a traitor who
seeks to gain from his treachery, but Henryk?

Henryk was as brave as a lion, as noble in his heart of hearts
as the hero of an epic poem. If he lied, then it was from an excess
of feverish thoughts, malignant infection or fantasies of the
imagination. And yet, at the same time, he possessed one feeling in
his life, one sacred thing, which—in the eyes of some very harsh
judges—would absolve him of sins a hundred times worse through
the intervention of sacramental grace: I can vouch for the support
of women at least when I state that Henryk loved his mother! Filial
love shone like the polar star of salvation above the tempest of his
reckless follies, passions and errors; guarded him from ruin; and by
its inspiration guided him towards virtue. You had to see him with
this mother to fully comprehend the background to his excesses,
the real background to so many entangled arabesques. Whenever
her pleasure was at stake, whole days of heavy drudgery were but

moments spent at the most delectable feast. Whenever she fell sick, whole nights without sleep could not weaken his solicitous care. For his mother, he would have renounced everything. Through his mother—even if the flame of religion were to be extinguished in his heart—through his mother he would have understood God. Oh! What a good thing it is that we shall never meet again, Henryk! You have remained in my mind so beautiful, so sanctified, so redeemed of all your sins and imperfections. Oh, what a good thing it is, Henryk! Perhaps if you'd lived you might have changed, loved yourself a little more or fallen in love with another woman; lost that youthful audacity of yours, despaired of people, begun to doubt your own strength—and then you might have walked more reluctantly along the path you once trod with conviction, and done out of vanity what you were accustomed to do only out of zeal! Perhaps you would have marred yourself in my eyes with your first success, poisoned yourself with your first taste of bitterness, tried to clumsily correct your first mistakes; but I liked you so much in the simplicity of your bad and good nature, in the richness of your light and the blackness of your shadows! Oh! What a good thing it is, Henryk, that we shall never meet again! May the sign of the Cross, the radiant song of the sun, shine on your memory and remain with you always…

Leon the Methodist[15] had a tender loving heart, an imagination uncommonly easy to engage, a mind singularly industrious and courageous; hence for everyone he became "the Methodist." In reality, these worthiest of qualities made him so fearful that—caterpillar-like—he spun a thick cocoon around himself of cold common sense, calculation and indifference. He spoke very little, never referred to himself, hid his more vivid impressions with grave-like secrecy, discharged the minor formalities of his daily life with constancy and precision—and guarded against enthusiasm, as if it were a crime. On the other hand, his every action was a perfect contradiction of outward appearances. He was the calculating one—yet he pinned all his hopes for the future on his own heart and efforts. He was the indifferent one—yet his powers of survival were derived from feeling alone, amid all the difficulties he encountered, straitened circumstances and the self-interest of the social caste that surrounded him. Whenever we women challenged him about the contradiction between his maxims and their content, he would solemnly prove that there was no such contradiction—that the words we threw back at him were but the words of poetry, whereas the mathematics of reality unfolded according to different laws. And was not mathematics the most ideal of all branches of knowledge? And did not poetry follow mathematical principles in its rhythm and harmony? What was to be done? His, it seems, was the fate of so many of our good people. A hundred times better than the world—yet as other, completely different beings, they are afraid of offending the world with their condemnation and prefer to adjust themselves to its demands. The world wants numbers? They write numbers. The world fears bright colours? They cast off the fair apparel of their youth. The world has a dictionary dating from time immemorial? They learn every expression in it and then think they are free to expound their own ideas with those half-baked phrases, able to fashion themselves comfortable garments out of that rotten material, of which every one of them gradually begins to feel the lack; they imagine that in the final reckoning the same sum will fall to them as to others. Poor dreamers! Oh! But don't be scared of your own inclinations! Don't believe—though you may hear it repeated everywhere—that love is a delusion, zeal mere feverish excitement, noble-mindedness an arithmetical error, beauty only an ideal. You know better, because you do love and believe! Your native enthusiasm is your one and only religious rule; do not resist this hallmark and anointing with the chrism. If it were not for enthusiasm—given how today's minds are crumbling into individual fantasies and philosophical systems—human beings would doubt even the teachings of the Gospels, happiness, everything. Arching above the great flood of our virtues and notions, enthusiasm is God's only rainbow, able to unite our scattered emotions into one radiant sign of light and beauty. Where are you now, Leon? Cast off the tight shell of unbecoming reason! Love, rejoice, weep, be entranced in harmony with the inspiration of the present moment! For I tell you—your instincts are pure and righteous: whatever you love will be good; whatever makes you rejoice will remain your strength in life and memory; and whatever makes you weep you'll clear all the quicker from your path. And whatever excites you and carries you away, you will fulfil more easily and attain more swiftly. Cliquish opinions, social prejudices can be no law to you, young athlete; your duty is precisely to fight against them. Don't push yourself forward among decrepit old men; don't adopt the language of men of experience; don't sow the soil of your future with such a miserly hand that you have to beg for concessions, grovel for a word of praise, tend every tiny seedling. It will do you no good, Leon. Respect the old men—for they too were once young—but live now in the springtime of your life so that one day you may be respected for it. Take the advice of those with experience but remember that experience is the collective wisdom of all our pasts—with the exception of the present moment; remember that experience has its judgments and its idea of everything that has already occurred, but it has no idea of what is going on inside you. And when you scatter the seed—cautious sower!—don't be afraid to cast whole handfuls of bold wishes before you, for scarcely the hundredth seed will take root if you take too few in your hand— and what will remain in the ground after the driving rains and icy gales? God be with you, Methodist! And may a lover's smile, the gold of hard-won earnings, the happiness of your dreams—also shine upon you. And may Satan and all his lesser devils begone from you! Away with duplicity and faintheartedness! Away with asceticism and cold calculation!"

Of Edmund, "the Mystic,"[16] our Emilka would always say:

"My God, how unjust people are! What do they want of this boy? He has drawn them so many lovely pictures, uttered so many lovely thoughts, and yet they insist on urging him to do more and upbraid him for his idleness and lack of practicality. Besides, they ought to be content with what someone brings them, especially when it is a good deal more than those who never bring anything, or even take away from society's shared coffers. But, as far as I can see, society has grown capricious. A person comes along with his heart in the right place and they ask: are you talented? A talented person comes along and they cry: is your heart in the right place? They just keep demanding and demanding."

"But my dear Emilka," I once said to her, "what is to be done when society absolutely needs people who have both heart and talent?" "If it absolutely needs them, then be in no doubt, Gabriella,"[17] she replied, "that God will send them. If, on the other hand, they are not absolutely necessary and only society considers them to be so, then society itself should strive to make it easier for them: embrace talent with love so as to awaken the heart; support a kind heart with general understanding, so it may gain the inspiration of true understanding. But always demanding, insisting, censoring teaches no one and improves no one."

I did not deny such valid observations. However, it did not surprise me at all that people clamoured for Edmund to perform great deeds. Indeed the man had a great talent for drawing and often brought us his distinctive, marvellously delineated sketches. He possessed the great gift of eloquence and often recited captivating things; yet behind these talents there stood a vain and empty man of fashion, a shaky, pliable reed. We gave him the name "Mystic" because that year he actually believed in ghosts, miracles and mesmerism. The previous winter he had been an ardent Hegelian; the coming spring he might turn into a solid man of reason. His mild sensitive nature always sought a balance with the elements surrounding it. This quality of assimilating, adapting his inner propensities and convictions from the outside in, was an entirely original eccentricity—even for him. He was often reproached for it, but I would stand up for him because I saw gain in it for ourselves—it was as though someone new visited us every few months and read us a completely new book, yet always written in an elegant style.

Teofil was referred to in our circle as "the Kid,"[18] not because of his age for he was older than the rest of us, but because of the unruly boorishness of his manners. He would slump across every table, sprawl on every settee, shout at the top of his voice whenever he spoke, loved cakes and sweets or amusing himself with a balloon or trapping a fly under a glass. And yet at the same time— as though atoning for all this—he was infatuated with the oldest, most extraordinary and most difficult of sciences: numismatics. He would have sat still on his chair for hours on end—bolt upright like a schoolgirl—in exchange for one tarnished little coin, or risked freedom and limb treading the most dangerous paths in search of some rare medal. He had such respect for the thoroughness of collecting, such artistic love for his subject, that he once relinquished a curious specimen of his own so that a richer collection might be complete. Teofil's claim to the world of scholarship and his ineptness in social life provided the most comical contradiction— he was like a living charade to which few could guess the solution. Some accused him of feigning, others of coarseness, yet at the same time he remained both a kid and a numismatist. Besides, his was the best and kindest of hearts. You could rob him of his overcoat or his watch, his time or his cheerfulness; you could exact from him sound advice, a good turn—or even a coin that was in current circulation, provided you did not give away an antiquarian one: all this he would grant you, he'd let you have anything you wanted, though he might pull a face depending on his mood. But despite his apparently inoffensive nature, Teofil had many enemies—as a child sometimes does and especially a child who is spoilt and likes to talk all the time. He always uttered whatever came into his head. And because he was a wit and a joker and met many different people, he was always thinking up caustic remarks about human stupidity, vanity, insincere politeness, amusing intrigues, which he formulated for his own entertainment but which often offended his listeners. Teofil, however, never harmed anyone—though other people harmed him terribly.

Benjamin was the last to join our circle of friends. His nicknames had no intellectual meaning and referred only to external circumstances. We called him "Humboldt" because he had been on long journeys to faraway places, and "Baldie" because he was already bald. He was first introduced to us by Teofil. They had made their acquaintance in the shop of an antiquarian dealer, discussing some numismatic curiosity; later, various incidents drew them ever closer until at last Teofil introduced him to our circle, recommending him as a man who could swiftly decipher the worn Greek inscriptions, or boldly defend the tarnished reputation of his friends. Both the one and the other were quite true; Teofil himself had experienced both the one and the other, and so a place

was immediately found for Benjamin by our beloved fireside. Our
evening conversations were soon enriched by facts about Spain,
Italy, Turkey, Persia, Egypt. Benjamin was a fine storyteller and—
for a traveller—displayed an unusual modesty. He almost never
brought himself onto the stage. He rarely reminded us that "I was
there, I saw it with my own eyes." When he described a place
or its customs, it was as if he first quoted fragments of works by
other authors: all trace of the individual observer had vanished,
while the images he presented unfolded one after the other with
daguerreotype precision. We could make out the shade of the
tiniest leaf, the smallest blade of grass, the play of the sun's rays,
the phantasmagoria of cloud formations—more even, for in those
images we could hear the mingling sounds of nature and the roar
of beasts of prey, the mysterious droning of midges over famous
waters, the warbling of a little bird among famous ruins, the song of
a young girl beside a forgotten grave—everything, but everything
except the echo of personal lived-through impressions. Benjamin
never embellished his tales with his own lyrics. Felicja was the first
to notice this, her opinion of the balding Humboldt being somewhat
harsh. She could not forgive him the fact that his personality never
made itself felt in his detailed objective accounts, even if only to
complement them—just as in real life he was unable to lift the
power of his spirit beyond the fulfilment of conventional duties and
inspire it towards more creative action. Felicja explained this lack
of initiative, of enterprise, of personal control over circumstances
and events—given Benjamin's undisputed high abilities—as
nothing more than a large dose of idleness. And in Felicja's book
idleness was the worst sin of the contemporary world. As far as I
was concerned, I admit I formed more flattering conclusions about
our new friend. I read in his handsome—though somewhat worn—
facial features the history of deep thought, violently repressed
emotions, strenuous undertakings carried out with determination.
I would have vouched even that his deathly composure was a
strength of his manly character, his apparent mediocrity a sign of
well-concealed superiority and his idleness—as Felicja called it—
nothing but a vehicle for the fulfilment of visions and purposes
that were as yet impenetrable to us. What did it all mean? You will

see. Benjamin began his series of tales—spun out throughout that whole winter and woven into the conversations of our shared life of trusty companionship—with his own biography.

I remember one occasion, it was in December—a hideous time to be outdoors: wintry gales were chanting their piercing *requiem* for the earth as it lay under shrouds of snow—and I say shrouds not swathes because the snow did not fully cover the ground; it lay in torn dirty patches, scattered here and there as though the poor earth, like a gypsy beggar-woman, had nothing else in which to wrap its scabby limbs. It must have felt so comfortable and agreeable in each other's company, because we travelled from different parts of the city to gather at Emilia's fireside, despite the cold and mud. The conversation would proceed seriously—then rush ahead wildly or leap cheerfully in the air, until at last it latched onto that inexhaustible age-old subject: love. Edmund was teased about a particular, very beautiful lady. He denied it. Without thinking, I threw in the remark that everyone who fell in love seemed to follow the strange custom of keeping it to themselves—as though it were a sin.

"As though it were a sin? What sort of comparison is that?" Augusta seized on my words. "You mean: as if it were a treasure, a hundred-carat diamond discovered in some mine where most people—after years of hard labour—find only twinkling little seeds? But if they were to catch but a glimpse of your riches, their jealousy would be aroused; a glimpse of your diamond, and their disbelief would cry out. And perhaps in order to test it, they would light a great fire and hold the curious stone in the flames to see if it would burn to nothing."

"However, I would not wish such a discovery upon you, Augusta," said Tekla.

"And why not?"

"Because it's too dangerous."

"What do you mean: dangerous? And what about happiness, my dear? Oh just give me, give me one moment of love! The world is so dull and distant, so caked in mud. Every hour of our lives involves hard work, an obligation, the force of habit. Tomorrow is just like yesterday and yesterday just as intolerable as today. I have to think: two plus two equals four. Should I wear a woollen dress or a silk one? Will dinner be late or early? Is that poor man hungry or drunk? Is our new guest angry or stupid? I have to put my thoughts into these hideous detestable words. Love! Ah, love!"

"Hashish! Ah, hashish!" jibed Felicja.

"A somewhat exotic remedy," added Seweryna. "A stiff glass of vodka might suffice!"

"Stop blaspheming, you women!" Edmund leapt to Augusta's defence. "Augusta is right. Without love the world is dull and filthy. Love says: I am the everlasting that preceded the beginning—the constancy in infinity, the brightness in light, the breathe in the air, the fragrance in a flower, the pinnacle of eternity, the ring in a voice, the seeing in sight, the wisdom in reason, the grace in beauty, the power in strength. I am that which is!"

"I am an Indian god and the creed of Brahma," concluded Albert facetiously. He knew the passage better than any of us, taken as it was from the Hindu holy books, though somewhat modified.[19]

"Your unchristian use of the word is now quite clear," said Anna. "Love is indeed all the things it is deemed to be by Edmund's lips—except that the individual feeling that Augusta claims for her amusement is not the whole of love; it is but one ray of light in the sea of love, one truth in the entirety of wisdom."

"Would God grant that it were!" Leon muttered in a sceptical tone.

"You doubt it?" asked Jadwiga.

"I have never seen it," was his brief reply.

"What do you mean: never seen it?" Jadwiga inquired in a more spirited voice. "Just recall whether you have never seen young people content in their mutual feeling, and—because of that very feeling—bolder in their pursuit of the good, more noble in their ideas, more conscientious in their chosen walk of life."

"I have seen very few people for whom their mutual feelings did not pose an obstacle to such qualities."

"Leave Leon alone," said Augusta gaily. "He already knows he said something nonsensical, so he'll defend it all the more stubbornly."

"Excuse me, ladies, there is no obstinacy or nonsense in what I said. I can prove it to you quite easily by means of arithmetic. I ask you simply to calculate carefully: how many people you know who are in love and who are also good for nothing; how many who have slithered—because of love—into selfishness when they were once prepared to make sacrifices for others; how many have persevered with good works whilst remaining in love? Compare the overall totals and just tell me whether I was so very wrong when I suggested that only a select few are not hindered in life by love."

"And yet it can be such a great help to them!" cried Jadwiga.

"Speculation is not my business. I note only the facts. But if I am also permitted to follow the logic of my deductions, why should I not say that if it were not for this one weakness, certain chosen people might be entirely saint-like? The apostles, after all, had no wives or lovers."

"Because it's easier to become a saint when you've got no wife than when you've got one!" cried Teofil, who was sprawling on the carpet.

"But what is easier is less beautiful," said Edmund.

"You are right," said Henryk, "what is easier is less beautiful, and what is less beautiful is also less truthful. It's supposed to be a great virtue to deny myself everything: while I am alive I flee from the earth so that when I die I'll go straight to heaven. I would bar the gates of heaven to such cowards. Go! Live in the world, gather everything to your breast, consecrate everything with your ideas, and then I shall open the gates and you will have salvation—but I shall not admit you so stripped bare and naked. With your theory of holiness, you make it some religious rule worthy of the Knights of the Sword.[20] But I want holiness to be the rule for all humankind so that the most ordinary person might live as a saint—and not only those who grow up in unnatural forced conditions. I want..."

"It's very gracious of you to say 'I want!' and not 'This is how it is,'" interrupted Leon.

"You're wrong: what I want is already how it is, whether it's the need of the times or the need in my own soul. I am madly in love and yet nothing hinders me in my scholarly work. I shall have a wife and children but I shall never refuse help to my neighbour. I shall maintain relations of mutual cooperation and friendship with the companions of my youth. I shall buy land and found a factory. And so I shall trudge through the snow in search of knowledge and glory, even to the pole itself like Ross or Parry.[21] I shall throw a wild banquet for myself and sprawl on cloth of gold, velvet, satin—like Teofil on that carpet—and if the need arises, distribute it all among the poor. For the sake of each one of you I would run through mud thicker than you may find anywhere, freeze in a gale colder than the one you can hear now. And I would do it all too, my Trappist friends,[22] if this were all it took to make noble-mindedness, disinterestedness, good works the exclusive privilege of celibate men. So may all our married citizens and fathers of families sleep peacefully in their egoism—may they even deceive you, injure you. The sacrament of marriage in our opinion gives them the absolute right to do so."

"Hey! Steady on, steady on!" cried Teofil laughing loudly.

"You really have galloped ahead," Emilia echoed Teofil. "Family relationships exonerate no one from honesty and kind-heartedness. Leon only wanted to say that they render us less equipped to perform extraordinary virtues, acts of self-sacrifice and magnanimity."

"What are you babbling about extraordinary virtues?" Henryk retorted in disgust. "What are these extraordinary virtues? If you mean those that we rarely see, then all virtues are immediately extraordinary—for today I do not encounter 'ordinarily' either straightforwardness in our daily affairs, or commitment in families, or exemplary living together in marriage, or orderliness and diligence in the running of our farms. Every good is extraordinary. But if by 'extraordinary' you understand some kind of 'supernatural' virtues, you have expressed yourself badly, Emilia. Such virtues do not exist; every virtue is natural to every human being and every virtue is the duty of every human being."

"Good for you, Henryk!" applauded Augusta.

"In a hundred years' time maybe!" concluded Leon.

"But I can see that you'll never understand one another," said Albert in a more serious tone. "You've got it all muddled up. He talks about one thing, she about another. First you should thank Anna for saving you from many nonsensical claims, when she made the distinction between universal love and individual love; later, you'll thank me for saving you from many more, as I remind you of further distinctions. You call 'love' any exclusive liking of one person for another. Remember that this kind of love still requires a proper definition: there is love which is affection, love which is passion, love which is pure fantasy. In real life the first translates into something sacred, the second into unhappiness and the third into sin: which one are we talking about here?"

"Once the philosopher pipes up with his *distinguo*, I wish to add nothing more," Augusta responded.

"Why not?" objected Seweryna. "Do you really accept no *distinguo*? You'd lump them all together? Sacredness, unhappiness, sin?"

"What are unhappiness and sin? Nothing but your well-argued prejudices and angry resentments. True, people who are in love are often unhappy, sinners even. But why? Because when what they are on the outside endures a thousand malicious rebuttals and they become incensed by the thousands of missiles thrown at them, then they are bound in the end to suffer and sin. Their sin, however, will be a condition wholly foreign to the nature of their feeling—the result of other flaws and perversions, but the feeling in itself will always be a virtue. The Italian who murders his rival in a moment of jealousy, the daughter who secretly leaves her parents' home for her lover, the wife who betrays her husband—all perpetrate terrible crimes, storing up for themselves sin and misfortune in life with full hearts; but they do it because of secondary factors, go astray because of a coincidental defect in their characters. For them the one moment of truth—perhaps the one moment of redemption—is precisely the moment of heartfelt love."

"It seems to me, Augusta, your last *distinguo* is even more subtle than the distinctions made by Albert," said Seweryna.

I, Gabriella, then made my own voice heard. "Ladies and gentlemen, what's your position? Decide on something concrete so I may know with certainty whether after today I am free to love, or not!"

"Well let's get on with it then," cried Teofil. "Cast your votes! The emancipation of love is at stake. Who's for and who's against? You declare first, Gabriella!"

"But you have to have someone who can accept the ruling. I'll be your plebs but you, Teofil—as the Kid—must begin. At Senate meetings, the youngest always speak first. There's none among us younger than 'the Kid.' So hurry up and cast your ballot."

"I cast it white as snow. So many beautiful medals have been struck in love's honour—it must be a feeling worthy of immortal praise."

"Now it's your turn, Emilia!"

Emilia accepted the motion in favour of love but with Albert's amendment. The others, much the same, threw in their own reservations. At the two extremes there remained Seweryna with Leon and Augusta with Henryk.

"What does this mean, Humboldt?" I said turning to Benjamin who sat alone in a corner of the room. "What does this mean? Even during such an important debate—you don't emerge from your silence. A firm majority has already been declared, I know, but your voice could well add many new things, clarify a position thrown open to doubt. Try! Perhaps you'll draw followers away from one camp or the other?"

"Let me be. I'd rather not say anything," he answered in a sharp, clipped voice.

"I was quite sure," Felicja then spoke up, "that if you'd sought his advice regarding other people's opinions about love, he would have quoted you every law and aphorism of every celebrated sage or poet from Confucius to the new civil code, from Solomon to George Sand; he would also have told you what views the Turks had on such matters, or the Red Indians, or the Hottentots, or the Greeks—but he would not have wished to tell you his own view."

"Why shouldn't I have wished to tell you? The matter is quite simple: I myself don't have an opinion. But I was also not minded to express one. I simply didn't wish to speak."

"You often slip into that accursed sickness of silence!"

"Why do you always have to oppose him, Felicja? Maybe he really is sick," Emilia stood up for him.

"Or lazy," the former retorted.

"Not sick and not lazy," said Benjamin. "I don't wish to talk because the wind is blowing and the fire is burning in the hearth."

"How odd: what've the wind and the fire got to do with it?" Felicja snatched at his words.

"I don't find anything odd in it," said Anna. "The music of the gale outside the window and the leaping flames transport the soul into a blissful state of reverie; we go numb on the outside while our minds dream a dream that is constant yet remembered."

"Sadly I can't accept that justification in its entirety," said Benjamin. "I do feel a sense of numbness, but I was not remembering a dream... Oh! I will tell you the truth. A morbid aberration—nothing more—once befell me, three years ago now, the consequence of a peculiar kind of accident."

"What a pity you've had such a fit today; would that you'd tell us about that accident," said Augusta.

"I could have told you before, recounted everything that happened to me, but it is too long a story."

"I love stories that are too long," I pleaded in a humble voice.

"Stories! Stories!" Teofil began to insist.

"I should warn you it will be my whole biography."

"Biography! Biography!" we all echoed Teofil.

"Well, alright. But wait a moment—I must recollect everything from the very beginning."

Benjamin covered his face for a moment with both hands, his elbows resting on his knees—and seemed to be pondering very deeply. Meanwhile we spread ourselves out into a wide circle, so that Benjamin, who until then had been sitting furthest away, was now the main link in the chain. Emilia threw a few dry logs onto the fire and a flame burst forth like a live flare. And when at last the flame lit up Benjamin's uplifted head, it seemed—through a strange optical illusion—that it blazed with youth, shone with happiness.

In that initial moment he shook it gracefully, jauntily even, as though he were attempting out of habit to toss back his lost curls, but quickly realized his mistake, laughed, stroked his bald head and began to speak:

I

IMAGINE A GREEN OASIS in the Sahara Desert. Imagine in today's world—a world of gold, silver, copper, rags converted into banknotes—a large family, poor yet happy. Into this family twenty-six years ago, at one o'clock in the morning, in the middle of the most beautiful August night lit up by the most beautiful full moon, a child of the male sex was born—the ninth child in the family. And yet—an amazing, extraordinary thing—it was received with such joy and blessings as might have greeted the longed-for first issue of a fading dynasty, the long-awaited heir to a vast fortune. But no! Such a comparison is blasphemy: the child was received with the same love as every child begotten in love. That child was me. No grievous accusation hung over the cradle that had been prepared for me. No complaint from an elder sister that there was new trouble in the house bringing fresh hardships; or from a brother—fast approaching his coming of age—that there was now another hand to wrestle with over his expected inheritance; or from my other brothers and sisters that there would be times when they would have to keep quiet, listen to reason and forgo affection; or from my mother that the new life she had created would diminish her own—that sleepless nights lay in store for her, suckling, weaning, the labours of rearing a child; or even from my father that times were hard, that it would be tough to raise me—that he no longer had either the strength or the means to contemplate my future profession. It was an amazing thing—a hundred times amazing—that there was none of this.

My mother and sisters had made me napkins from old underclothes. As a surprise, one of my brothers had made a new wickerwork cradle. And my father, when the good midwife brought me to him on a pillow, made the sign of the cross over me: "Unto the world a child is born": these were his only words. And with tears in his eyes and a smile on his lips he hastened to his wife as fast as he could, kissed her hand and did not leave her until she had fallen peacefully asleep, weak but still radiating joy of ineffable sweetness, her newborn babe by her side.

So that was what my birth was like. For a long time I did not have a name: I was called "little one," "little son," "poppet," while family conferences about what I should be called dragged on for ages. Teresa, the youngest before me of my brothers and sisters, was to settle any doubt. When one of our older brothers told her the story of Jacob's sons from the biblical scenes on our old icons, she was filled with such affection for the youngest son that when the evening conversation turned once more to my approaching baptism the little girl, seated at that moment beside my cradle, solemnly raised her finger and announced in a resolute voice:

"You, little one, will be Beniaminek."[23]

From that moment on I was called Benjamin.

Kind Terenia! They had forgotten to tell her that Benjamin was initially called "Benoni" in accordance with his mother's preference and that Benoni meant "son of pain"[24]; but my mother and brothers and sisters seized on Terenia's idea because it appealed to their hearts, and my father too sanctioned it—for it was the name of his own great hero, his ideal among famous men: Benjamin Franklin.[25] From his veneration of Franklin you can surmise my father's whole character, even if you are only slightly adept at reading those hidden—yet always logical—links between a person's tastes and sympathies and the essence of their nature. As to myself, I possess—in this respect at least—an instinct that never fails. Once, on a visit to the Louvre, I saw a handsome young man pause for a long time before Velázquez's *Cato* and study it with the calmest of faces while Cato rent his breast, bloodily, horribly. [26] I said to myself at once: "that is an evil man." And my words proved right: he was an anatomist of the human heart. I encountered him later in a court of law as an interested spectator, when he gave witness at the very last moment against the accused—a man unjustly accused, as far as I could judge in all conscience. But to return to my own biography: now you know under what influences, into what kind of atmosphere, as it were, I landed on this earth—descended in accordance with ancient notions, entered in accordance with more recent ones and was reborn in accordance with those that are the closest approximations to truth. How I was lulled to sleep, rocked and caressed for so long without my knowledge; how I unfolded in that warmth of emotion, that sunny day of happiness; how the whole essence of my being was saturated with that many-sided universal song of love! Oh, if only I could remember! But I can't, I don't remember anything. And yet that was already my life, already the cause of later successions of events—the parent of all my moments, of all my years to come. When I became conscious for the first time of the world around me and gazed about at it, the fruit was already lodged deep within my soul; and that fruit became for me what they call one's inclinations, my character, my nature. Everyone loved me and I woke up loving everyone—but loving was an indispensable necessity of my organism, just as one breathes, eats, drinks; there was no past for me before my loving, just as there was no beginning before God. But this was still not enough: every member of my family also loved—apart from me—the whole of existence in all its different manifestations, in all its different shapes and forms; and there was something beautiful, sacred in their choice of these forms and manifestations. And they each loved one thing in particular as though it were their special possession. But you must understand this in the literal sense: loved, not liked.

My eldest sister Julcia loved Ukrainian ballads, and my brother Adam loved the blue eyes of the daughter of our closest neighbour, and my brother Józef loved the soil that he cultivated, and my sister Ludwinka loved flowing water and wild flowers growing unpicked in the meadows, and my brother Karol loved his dog and horse and double-barrelled gun, and my sister Bronisia loved the stars and the sky, and my brother Cypian loved paintings, and my sister Terenia loved novels, and my father loved books, and my mother loved people. And so my first impressions of the world were composed of the impressions they each favoured.

The earliest picture in which I recall my sister Julcia is of a wooden bench beneath an open window. The day was warm yet overcast as though someone had poured molten lead over the sky. Julcia—bent over her needlework—was singing such a moving song and in such long drawn-out tones that grew more and more melancholy and seemed unable to melt away into the heavy air—rebounding only against my legs and chest as I sat beside her. And I began to weep. Julcia looked at me and fell silent for a moment, but in that silence my tears—soft to begin with—erupted into genuine sobs of pain. Then my sister pressed my head against her knees, stroked and fondled my hair with her fingers and began to sing again. And I began to weep again ever so softly and felt so good shedding those tears, such delight as I never felt even when my little bird—my happy linnet, a present from my old nurse—fluttered its wings at me every time it saw me from its cage.

I first remember Adam coming into the room with a snow-white girl, dressed all in white.

"Who's that?" I asked him.

"Your little sister," he answered with a smile.

"Our little sister, Adaś?" I repeated, surprised. "But how come I don't know her? Where was she?"

"Eighteen years ago she was still in heaven!"

But when I looked at him and then at her in disbelief, he said again: "In heaven. Look into your little sister's eyes and you'll see sapphires, bright and pure. Is heaven any different on the clearest day?"

I looked. The girl blushed and burst into laughter and I shouted for joy.

"Ah, you're right, Adaś. It's just like our little sister's eyes."

"Don't ever say 'our' to me, Beniaminek. Because she's your sister and the sister of your sisters—but not *my* sister. Remember: not *my* sister."

"Then you must be all the poorer, Adaś, for having one less sister."

"Me poor?" My brother turned with a smile to the girl in white, though the words faltered on his lips. The girl wound herself about my brother's arm like a coil of wild mallow, her head lowered—and yet she answered him swiftly without thinking twice, in a voice surer than that of her interrogator.

"No, you are not poor, Adaś, you are very rich."

"How happy I am," he added as though the words came from somewhere deep in his heart. And then, I don't know why, he took my hand and squeezed it with such a tender, tremulous and (thinking of it today I am free to say it) *passionate* grip I even forgot to ask him to explain his words, which to me were quite incomprehensible. Later, even a short while afterwards, I was to grasp the full sanctity of their meaning. Love in our family was never a secret kept well hidden by the decorum of polite society; nor was it something shocking, carefully concealed from the eyes of children. Love for us was the happiness of life, that most beautiful of divine truths. It walked with head held high amid sympathy—amid the modest respect and esteem of hearts bound by friendship and good will. Once when Waleria had been reading Bohdan's poetry,[27] Adam drew close to her and taking her golden head in both hands planted a kiss upon her slightly parted lips; but when Waleria went bright red from forehead to shoulder because of that kiss, when she flung herself involuntarily towards my mother who was sitting beside her and hid herself like a little bird in her embrace, none of us as much as smiled—I can still remember it today—none of us ruined the lovers' moment of happiness with our jokes. Only my mother gave Adam a sign to bow his head before her and then—still clasping Walerka to her bosom—she placed her own kiss on his bowed head, a kiss so tender it seemed not to have been given but entrusted, sacred like a blessing, drawn from the depths of her own breast.

The most lasting memory I have of Józef is of seeing him in the fields among the reapers. He is laughing, binding the sheaves, chasing the other drivers home, their carts piled high with corn. He hoists me onto one of the loaded carts and I sit there beside him on my throne, and he shows me the land, the earth which is the kingdom of all people—my future birthright which I shall inherit and where I shall manage the work one day. And he names everything for me with delightful words: the rye is silver; wheat is gold; the blushing buckwheat, cloth of purple; and I believe they really are silver, gold, cloth of purple, and that the world possesses no other kinds. Along the way Józef breaks me off sprigs of coral from the rowan-trees planted by the roadside every few yards by our parents, while I grasp in my hand bunches of cornflowers, corncockles, heartsease, ears of ripe rye and unripe barley, mixing the white and the green tufts into different arrangements—now among clusters of rowan-berries, now among posies of cornflowers. And I feel that I have everything, and that nature in all her bounty, her beauty, her totality—that nature will always be mine. Only I do not say this to myself in words but in feeling, in deed, in that short moment in my life.

My Ludwinka, the least pretty, the quietest, most melancholy of all my brothers and sisters, I remember most clearly in a particular scene, over which my tiny head began to ponder perhaps for the longest and perhaps for the first time. At the foot of our garden, beyond a row of lush overgrown willows, there flowed a tiny stream. It had no name and was so narrow you could jump over it. Its bed was strewn with fine gravel which made you want to scoop it up and count the multi-coloured grains. Beside this stream, on the very edge of the bank, Ludwinka sat leaning forward—half her form was reflected in the water, while the waves tossed her reflection in a regular motion, continuously, peacefully, as though rocking it to sleep. Exhausted by running around, I knelt down beside Ludwinka and began to dabble in the silver ripples with a stick.

"Don't wake me, Beniaminek," whispered my sister in such a hushed voice I could barely hear her.

"Are you asleep then, Ludwinka?" I asked.

"Asleep, asleep, little brother," she replied in an even quieter voice. But I was watching her eyes and could see that although they were cast down towards the water, they were not closed or drowsy.

"You're joking!" I cried recklessly and hit out harder with my stick so that the water near the bank grew muddy.

Ludwinka trembled as though it were she I'd hit with my stick.

"You've woken me," she said very, very sadly. And I sensed at once that I had done something wrong, something of the very worst, injured someone who was already suffering.

"But you weren't asleep," I said in a last attempt to justify myself. "You were not asleep, Ludwinka," I implored. My sister did not reply. She simply took me by the hand and leaned over the stream with me, gently pointing with her finger at the water that was now calm again. I saw myself and Ludwinka. The image amused me like one in a toy mirror, but the more I stared at it the more I was slowly overcome by a feeling of drowsiness. But it was not a drowsiness of the eyes, of the body, because my were eyes wide open and my body held firmly in the same bent position—it was rather a drowsiness in the reflection itself, in some part of myself that had fallen into the finely broken waves and was undulating there in the crystal water monotonously, uninterrupted, unchanging. But then—directly above our heads—across the backdrop of the sky, with whose azure tint the stream's own colour seemed to flow, there moved a mass of silver cloud and ruptured the unity of the vision; my child's eyes pursued it at once but the cloud had vanished both in the sky and in the stream.

"But where is it, where is it, Ludwinka?"

Ludwinka was not watching the cloud. She had seen its passage though, and understood my question.

"Far away," she replied in the same tone as before, only this time in a whisper.

"Where's 'far away,' my Ludwinka? I don't know where you mean: 'far away?'"

Ludwinka became lost in thought—either about how to explain or about the content of her explanation, I don't know. After a while she shook her head as though trying to wipe away the remnants of sleep, or the remnants of impressions, and spoke in a more audible voice—but always in that muffled tone as though confiding a secret:

"You ask me, Beniaminek: where is 'far away'? So look: try to chase this water that flows so slowly, and you'll never catch up with it, never catch up with it. The water runs away into the San, the San into the wide Vistula and the Vistula into the deep sea. And the sea? I cannot tell you where that is. The sea is far away. But now—there at the end of the meadow—can you see how the sky touches the earth? Go and fetch me a fragment of that sapphire sky! Cross the meadow and the sky will be beyond the open fields; cross the fields and the sky will be beyond the woods; cross the woods and the sky will be beyond another meadow, then again beyond open fields, more woods, another stream. And where is the sky? I cannot tell you. The sky is far away. Far away. And now go and fetch the cage with your linnet—so well fed and cosseted during the winter! It's springtime now, Beniaminek—the flowers are in bloom, trees are turning green, hosts of birds are everywhere in song. Open the cage, little brother, open it—and you will see how the little bird that loved you so dearly, ate seeds from your palm, drank sugared water from your lips, see how it will fly away towards the spring, towards new flowers. And you will be left feeling despondent and perhaps ask: Ludwinka, where has my little bird gone? And I won't be able to tell you, Beniaminek, because the bird will be far away—oh, far away! Further away than the water you chase in the river, further than the sky you try to catch up with, further than hope, further than seems likely or possible. 'Further away,' little brother, is what abandons us in life, what ceases to love us." Ludwinka leaned again over the water of the stream—only her reflection trembled a little more than it did before, and a moment later was rent asunder as two large drops fell upon it. I looked up: Ludwinka's face was very calm but the long fair lashes of her grey eyes still shone with one last pure tear. Ludwinka raised her eyes and cast a long anxious, melancholy stare at the boy who was watching her.

"Beniaminek," she said in a more cheerful tone of voice. "Why ask where 'far away' is? Better run and play with the flowers. Flowers are always near at hand and often grow close to the ground, little brother." She lowered me gently from her knees but I did not run off as she advised. I walked along the bank of the stream and tried to see if I could reach far away—as far away as the sea or the sky. I walked on and on, beyond the garden, beyond the open fields, until our house was lost from sight. And when my little legs began to ache, when I saw ahead of me a dark unknown forest but still could not see the end of the river, when I could touch the spiky juniper bushes with my outstretched hand but not the wall of the sky, only then did I understand what was meant by "far away"—only then did I understand what was meant by "sometime in the future."

"I will reach there 'sometime,'" I said to myself, "sometime— when I am older." And so I returned, reassured by this design, and on the way gathered flowers for my sister Ludwinka. Suddenly, I showered her with the flowers I had picked as she sat in the same spot by the water just as motionless as before.

Ludwinka gathered them all up, gazed at them for a moment and then turned to me. "What a shame, what a pity," she said. "So many flowers, Beniaminek."

Then she chose the freshest ones, ones that would last, ones that had not wilted in the warmth of my hands, and began to plant them carefully one by one in the moist sand by the bank—as children plant out their miniature gardens that last no more than an hour. I helped her in her work. I—a child—had guessed her thoughts—the thoughts of the dreamer, the woman. Or rather: I had not guessed, I only felt what she felt. And when we had planted all the flowers, they shone with a new freshness.

"It will be better for them here," I remarked naturally. "Better than out there in the fields in the scorching sun—they'll even live longer."

"But when the time comes to wither, they will wither all the more sadly," she replied. And I did not inquire into the meaning of those words—for they were also the words I felt instinctively.

I have no special memories from my early childhood of my brother Karol, because Karol of all of us spent least time at home. In the division of labour on the farm, he was in charge of the woods—more as his unstated right than through any explicit agreement. I must have been nine years old already when a particular memory of him became firmly engraved in my mind. I still seem to see him today as a vigorous lad of twenty, sunburnt as a highlander, dark-haired, black-eyed, in his green baize hooded coat. He would whistle, and at his whistle a great black mastiff would come leaping towards him. Karol had called him Moloch, because of his colour—though he sometimes regretted having profaned this favourite and most noble creature with such a devilish name[28]; he even wanted to change it, but Ludwinka wouldn't let him.

"Let Moloch begin to be good—if only as an animal," she told him.

And Karol, however much he may have resisted others with his brisk defiance, never refused Ludwinka anything. Ludwinka was his chosen one, the most beloved of all his loved ones, and so Moloch remained as Moloch. And he was a dog of uncommon virtue, of rare strength and courage, with astounding instincts. He never bit anyone, but if he took a dislike to them he would knock them to the ground and hold them there calmly but forcibly until one of the family came to the rescue. Karol never trusted a guest who had been greeted in that way by Moloch. And if ever he wanted to say that someone was wicked, then he would declare: "Moloch would have torn him to bits—torn him to bits as he deserves."

I have never seen a more magnificent or gentler beast in the entire dog kingdom. There were times when some pampered canine would bark and throw itself at him, but Moloch just wagged his tail proudly, shook himself as if he were merely shaking off water or a cloud of dust and walked on unruffled in his solemn majesty. But please don't mock me, ladies and gentlemen, for telling you so much about Moloch. I have never in my whole life met a... *person* quite like him.

Ha! A person who—being one of the strongest—would never abuse his own strength. Some strong people are saints, but the strongest, the one who is strongest of all... anyway, perhaps you remember who—I can't remember, my memory has been failing me terribly of late. Yet it is a strange thing how well I can recall everything as it was then—all those earliest images of my life— how I look upon them with a clear eye and see them exactly as they were. Oh, that huge friendly Moloch! How he used to bound out of his kennel and rejoice to see his master! Rejoice—for I would never use the words "ingratiated himself" to describe Moloch. Moloch never "ingratiated" himself with anyone. Moloch would greet you, was pleased to see you, would romp and roll on the ground. Karol received this sign of Moloch's sincere affection with a smile, patting him on the back of the neck in much the same way as an officer might slap an old soldier across the shoulder, remarking to a fellow officer: "Look at this seasoned old campaigner!" Then Karol would shout "Zitta!" and a young mare would come charging out of our stable in leaps and bounds, lithe as a roe-deer, black as night, a real Turkish thoroughbred— already broken in and adorned in crimson trappings. My father had acquired the mare very cheaply by chance—still as a foal, still small and weak—from the military when they abandoned their local quarters. He gave it to Karol on condition he earned enough money to keep her himself. Later, this condition was to enrich me too—with the brand new cradle at my birth; for the youth who would not have begrudged his own blood for the sake of his horse, did not begrudge his time either. He learned the craft of basketry, made brooms and straw doormats and sold them in the neighbouring towns and villages and even sent the prettier objects as far away as Lwów.[29] Because of this Zitta always had plenty of fragrant hay, and the tastiest fodder, and when she grew up a saddle was also found for her. The mare also brought Karol lavish support: at Christmastime a few bushels of oats were added to his stores and before a year was out, on his birthday, his sisters hung by his bed the crimson trappings that were to suit Zitta so well. Napoleon, who sent Lefebvre[30] his princely title inside a packet of chocolate, could not have brought him a handsomer surprise. Karol was beside himself with joy, for he loved his Zitta like a true Zaporozhian[31;] he fed, watered and groomed her himself, and would never have sold her for all the treasure in Galicia and Lodomeria.[32] Zitta was his jet-black she-eagle, his wild Mooress, his own burning fire spell-bound within a horse. And it was obvious too how Zitta looked at him with a knowing eye—strangely detached from the rest of her head by its gleaming whiteness. How she rested her head on his shoulder with a kind of oriental voluptuousness—soft, graceful and passionate! How she would come running from afar at the sound of his voice, but with easy strides, nimbly, swiftly—you really could not tell if her hooves even touched the ground! Ah Zitta! Zitta, I dreamed about her not long ago. Say what you will, ladies and gentlemen—but after that dream I felt happier and younger for the whole of the next day! And so, to return to the moment I spoke of in my reminiscences: I can still see Karol amid his most beloved possessions, though I forgot to mention that he would also have had his double-barrelled gun[33] on his back—his rifle that was like a precious plaything, bright and shining, light to carry, like a woman's favourite jewel, yet sure, unfailing, as though it fired of its own accord to hit the target—all the marksman had to do was to take it in his hands with his eyes closed, and release the trigger. Karol, who liked to call everything by its proper name, had his own name for it: "Mistress." Once when he began to speak of her perfections, of her song that was the sweetest music to his ears, a gentleman who was not well acquainted with him inquired: "And does the young lady live far from here?" Karol then introduced the "young lady" with the utmost seriousness to the inquirer's utmost surprise. "Well, my lad," he cried on that day. "Will you come with me?" I responded by stretching up my arms as fast as I could to grab the saddle but found it too hard to jump on without a stirrup. My brother smiled when he saw my efforts and whistled in his characteristic manner. At the sound of his whistle Zitta knelt down and stretched her sinewy neck towards me so I could put my arms around it; and when I had clasped hold of her and thrown myself on her back, Zitta sprung to her feet powerfully tossing her neck as if trying to adjust me more securely in my seat.

"Wrap him in your greatcoat so he doesn't freeze!" cried my mother who was watching from the window.

"Yes, yes, never fear!" called Karol and sat me in front of him. He pressed me against his chest with one arm and tugged the bridle lightly with the other. At this sign Zitta moved off, as did Moloch, and a few minutes later the house and village were lost from sight.

It was a beautiful day, so frosty the snow crunched beneath our feet—but so bright with the sunlight, so sparkling with diamonds that we were almost blinded. I sped along with my brother, rode until at last we entered a forest. Amid the dazzling whiteness all around, I could not absorb enough of the rainbow-tinted glints of colour flashing among the branches of the trees scattered along our way, or of that jet-black Zitta, or of black Moloch. Suddenly Zitta pricked up her ears. Moloch stood stock still, his fur on end. My brother's nostrils flared. Then he smacked his lips as if trying to kiss the air and stopped the horse.

"What is it, Karol?" I asked.

"Quiet, quiet—it's a wolf."

I had only heard about wolves from Terenia's stories. Her stories were terrifying but my curiosity was great. My brother leaned forward, looked me in the eye and then moved the arm with which he had been holding me further to the left. I returned his gaze with a look that was calm enough; but I cannot honestly say something was not pounding violently in my chest beneath my brother's arm.

"Good, good! Not bad at all," Karol whispered to himself under his breath. Then he added in a louder voice: "We're going to kill a wolf, Beniaminek!"

"How come? Am I going to kill it?"

"You too, my lad. Only be careful—be on your guard!" He drew his shoulders round me. "Good." He held his gun and aimed. "Now put both hands here—grip where I'm gripping." He placed my fingers on the cock of the gun and only then laid his own finger on top. Whilst we were making these preparations, the black speck that we had seen in the distance had been drawing gradually closer, majestic as a monarch stalking the boundaries of his kingdom. The wolf was huge. Moloch snarled. Zitta snorted. Karol cried "Psst!" and once more everything fell silent. But the wolf advanced fearless and unperturbed. That wolf—we learnt afterwards—was notorious in the district. Only a few feet from us, it sprang an enormous leap. Moloch was unable to contain himself and also flung himself forward, but Karol yelled again—"Down!"—and Moloch dropped down, whimpering furiously and scrabbling in the snow as if in despair of being humiliated. The wolf stood still. And at that moment my brother pressed my finger. The shot rang out and the snow turned a reddish hue. But suddenly, before we could take it in with our eyes, the wounded beast flew straight at Zitta's breast; the mare whinnied in terror and reared so violently to one side that I—who at that moment was clinging neither to the saddle nor to my brother—fell like a bullet to the ground. As I leaped to my feet the tiniest details of the scene that now presented itself to my eyes became implanted on my memory for ever. I carry a number of such scenes in my soul; without my knowing it, they have become imprinted there so precisely, so powerfully that I am amazed how they come into my mind complete in every shade and detail, as though they were happening again. In this scene for instance, I can perfectly picture not only my brother, who jumped down from the saddle, stood in front of me and gathered me up with both arms to shield me from danger against his own breast; not only Zitta struggling on her hind legs under the powerful paws of the wolf which—though assailed by Moloch—still clung to her breast-plate; not only Moloch, who had buried his face in the shaggy coat of his adversary and sunk his muzzle so deep into its mutilated flesh he could hardly even see it; not only the wolf, raised on its hind legs and turning on its enemy with a violent craning of the neck, but also its flickering blood-red stare, the dirty yellow sheen of its coat—I can still see all its teeth in its wide open jaw and could draw them here and now for an anatomist without omitting a single one. After the first anxious moment, Karol moved away from me, picked up his gun and with the utmost sang-froid handed it to me again. He took aim with a single sweep of his eye, jerked my finger and the wolf had no time to even draw breath. My brother went straight over to Zitta, applied a cloth to her wounded breast and tied it in place with the bridle strap. He stroked Moloch, gave his ears a pull and kissed him on his broad forehead. Then he sprang lightly into the saddle and whistled again for Zitta to kneel before me. The whole way home we talked about what a lovely rug the wolf's fur would make for our mother's feet and many other things. The only word that never strayed onto the lips of either of us was "fear." Karol did not mention it, did not even ask me about it. He let me feel the happiness of my first conquest as my natural possession, an event rightfully due to me as a human being. After that my brother took me hunting more and more often, and when I killed my first wild boar he hugged me for joy—but hugged me because it was a choice male specimen in its prime, not because I let it charge within five feet of me and then aimed with such accuracy it was as though my desire alone had guided the bullet.

My sister Bronisława cast but a single word into my life. I don't remember which birthday it was: it happened—or so it seemed—at that moment of my development when a human being first begins to raise his head and gaze into the sky. I was sitting in the late evening on a stone beneath a broad, shady lime-tree that grew in the middle of the yard. Bronisława was sitting beside me. Neither of us spoke. But the air, the earth, the whole sky spoke to us in the distinct yet unexpressed voice of insects swarming above the grass, frogs croaking by the ponds, leaves trembling on the tree in the cool breeze. The moon was full like on the night I was born—the stars so paled before it that only a couple flickered somewhere far away from it. White clouds scudded across the deep blue firmament, like the frolicking white-fleeced flocks of an unseen shepherd or a flight of snow-white doves—or dissolved into the silvery feathers of swans sailing on water, or eagles soaring on high. From time to time a boat full of mysterious figures would glide past, or an angel in a long trailing gown—for what things did I not see there! Until my sister took my hand.

"Benjamin," she said—for she alone among my brothers and sisters never used the affectionate form of my name. "Benjamin, do you hear?"

"Oh! I'm listening all the time, sister. It must be the meadows and trees playing their music."

"Benjamin, do you see?" she asked again and pointed upwards.

"Oh! I am looking all the time, sister. It's more beautiful than all Cyprian's pictures put together."

"And do you feel anything, Benjamin, in your own chest?" And she placed my hand on my heart.

"I feel," I replied after a while, "that I feel good—like when Julcia sings, when Mother puts me on her knee, when Karol sits me on his Zitta. Better even, because it's like when I cry when I'm not upset, when I feel so happy I cannot laugh, when I want to clutch you all in one big embrace and take in everything in the world in a single glance. But put altogether it's... I can't tell you, sister, what it is."

"I will tell you, Benjamin. Only remember it for all your life— what you are about to hear now, in this moment. What you see before you, what you sense inside you, everything that's melodious, beautiful, bright, clear, happy—all this is God..."

I treasured Bronislawa's words and kept them all my life, just as she had commanded. I have turned the pages of many books—wise and not so wise, harkened to many truths and untruths, indulged in still more dreams; but those words heard as a child from my sister would come back to me at any time and after any ordeal. The future course of my soul unfolded upon them: I may have denied myself but I never denied them. Though I was troubled and hurting, and though I might not feel it myself—I could always see that everything melodious, beautiful, bright and happy was God: that wisdom was God, happiness was God, love was God... That evening spent with Bronisława sitting on the stone under the lime-tree was my life's prayer of initiation.

If Karol and Bronisława have left their imprint on my past in such distinct yet unique memories, then I seek in vain for any exclusive incident in my early childhood that might single out Cyprian or Terenia. Yet I see them in every hour—they live on in my every reminiscence. Cyprian would paint me pictures or show me pictures painted by others. Terenia would tell him—and me—marvellous stories about every one of them; but if I were to repeat to you now the ones that made the greatest impression on me, then there would be no end to them today or tomorrow. I only stopped listening to them when I was fourteen years old—but when I began listening… I truly cannot say. At the same time as I heard the names of everyday objects that surrounded me, I also heard thousands of other, strange expressions, such as "enchanted princess," "handsome knight," "wonder-working signet-ring," "magic castle," "underground palaces with diamond-studded walls," "fiery spirits flying on the clouds"—and it all somehow formed part of my own nature, not as superstition or weakness of character but rather, I would say, as some strange power for creating my own fantasies. One day, when I have discharged myself of this tale of my life—conjured up according to your own wish—and when we are assembled again beside the warm fire for a friendly conversation—and so long as the wind is not whistling and howling outside—then I will tell you one of Terenia's fairytales. I am sure it won't bore you, Henryk, Tekla, Edmund. Those who have no knowledge of life—like those who have known it to the point of losing all hope, to the point of regaining a child-like composure—are those who enjoy listening to wondrous fairytales. Is that not true, my dear friends? Oh, those tales! And those pictures of Cyprian! But Cyprian is already finding his way into my extravagant biography… and yet my thoughts and words still flee back to an earlier era, to my earliest and most sacred memories.

You have already heard something of my father—my father who was so serious, so learned, so kind and mild. In our frugal little home he had no separate study for his books and papers, yet whenever he sat down to read everything would fall so silent you could hear a fly buzzing—through no command of his, no sense of compulsion, but through the simple compliance of things and habits. This was the atmosphere in which I grew up. And I don't remember anyone even ordering me to be quiet. Whenever my father spread open the pages of a book, my mother would cross the room on tiptoe. My brothers and sisters and brothers would usually go outside or a sister would sit quietly in a corner with her sewing. One day I too remained indoors, gingerly leafing through the pages—lest they should rustle at all—of an old *in quarto* album in which there were pictures of the former kings and queens of Poland.[34] Oh dear God! How well I recall it! Cyprian would get angry at these images, in particular the fact that Wanda[35] had been given a pointed wimple and Jadwiga[36] an enormous ruff that made her bend forward like a hunch-back crushed by its weight. But I was a less severe critic—every day I had something new to amuse me: the mice gnawing at Popiel,[37] Wiśniowiecki's enormous wig,[38] the chains of the Zygmunts,[39] for I should confess that I also regarded them entirely from my own separate perspective.

On that particular day, however, I had half completed my examination of the book and begun to stare intently, not at it but at the face of my father who was sitting opposite me—for my linnet had begun to sing in its cage hanging on a branch outside the window. I felt a huge desire to run out to it but was afraid of disturbing my father, all the more so because it was hard to open and shut the door, and—who knows?—maybe the latch had been set too high for my hand to reach. Watching intently all the time, I noticed how my father suddenly frowned and how a forbidding expression spread across his face as if he were angry with someone. Then he rested his head in his hand and stopped looking at his book for a moment; but in that moment his angry expression became transformed into one of deep anguish, and a loud heavy sigh wrenched itself from his chest.

"Father, father, what's the matter? Is something hurting?" I asked at once, running over to him.

My father smiled sadly. Even today I cannot properly express the bitterness of that smile on his manly countenance, full of strength and kindness. For my father was a remarkably handsome man. I have never come across another equal in age yet equal too in youthful vigour and lively physiognomy. He had an oval face— slightly pale and yellowish, a Roman nose, very black eyebrows and glossy raven-black hair that was already speckled with silver and receding from his forehead. His eyes, half covered by protruding lids, expressed a grave thoughtfulness and certain strictness. On the other hand, there was so much sweet warmth in the contours of his mouth, so much tenderness that we children were never in the slightest afraid of the strictness of his stare. No one ever frightened us by invoking our father's wrath. So you can imagine what sort of impression might have been made on me by such a bitter smile on those usually kind, mild lips.

"Father, father! what's hurting you?" I repeated on the verge of tears.

"That's what's hurting me." My father pointed to his book.

"Vile, nasty book," I cried and threw it on the floor in disgust.

"You do wrong, my son," he replied, calmly picking it up.

"So what is it, father?"

"History."

"And what is there in this history?"

.... [40]

"Ah, my little son! Everything that no longer is, everything that is, everything that has yet to come—you will find it in books just like this one."

And when I expressed astonishment, my father showed me a page on which there were different little signs and told me that one day, with the aid of those little signs, I would be able to learn what the dead had accomplished, hear what people had spoken of the longest or from the earliest times, see to the far corners of the earth and sky and into the depths of the human soul. I learnt the little signs as fast as I could—my father indicating to me their use in a very peculiar way. I remember him making me put together for the first time the following words: "Mother loves you." Then he took away my ABC-book and told me to close my eyes and imagine Mother in the moment when she stooped over my bed in the morning and woke me with a kiss, wishing me good-day. Later he promised me that in certain letters I would see flowers, trees, fruits—and then he made me read the word "garden." Later still, when he gave me the word "star," he reminded me of how it twinkled high in the heavens as a trembling point of light, and yet of how a star too was a world. And in that way he taught me to read every word as an image, feeling, thought.

But my friends, you must be wondering why I have not yet mentioned my mother. Ah! For she was present in every one of my memories. I have felt her presence so much—it seems I have been talking all the time only about her, or talking to her.

Mother......... Do you have any idea why I step aside with such respect and bow my head with such reverence when a woman in her declining years walks past me? Do you know why in church—and especially in a small impoverished country church—tears well up in my eyes when I see from a distance a female figure kneeling at the foot of the altar? Do you know why I can never walk past a beggar without stretching out my hand to offer him alms, past an unhappy man without wishing to turn to him with thoughts of comfort, past a weeping child without consoling it with an affectionate word, without taking its hand—without warming it in winter against my own breast or sheltering it in summer from the danger of being knocked down by an oncoming cart? Do you have any idea, why? Because I had a mother!... because in every such moment I see her always before me—loving, angelic, imparting her blessing... doing everything just as I myself had grown used to doing when I was still with her. Oh! To be sure—whenever the blessed days of my early youth unfold in my memory, whenever I contrast them with later days... But you do not want some lyrical elegy. I mean only to satisfy your curiosity regarding the events of my life. But please allow me one moment of eccentricity.

Have any of you ever dreamed that some hand pushed you off a very high and very steep mountain, a mountain such as the one from which Christ surveyed all the kingdoms of the world and all the treasures of the kingdoms, and toppled you into the abyss? Let us say the hand of Satan, whom you—who are not Christ—had trusted as a god? Remember the sensation of falling, ever slower, ever heavier—the earth has already vanished from view, the sky is visible only through a tiny crevice. But the sky too will vanish.

And it grows darker and darker, more and more terrible. And you know that as you fall down, somewhere at the bottom, you must be smashed to smithereens—only you cannot see the bottom, cannot see it! Oh! Then, after the first moment of being dazed, there follow long moments of frantic despair: it is time to recall every lost joy, all your hopes, all your deeds, all your high-minded intentions, all your perhaps great—and perhaps useful to the world—talents that are fast disappearing now without a trace, do not even exist anymore, though we still exist. And at this point, as if to sharpen the torture, the image at which we marvelled on the mountain-top spreads before eyes like a phantasmagoria of hell; and though we have recognized Satan, we feel we would sacrifice eternity a second time in exchange for a single moment such as that. For only now does the vulture of regret tear great chunks of flesh from our hearts: if only we could have died before; why did we not smash our brains tumbling from this mountain? But then there follows another agony—for then we see with utmost clarity every frail herb that we might have grasped while still descending; we weigh up any means, any likelihood of rescue; persuade ourselves that if it had not been for one false step, one move, one thought, we would not have fallen, we would have struggled to our feet. But now it's all in vain, now we cannot reverse the laws of nature—we were hanging heavily over the pit, and now we must fall, fall, fall! Only one future remains to us, one hope: to be shattered to pieces there at the bottom and finish it once and for all, to fall, to not live. Our whole despair culminates in this wild frantic impatience, yet the abyss is deep, Milton's abyss, into which we must fall nine days and nine nights.[41] And so, at last, impatience consumes itself. The human has become as stone, knowing and remembering, but no longer in agony, no longer in despair. And the human stone, as it descends, does it lighten the darkness—even there in those depths—with a final spark in its final destruction?... Ah! forgive me, forgive me, ladies and gentlemen, I was to speak of something quite different. Forgive that dream, that abyss, those things which are unlike anything else—though very like the things I have felt in my waking. But may fate grant you happiness and prosperity! I am eternally grateful that no one has understood me.

But on the other hand, you have understood my childhood and the nature I possessed in those days. You know I was born loved, and grew up as a loving child: love and affection, always love and affection—that was the entire summation of the education I underwent. As it happens, I also studied mining and when I was seventeen I became a mining engineer.

My seventeenth year also marked the beginning of a bizarre tale of highly amusing events—you will laugh heartily.

II

CHRISTMAS EVE WAS BEING CELEBRATED at my parents' house. We children had travelled to be with them since not all of us were still living under the family roof. My two married brothers, Adam and Józef, lived in faraway parts. Three sisters had also got married: Julcia, Bronisia and Terenia. Karol was serving with the army in the Kingdom[42] and had come home for a short time on leave from somewhere near Lublin. Cyprian had written his last letter from as far away as Rome. I myself was on my way back from Hungary. Only Ludwinka had remained with my parents as their angel of solace—my Ludwinka, forever pale, forever sad, as if always yearning even in her moments of joy for some unattainable happiness. I think now that Ludwinka must have lived with some secret suffering hidden deep in her soul, just as her beloved flowers often grew for a long time with some poisonous insect hidden in the shadow of their leaves. I certainly cannot vouch for it though, Ludwinka never complained to anyone.

The long table had been laid for the Christmas meal with a white tablecloth, and fresh hay spread underneath it; and when the first star began to shine in the sky we all gathered around to the ringing of a little bell: parents, children, grandchildren, domestics, labourers.

My mother took the wafer and handed it to my father. "To this year of our Lord!" she said in a voice that was solemn but trembling with emotion. "Husband, all my children, I wish you this year of our Lord! To this year of our Lord! May every one of you, one day, thus break the bread of God—with the hands of valiant sons, happy daughters, beautiful grandchildren, loyal servants. May another hand, one day, thus pass you the holy wafer as I pass it now to your father—a hand that will have leaned for long years on your own in never-disappointed trust."

"Amen," we all answered. My parents broke the wafer and then my mother came up to each of us in turn, starting with the eldest and working down to the youngest, giving us a portion of the wafer and then receiving back from us a part of each portion. But when it was Terenia's turn to extend her arm, my mother drew back a little and tears sprung to her eyes.

"No, it's the turn of my distant son," she said. "In Cyprian's name and with my blessing let us keep this piece of the wafer until his return." And in keeping with her words, she went to put it aside...

At that moment the doors were flung wide open. Someone stood on the threshold...

"Mother, your son has returned to claim his share in the family happiness," announced a voice so familiar that every breast resounded with shouts of joy.

"Cyprian! Our Cyprian..."

Indeed my brother Cyprian—painter, wanderer, artist—had returned.

Albert, Philosopher! Tell me, is there such a thing as intuition?... Ha! it's just as well for you that you are nodding your head so solemnly and giving an affirmative answer, for I was about to fire at you another question: why did my heart contract in pain when Cyprian entered the room? That was precisely what it was, ladies and gentlemen: pain. Even though in that first moment I could not distinguish it from my great feeling of joy.

To greet my brother—the companion of my childhood thoughts and games—after several years of separation, to greet him with a tear in my eye, trembling hand and pallid brow, seemed to me then only some new way of expressing my feeling of happiness. A strange way nevertheless... Later on I realized more precisely what it was, and today I can say for sure that it was nothing but the pain of a terrible dread.

Cyprian embraced first my mother, kissed first my father's hand. Then my sisters flung themselves upon him one by one; those with children held them up to him so they would be the first to receive a kiss, so he would greet them better. I was the last to draw near.

Cyprian clasped me round the neck but before he pressed me to his chest, he stopped as though surprised by something. He stared fixedly at my face while his hands became almost rigid on my shoulders. And thus he held me for a while at arm's length; thus he went on gazing at me. And such a strange smile of fascination shone from his lips that I, not understanding it myself, smiled back at him, freeing myself as though by force from the sense of division and discord that had been thrust upon me.

"What's the matter?" I said. "Is Benjamin the only one you don't recognize?"

"Oh! Mother, how wondrously beautiful he is!" cried Cyprian to the woman who stood behind him, averting his gaze a little.

"Then why don't you want to greet me?"

Cyprian greeted me more joyfully perhaps than he had the rest of our brothers and sisters, but was it any more sincere?... I do not know. It was not without a certain reproach that I said: "You seem more like a painter at this moment than a brother."

"Very true," he replied in a hushed, clipped voice. And again he stared at me.

For in those days I suppose I was rather beautiful, very beautiful in fact. You would never credit it today, Anna. You would certainly all refute it. Today my eyes are sunken, watery, lifeless. My hair has grown thin, even begun to go grey, I believe. The skin on my shrunken cheeks is scarred by hideous furrows. My complexion has not gone black or ashen but merely dried up like a grubby piece of paper. And my lips have become so twisted in such an habitual smile of distaste that happy people find it a bore to look at me. How is it that a man can grow so old in only his twenty-sixth year?!... It's true, is it not, ladies, that something is not quite right? Ha! At least I can comfort myself by saying that I was beautiful once upon a time... beautiful... beautiful...

Every time Cyprian glanced at me, some brighter thought seemed to pass visibly across his face. Sometimes he closed his eyes as if he was trying to examine that thought better inside his own head; sometimes he appeared to be angered by something about me, and then he would knit his brow, bite his lips. This latter change to his features became more and more pronounced as the festive supper drew to its close, for I too had begun to regard him with more studied attention.

Once the initial elation of our mutual greetings had died down and once Cyprian's face—enlivened by our embraces and flushed from his sudden transition into the light and warmth—had begun to resume its usual aspect, I was gripped to the core by a sudden chill, for I had observed the marks of a terrible devastation.

Cyprian had inherited my father's facial features but the fair hair and white complexion of my mother. Now those features seemed thin and stretched out of all proportion. His skin, once so fresh, had acquired a chalky, deathly pallor. The sockets of his eyes had grown larger indeed, and yet his eyes had fled somewhere deep beneath his brow. His hair had gone grey, yes, even more so than mine has today. His nose had become terribly bent, his chin protruded sharply, his bony cheeks projected almost though his skin.

My mother was eyeing him with concern. No doubt he must have noticed this, because having remained silent for a while, seemingly weary, he again livened up, began to talk in a loud voice and told us thousands of small details about his journey. It was clear Cyprian wished to deceive that enquiring maternal gaze—unhappy yet unerring—with torrents of words and impulsive movements. His ailing disposition nevertheless got the better of him for a moment—he broke off abruptly and burst into the cough he had been suppressing for a long time.

An anxious stir arose amongst the women. Cyprian motioned to them with his hand to leave him alone. He covered his mouth with a handkerchief and then steered the remainder of the attack into an empty smile.

"It's nothing, nothing, I only choked," he said quickly, thrusting the handkerchief into his pocket.

I was sitting right beside him and I alone noticed there was blood on the handkerchief.

"I consecrate this glass to your peace of mind!" he went on jauntily.

"Better drink water," I whispered to him quietly. But when I reached for the carafe, I brushed against him so hard, though quite unintentionally, that all the wine in his glass spilled onto the tablecloth.

Cyprian turned to me with an impatient movement.

"You are a little clumsy, little brother. That's a shame." And he stared at me with a look of distinct dissatisfaction in his eyes. I withstood his gaze.

"Have some water," I repeated half as a plea, half as an order.

"I shall drink whatever you wish, Beniaminek," he replied, his face brightening slightly with a smile. "I shall drink vinegar and even bile, for once again you are adorable, but you must heed one piece of advice…"

"Three pieces of your advice, Cyprian—only you must accept two words from me. You're ill," I whispered in his ear.

"We'll discuss that later," he said in the most indifferent of voices and banged his empty glass forcefully on the table in order to smother the words he was exchanging with me.

"My advice to you, Benjamin, is this: that above all you should be happy. I'm telling you: absolutely happy. For if you're not, you'll become ugly, so ugly that even Ludwinka, who loves everything that is unhappy, won't recognize you and will turn away from you in disgust."

My kindly sister denied this with all haste but Cyprian would not give up.

"I can prophesy with complete certainty in this respect," he said. "As a painter I have studied different transformations, the effects of different impressions on different facial features, and I can swear to you that Benjamin will become horrendously ugly if he experiences unhappiness—because his face is created to reflect only joy…"

Oh! Then I took up arms to defend myself!

"You observe my face joyful at this point in time," I said, "perhaps still childish even. But how can you be the prophet of my feelings at different moments, of my face in a future that is still unknown? Am I so weak and sickly? And yet not so long ago you were praising my beauty? What beauty? Do you mean the beauty of the plants, which varies according to their species and colour, health and robustness? And I thought you had read at first glance the secrets of my soul written on my brow and seen in them the reflection of your own being. You greeted me with that artistic word "beautiful," but now I see that all you had in mind were lines and colours."

"Be angry, be angry, my child." He answered my accusations with a smile. I was not angry, but I felt terribly sad.

"Cyprian," I said after a while. "Even if your prediction were to come true, it would be of no consequence as I shall challenge unhappiness to the fight. I will be uglier but I will be a better person."

"In your unhappiness?"

"Yes, indeed! In unhappiness, when I test all my strengths, when I exert all the rights of my humanity—for the struggle against unhappiness is our supreme right, the struggle against unhappiness our supreme strength!"

I said something or other along these lines and more in the same vein, but now I cannot recall a single word. And though I would like to make up for my lack of recollection with inspiration, in truth I find that harder still: I cannot find either in my feelings or in my mind anything resembling the blessed dreams of my former fresh imagination. I raised unhappiness to the power of an ideal. I composed a hymn in its honour, and in the final thought of the final stanza I pressed the most proud-spirited of challenges to the adverse blows of fate. Madman that I was!...

Cyprian listened, watched me, smiled. And when I had finished he ran his long white fingers nonchalantly through my hair, which in those days fell onto my shoulders like that of a highlander.

"What a child he is! What a beautiful child he still is," he said as if talking to himself. "He does not realize that the human creature in its superiority possesses only the power to consume, the ability to enjoy happiness—the power to create pleasure. And yet he has heard, albeit from his mother, about a ninth heaven where the elect rejoice throughout eternity face-to-face with God... The struggle against suffering... He imagines that this will be a moment of improvisation such as he has just composed for us—a play of nerves, a quickening of the blood such as he has just experienced. My dearest loveliest child, it will be something of quite a different nature"—and now his fingers fondled the full length of my hair. "It will be this hair,"—he went on—

"this miraculous hair, radiant with the light of the sun, become thin and grey from endless nights without sleep; it will be those thoughts, shimmering in your brain today with all the colours of the rainbow, finding themselves caught up in the calculation of events, actions, probabilities, falsehoods; it will this breast, breathing today with the fullness of life, hoarsened by coughing, wracked by asthma; it will be that glassy-black eye clouded by a web of tiny blood vessels and shot with gall; it will be sickness, numbness, some great trouble over a fortune, over a woman, over some life-plan perhaps, but it will not be a struggle against unhappiness as you imagine it, Beniaminek. You imagine unhappiness looks like a white angel draped in black crêpe with a burning sword in his hand, and thus you would like to contend with him. Oh, I can well believe you might not grow ugly then! But I can tell you that unhappiness is no angel. Unhappiness looks like a dog that bites you stealthily, like a bigoted old woman slandering you in her piety, like a ragged Jewish moneylender clipping his coins and tampering with every gold piece of your life. Unhappiness looks like a drunk at daybreak, a hideous bat, a pool of filthy muck, an abscess under your fingernail, a soiled handkerchief. Fie, fie! Listen to my advice. Better to be happy, Beniaminek!" And he concluded with a loud laugh and a suppressed cough.

None of us laughed in reply. We all felt crushed by the weight of his strangely ironic words. Bronisława simply said: "You have expressed a great truth, Cyprian, in a rather comical way. But next time, don't dress it up in such horrid old rags because the children are frightened." And she bent over her small son who was leaning against her knee—a beautiful little boy with a broad pale brow and great dark eyes. "Unhappiness, my Bohdan, is a very ugly thing," she added. "Because unhappiness is both the evil that is done and the good that cannot be done—your own sin and the sin of others, of your brothers. Shun unhappiness."

The boy was lost in thought. After a while he answered. "Yes, mother, I will shun it."

Without saying anything, I indicated him to Cyprian. Cyprian understood the hint but merely shook his head, watched a little and then said casually: "That's quite different. Bohdan is older than you are: he today, you tomorrow."

There was no way we could understand one another.

The evening eventually came to an end. Everyone went to bed in the place prepared for them by Ludwinka's efforts.

Karol, Cyprian and I had been allotted the little room in the attic. Cyprian lay down first and ordered us to blow out the candle. Since he was exhausted by his journey, sick even, which was obvious from his face, we did not want to deprive him of essential moments of rest. We both followed his example, leaped swiftly into bed and fell asleep still more swiftly, drifting into that delicious, blessed first sleep that you experience every night when you are still young and undisturbed. At least, that was how I fell asleep.

Suddenly, a few hours later perhaps, I was woken by a bright light. I stared before me. Cyprian was standing by my bed.

He was holding a lighted candle in one hand and shielding the flame with the other so that Karol lay in shadow and all the light fell on me. Beneath his dishevelled, unbuttoned shirt I could see his sunken chest and all the bones drawn with anatomical precision below the skin. It was how you might imagine a skeleton with only flesh-coloured membrane stretched over it. Yet all the life from that corpse-like chest had fled to the face, as if to compensate for it. At that moment it was a face restored to first youth though the play of nerves and muscles—eyes gleaming with a warm glow, lips swollen and purple from a fresh rush of blood, forehead radiant in the reflection of some unseen star. In a word, it was the head of one raised from the dead resting on the shoulders of a corpse. A staggering contradiction, outrageous yet miraculous.

Bound by its spell, in the moment of unexpected awakening, I was unable to summon words to question my brother. I merely wiped my eyes, sprang to my feet, and then sat down again on the bed. My brother pushed me gently back down onto the covers and signalled to me to keep silent.

"What is it?" I inquired at last.

Cyprian frowned a little and sat down on the edge of my bed. He still had the candle turned fully on my face but said nothing in reply.

"What is it?" I asked for the second time.

Again he was silent. But after a while he avoided my question with one of his own: "What were you dreaming about?"

"I can't remember anything," I replied, for that was the truth.

"That's very bad, Benjamin. Try, perhaps it'll come back to you."

"Really, I can't remember. Not a thing."

"And I'd give my left arm, as far as my elbow, if only you could."

"Don't wait for me, Cyprian, because you'll catch cold again. How can you get up on Christmas night with that cough, wander around barefoot and not even throw a coat over yourself?"

My brother hissed and bit his lip.

"I asked you what you were dreaming about," he insisted again.

"We can talk about it but put on something warmer first or lie down beside me."

"Listen, Benjamin," he said with suppressed but obvious impatience. "The Alpine cold, for God's sake, never harmed me! I slept several times under the snow. I have been in mountains where the breath froze in my mouth and yet I always returned healthier and more invigorated. But one day when I was incensed about something, the blood gushed at once from my nose and mouth. So I am warning you about this infirmity of mine, little brother: don't make me angry! Because you see, my dear," he went on, sensing my surprise and anxiety, "there are moments in life that should not be squandered on trivial impressions: 'But you'll catch cold'—'But eat'—'But drink'—'But this, that and the other.' I cannot abide all this worthless solicitude! If you fritter away your feelings on it, then you'll lack heart in times of crisis. I care now—as a matter of life and death—about summoning up your dream-phantom; in my head I have the future, I have glory! And all you do is remind me of my cough, and if I'd only let you, you'd start offering me elderberry tea! Are you some lovesick German woman, a hospital nurse? You're unbearable!"

"I am not going to tell you anything now," I replied. "It would be better if you just said what you want."

"I want to see what you were dreaming about?"

"What a strange man you are! It would easier for me to make up some dream from inspiration."

"Why yes, indeed! Please go ahead..."

"So listen. I was dreaming that I was descending into a deep cavern with a lamp flickering in my hand. In the cavern there was such great treasure that..."

"You're lying, Benjamin. I can remember your dream better than you. Just reflect a moment: did you not imagine that you were an Ancient Greek in those beautiful days when Greece was young?"

"Oh no, you can be sure of that! In all my dreams of past or future I was and always will be a mining engineer from the Tatras, the son of my own fathers."

"Are you really so sure, Benjamin? Perhaps you also dreamed you were a poet. But let us understand one another correctly: not a poet with a pen in his hand, with fingers stained in ink, bent over a wooden desk—and still in his dressing-gown and slippers at that. Oh, no! Perhaps you dreamed you were a poet in ancient times when the earth was still young, dreamed you held in your hand a seven-stringed lyre. And above you there was nothing but the sky and all around you—instead of four walls of damp brick—boundless open space and a wall of human breasts pulsating with life. And then you sang your great, resounding, fearless song—and the people listened, felt, believed. They laughed and cried and rung their iron swords to the rhythm of your song. And the song was all yours, Benjamin, and the Olympic wreath—for though you sung many songs for the crowd, you alone were victorious; the crowd of common people fell at your feet while your fellow masters humbled themselves before you. Well what do you think? Would it not be worth dreaming such a dream? Even to then fall dumb forever after…?"

"You have spoken true, brother. You can recall my own dreams better than I myself. I have sometimes dreamed the poet's dream but without the Olympic wreath, without rivals humbling themselves before me, without crowds at my feet. I dreamed only that the hearts of my fellow human beings would beat rhythmically to the pulse of my own blood, that every feeling cast into creation would radiate in my own feeling, that I was one with all beings and all beings were one with me—not below me, not further away, but just here beneath the touch of my brotherly hand, in the very sound of my song."

"Good, Benjamin, good. But the sound of your song is still not the totality of your life. You are young. Youth in itself is power and potential. You are bound to make use of it, one way or another, bound to expend your surfeit of energy even on frivolous things. To satisfy the demands of your violent impulses, you have to create a fitting madness—for your arteries are all swollen, flowing with red-hot juice like scalding lava; if you don't channel your surfeit into the pleasures of the world, then nature will step back and poison the inner depths of your soul. You must let yourself go, Benjamin. Did you not have such a dream? Perhaps you also saw yourself riding a golden chariot, slackening the reins of your gallant steeds and charging to the winning-post alongside the most renowned heroes of the chase. You are so young, so inept—better give up, for a thousand eyes are upon you! There sits a row of women. And here are the elders who will solemnly scold you for your imprudence, and there your young companions who will mock your premature vanity. Give up! You should still be in the *gyneceum*, being nursed with sweet songs or separating out the coloured threads on the loom. Give up! You child, you weak ridiculous man! Your head reels and your hands are faint and feeble. Ha, perhaps you've already been told that before! But you did not want to listen. Your brain began to boil in your head from the confusion, the clamour. Your hands tremble as you grasp the reins; you are almost mesmerized by the eyes of the spectators—the more there are, the better. You've boarded your chariot and are flying. Your horses froth at the mouth. Covered in a cloud of dust, you cannot see the sky. You are racing against space itself. Will you escape it? Outstrip it? And can you hear how they laugh? Oh the mockery of the common herd is like a harpy[43] gnawing at your heart, its insulting laughter a burning iron beneath your skull! Hurry, hurry! Because that chariot bedecked in purple will overtake you, its white horses streaming through the air like flying arrows. And do you hear the applause? Do you hear the cries of triumph? Hurry, hurry! There, opposite you, sit the judges watchful-eyed, the finishing-post is already near. A sudden rush of air stems the voice in your chest. You try to scream; if only you could scream, your steeds would gain new strength. Ha, you have screamed and you are at the post! You are the first. Gaze now at the spectators and laugh at those who doubted you! Take your prize and walk from the lists with head held high, with pride in your eye, and listen how the words pass from mouth to mouth along your way: 'That's him, that's him, the victor of the hippodrome....'"

My brother fell silent and stared at me. I must confess to you, ladies and gentlemen, that when anyone spoke to me in those days of horses or horse racing, of such sudden fluctuations in hope and doubt, then it was as if they were shuffling cards and jangling stakes of gold before the eyes of a card-sharper. A warmer feeling came over me. I began to laugh. Cyprian ran his fingers though my hair and spoke again. But this time his voice was graver, deeper, even trembling a little now and then.

"Maybe you also dreamed, Benjamin, that your head was sprinkled with Arabian scents, your tunic woven from the finest Sidonian wool, your brow adorned with a crown of roses—and that that brow was resting in the lap of a woman. But not that of your mother, oh no! Not of your sister, nor even yet of your lover... Benjamin, do you understand that moment when a woman is not yet your lover, but already in love and loved? Do you understand that moment? And have you seen such a woman? A beautiful woman, strong in passion and inviolable in her soul? On her forehead such power of thought that she would be capable of steering Athens.[44] And yet on her lips such rapture. In her gaze such burning, penetrating attraction... Have you dreamed of her? Eh, what do I care for the ceremony of conventional marriage! What do I want with a virgin who coyly lowers her eyes as though she were nodding off? Innocently laces her lips and gives me nothing in life except the rights stipulated by the law-book? Oh! How different is my beauty from that petty little soul pasted together from the standard moral prescriptions! As different as lightning from a candle-flame! You too, Benjamin, have dreamed of one quite other. Her eyes, cast down, are like the too dazzling ray of hope or memory and thus shaded over; her blushing cheek is but her blood, the life that rushes violently to the surface from her brimming organism; and her love!... You did not know your own power, did not understand the world, had no sense of God until she fell in love with you. Beauty, happiness, a miracle—such is her love. Believe me, brother! Such women do exist. You may meet one. And one day you may long to die in her arms, even if you are happy, in order never to be otherwise. And do not call this kind of happiness sensuality, or your bliss dissipation. Sensuality is but the most bodily form of the ascent of human nature towards the fullness of Divinity—in body and soul. Bliss itself will stand witness against dissipation. The sensualist does not feel or the libertine enjoy as much as you will feel with all the powers of your soul, as you will enjoy with all the virility of your young strength. And if you were not to receive recognition every minute of your own worth; if she were not the Medea who commands the elements—but the Medea who would never commit a crime because she would always be loved[45]; if—after resting your head on her soft cushions—you were no longer hard enough to sleep in your Spartan discomfort[46]; if she were not to spit from her pampered lips in time of need at the tortures borne, her tongue drenched in blood; if you both were to lack the imagination that turns every golden kiss into poetry, or the bold thoughts which draw strength from every moment of joy, which always reveal a new truth or create a new means to happiness; if you were not so powerful in spirit, not so elevated by your intelligence, not so noble in your confession of your self-belief—then you could not be so happy. For happiness—listen! Let yourself dream of it at least, Benjamin!—happiness is given only to those who know how to suffer most humbly for the good of their neighbours—or how to press most passionately their lover to their breast."

Cyprian again fell silent, though I was still listening to him. My head swam with strange wonders as his words coursed through my veins with my life-blood. And yet I felt the need to resist these thrilling sensations.

"Tempter!" I whispered under my breath.

My brother leaned forward and kissed my forehead. But the candle he was holding suddenly began to flicker, fell to the floor with the candlestick and went out. I seized Cyprian by the hand. His hand was cold as ice. I screamed. Karol awoke, quickly sprang out of bed and relit the candle. By the light of the candle we saw Cyprian hanging over the end of the bed, unconscious. Large clots of blood were pouring from his mouth. He was a ghastly pale yellow. I thought he was already dead. At that moment the church-bells began to ring out, summoning the villagers to midnight mass…

Please excuse me, ladies and gentlemen… I must take a little rest. As I recall that image, it seems more terrible to me now than it did even then.

❧ III ❧

AND THAT WHOLE GRUESOME INCIDENT: have you been wondering what reason lay behind it? What goal inspired such an outburst?... Cyprian required my features to complete one of his paintings and had been studying and arranging them to reflect his artistic aims. My brother Cyprian was an artist, a great artist.

I will tell you one thing however: if I had to bestow a blessing today on my most beloved child, as was the custom of the ancient patriarchs, and if I believed in the infallibility of my blessing like people believed once in the supernatural power of chants, then I would raise my eyes to heaven over the head of the child kneeling before me and cry from the depths of my soul: "May God remove all artists from your life's path." Ha! Now you are ready to be angry with me, all you lovers of beauty and art! But I am not talking about you. Art and beauty absorbed usefully into life belong to everyone—to me, to you, to all people. But to be an artist is quite a different thing from being a consumer. To be an artist means no more than to be endowed with a certain amount of brain-matter that creates a certain protuberance in a certain place in the skull. Nothing more, believe me! Someone who uses or enjoys something must have the heart to love the thing they use or enjoy. Loving never shuts itself away within itself; loving sheds light into infinity with good impulses and noble deeds. But an artist does not love, he creates. Work after work falls from him; moment after moment descends into space, is encased in forms and shapes and remains as dust, as emptiness, which even the wisdom of Solomon cannot fill until it is inspired by another person's feeling, until another's enthusiasm awakens and propels it into the infinity of life. An artist only creates. He creates, however, because he has talent and must create, because his entire being and organism demand it, because the bee must produce honey, the flower give out scent, the water flow in the river. But how does he create? For what purpose does he create? What sets him apart is not some special artistic nature. Sometimes he creates by terrible means: in order to paint the dying Christ, he nails a living person to a cross and fatally wounds him by thrusting a sword into his side. In order to sing a song of love, he calmly rests his ear against the shaken breast, tunes the bloodied strings of the sufferer's heart and manipulates them with his marble fingertips till they bring forth an artistic sound. And when they do bring it forth, even if all the strings break and become entangled, he tears away his fingers and transfers them as swiftly as he can to the ivory keys of the piano—or maybe the hairs of his bow—and whatever he has overheard, he reproduces exactly; whatever he has used to stretch his memory, he uses to augment the echo of the wind and brass. Sometimes the artist will invent the impression of a sound from within himself, sketch for himself an image seen nowhere before! Oh that is even more dangerous! For you surely realize he is not able to immortalize it as mere love and emotion, he has to capture it in physical shape and form, thus ensuring its finiteness. So he seeks form as well, chooses his conditions, tests his idea—and always on living specimens like when doctors try out new medicines... though doctors do it only on animals... Well, what of it? Are we to hurl curses at the artist for so doing? And suppose he were to give you in exchange for your blood and suffering some great work of art? The most beautiful picture? The exquisite melody of a song? Well? Would you curse him then? Oh no! But just make sure that those whom you love steer clear of artists... Look, what a splendid fire we have! Exuding light and warmth. A splendid fire! And yet gradually, you have all moved away from the hearth leaving a wide empty berth around it. The genius of an artist is like a fire. Cast into it whatever prey you will, but don't discard the golden happiness of your friends or hearts that beat with love. Or are you some kind of latter-day Sabians or Guebres?[47] Worshippers of all that glitters? For I tell you that the dazzling brilliance of that genius has become for you like air, like food and drink. The gods have been debarred from nature, people nowadays no longer prostrate themselves before the sun, the moon, the stars—so you too should cut out the adoration from your enjoyment of art and beauty! Cast down the artists from your altars! Because your worship of them is only a new form of idolatry, of intellectual Sabaism. What is divine in an artist is what you give to him and he to you; what is divine in an artist must constantly be disengaged from him, so that it stands before you on its own; what is divine in him is what seeps out from his soul like black gold, coming to the surface to smoulder and shimmer only when it encounters your gaze, your minds, your feelings—and yet deep down inside him there is nothing more than a mass of black earthbound clay, of a slightly different type than your own. Yes, that's a good way of putting it. What's the use of judging, blaming, praising?—An artist is just a little bit different, and that's the end of it! Let whoever wants to, worship whiteness and condemn blueness! I harbour no grudge against Cyprian. Poor Cyprian! His wrecked life, the disturbed dreams of my youth! Could I have guessed it was all just a plan for a picture? When Karol took the fainting man by the hand and helped him back to bed, I felt nothing but the keenest pain. Later, when our sisters had been told and our parents come upstairs, I did not have a single free moment to escape into my newly wakened personality, a single flutter of my heart to waste on secondary impressions. We restored Cyprian to consciousness, saved his life. I would have transformed myself into each drop of refreshing water that restored his lifeless brow, into any word of comfort that calmed my trembling, frightened mother. I suffered on his behalf, on behalf of them all; I suffered with my own suffering. And there were times later in life when I even yearned not for past pleasures, not for my lost freedom, but to experience again that first pain. Such pain does not exhaust the spirit; while there is still hope of easing the distress of others, of enriching them, even if it means your own extreme poverty, then pain still has something with which to consecrate itself. But when it merely inflames us and even creates obstacles and scandal for others, then it becomes a true agony: horrifying, demented as a wild beast, godless as hell!

Cyprian gradually returned to himself, thanked us for our solicitude through his gaze and uncertain smile, but he was too feeble to speak. He fell asleep eventually and we took it in turns to look after him. I was the first to take up my place beside him but once the others had dispersed I did not want to let anyone back in. Sitting like that, sitting hour after hour in the most profound silence, I did not know myself by what train of thought I fell into contemplating the things Cyprian had told me before he fainted. And it was a strange kind of reverie. Sometimes I felt stifled, sick with yearning to the point of despair; later it was as if I had to rush somewhere violently, as if something would elude me by a split second or overtake me, as if I had lost patience with something, as if I couldn't break the seal of a letter I had been longing to receive, couldn't break or untie the rope that bound my legs. With a sudden reflex I clenched my hands together, interlocking my fingers so tightly all the joints cracked; then I clasped both hands round my crossed knees. I don't know whether it was the sudden movement that aroused Cyprian or whether he woke for some other reason, but when I looked at him he already had his eyes open and fixed intently upon me.

"Perhaps I've acted wrongly?" he said in his former kindly, brotherly voice. "The dreams I have planted in your soul were premature and you are already suffering."

"Oh why do you speak again of suffering?" I did my best to keep him calm. "Sleep, brother, sleep! I could not be happier, if it were not for your illness."

"If that's so, then all's well and good. I woke up with regretful thoughts in the very moment you wrung your hands. In what remained of my dream I was imagining I might be the beginning of your restlessness."

"My restlessness? Maybe. But let us think first of you, Cyprian."

"I'm the last thing you should be thinking about, my Beniaminek! First… I've already been anticipating what comes first. A pity too, because you will suffer a little, now or later. But it couldn't have been otherwise. My picture comes first and foremost." And with this utterance it was as though he cast off all responsibility from his conscience. "Although you will suffer," he resumed very calmly, "I will reward you for it. I will take you with your life, your youth, your dreams, the wondrous beauty of your features; I will take you, Beniaminek, and carry you into the world of happiness. I will place your head in the lap of the woman before whom I fell on bended knee when she first revealed herself to me. I will make you infatuated, I will pamper and fondle you!... Why are you staring at me so oddly? Or have you still not understood that I am talking about my picture? My picture represents all my knowledge and learning, all my passions, my ultimate hope! From the moment I conceived it in mind and spirit, I have felt it drawing into itself all my vital powers; on the day it becomes separated from me, when it stands apart visibly as a finished work of art, then you will be able to say, Benjamin: "I had a brother, Cyprian."

"What picture do you mean? What picture?" I kept repeating in the brief intervals when he stopped speaking.

"My picture of Aspasia and Alcibiades.[48] Why Aspasia? Why Alcibiades? Ask the Lord God himself for an answer to that! I once stood in ecstasy before a wonderfully executed image of Our Lady mourning for her son. I saw lips that did not complain, tears that flowed without knowing it, a soul liberated from nervous compulsion, an earthly existence thrust deep into the abyss of forgetfulness—I saw and understood everything. Then, suddenly, the figures in my picture obscured my vision. Perhaps some wise man can explain this sign to you with his law of ultimate ends; all I know is that I had been admiring holiness in the most terrible agony when holiness in the highest transports of happiness revealed itself to me; I know that I had been praying to the Immaculate Virgin of the Christians when a notion of the pagan past entered my soul and commanded me to paint it—commanded me in no uncertain terms to paint it; and from then on, my whole life has been the continuation of my work on this one picture, and not only of work at my easel. Everywhere and in every moment I collected colours for it, sketches, rearranged the composition in every kind of light, until in the end its subject took possession of me, seeped into me until I was saturated with it. And I began to live it—in the Athenian manner, in moments of pleasure, beauty and youthful strength... Oh! Yet it seems to me that people have regressed, become more backward, since today they dare to deny such a life ... Oh, yet such things, my Benjamin, the songs, dancing, clamour of a sumptuous feast, ethereal robes of fair-skinned women, ruby-gold liquids frothing in translucent glass, the heady perfume of flowers and perfumed haze rising from incense-burners struck from precious metal, the bright light of pure olive oil, bright light of priceless gems, and the brightest light of all: the gaze of beautiful eyes—yet such things are good! Oh, they are good, my Benjamin, because they make you happy! It is not possible that you should be repelled by them! And when your thought soars still higher in the sky, when you even outstrip all this in your desire for glory and beautify it with a moment of inspiration, when your own talent gives you more than the many things you have already, oh then indeed you will have no cause to bemoan your life, your love, your powers! Now I understand why the Athenians possessed such courage in the face of death, such courage as you will never find subsequently in the whole of human history. Only because they knew how to live! They lived to the full in all their natural inclinations, in the full potential of their nature! He who dies in the secure faith that he will go to Heaven has no courage in the face of death; he has only a great impatience to gain a better life. But the man who does not know what will befall him in the hereafter or is assured that nothing can befall him, who sees nothing in his passing away but the disintegration of his organism, the pain of sickness, the stiffness of his corpse and the ashes in his funeral urn, and yet strides boldly forward—such a man as he does not fear death. And I will tell you who in particular is able not to fear it: the truly happy man, and he alone! Believe me, brother, nothing reconciles humankind to the inevitable better than happiness. He who has happily made the most of everything, dug deep with both hands into the world's treasures or deep with his whole brain into the riches of the human mind, such a man will have no quarrel with destiny. In every human being there is a certain dose of commercial plain dealing: you take so much from nature—you give back so much, and it's quits. You take life—you give life back. You take it to enjoy it—you return it expended; the slate is clean, the sums perfectly balanced; who wants to haggle over any balance left over? But when unhappiness inserts a long row of terrible nothings, of doleful zeros, alongside the digit that stands for you—then it augments itself of its own accord, multiplying its value hundreds and thousands of times. How can I pay back what I have bought with my tears? How can I pay back what has cost me so much suffering? Give back what I have not yet taken? My convulsions are the swindling death duty I've had to pay for my tears and suffering—the toll for all my years of loss, calculated according to some false calendar bearing no relation to the size of my pain. If an unhappy man in a paroxysm of despair, in an attack of madness, fails to take his own life, then never believe him when he says he wishes to die. For it is precisely the unhappy man who wishes to live. The unhappy man clings to tomorrow with all the strength in his stiffening hands, for he is bound to tomorrow by something more powerful than hope itself: by his curiosity. But what kind of happiness is that either? The unhappy man fears everything; the unhappy man is the most despicable coward though he denies it before himself and others; the unhappy man, as death approaches, dies with a curse on his lips, hurling at God the sneering insults of hell and spitting upon an unintelligible, incomprehensible world which had given him needs but not the means to satisfy them, given him time to suffer but not one moment of joy. I will not die thus, little brother! I have been happy, I have loved, I have enjoyed, and I have created my picture: I have had everything and regret nothing."

As he spoke these last words my brother, who had revived and grown visibly stronger during the course of his speech, suddenly got up from his bed as if he were the fittest man alive and began to dress hurriedly.

"Aha, my Benjamin!" he called to me with a laugh. "You still haven't grasped half of what I've been saying! You still don't understand the first thing about me!"

"I don't understand you at all, you're right," I replied slowly, with deliberation.

"Because you don't understand anything, happiness or unhappiness. You're still a child!"

"You're wrong. It's only in your picture that I don't understand myself."

"But you would like to understand. You see: curiosity. The first step on the road to hell. And it seems to you, apparently, that you'd be up to wrestling with unhappiness, which is but the eternal, restless and never satisfied curiosity to know about life. Stop fooling yourself with these delusions! Go where you have to go, and be happy: experience and take!"

As you can see, ladies and gentlemen, Cyprian was beginning to act strangely. He was feverish. But why did I listen to him? Lend him my ear, pay heed in spirit? He in the meantime paced around the room talking to me, till he drew near a large roll of canvas that stood at the head of his bed, not far from where I sat. He touched the canvas and—an amazing thing—I shuddered as though, without any warning, I had felt its touch.

"Show me!" was all I cried.

Cyprian hesitated.

"She is here," he said quietly, "my Aspasia, I have her now." His chest swelled in a deep sigh, his brow shone with the mighty power of his thoughts, his lips fell open with words of love, with the promise of a kiss. "I have her now, she is here, close to both of us. Aspasia— my burning flame, Aspasia—my resounding chord, Aspasia—my delight in wisdom and wisdom in delight! My Aspasia! My lover who made me forever indifferent to the charms of other women, who stood before me in my childish musings and my restless nocturnal dreams as an eternal phantasm, a vision of the unattainable! My Aspasia!... My own!... But you will be hers! Oh, yes, Benjamin! I have emptied all the treasure-houses of my soul in order to compose this picture of a woman. Today, I cannot say whether she was so rich or I so poor, but I lacked the ideal model to create a lover worthy of her love. When she stepped down from the lifeless canvas, vibrant and resplendent; when she sat before me in all the majesty of our shared happiness, I retreated before my own power and my own incompetence. Having achieved so much, I began to tremble... for it seemed to me I would never achieve anything more. For a year I have been living in this terrible state of conflict, locked in battle with my unfinished work. Perhaps this is what sustains me, for it is already quite clear to me that when I finish my picture, my whole career will end and I will die. But, as I told you a moment ago, Benjamin, death does not frighten me. On the contrary, such long exertion has begun to take its toll—and yet, since yesterday, I find myself twice as happy! I have found him! I have found him! God himself has given you to me, Benjamin! How happy you are! How beautiful you will be by her side! All yesterday evening I studied the wonderful oval of your face and the vigour of your movements and the softness of your gaze and the tender outline of your lips... You countered me at times with an expression of anxious sadness. I cannot conceive of you as sad... No... Say what you will: sadness does not become you. You are made to be happy. Thus I lay in bed trying in vain to sleep as you kept flashing before my eyes in all the different transformations of your face, and I could not seize upon the right moment. Ha! Then I took the candle and went over to you, and again, again you were the one I'd been seeking for so long throughout the world. Beautiful! Oh, how beautiful! You had lain one hand beneath your head which was resting slightly thrown back; your other arm hung loose, stretched out along the length of your body; your white neck, lovingly turned on the potter's wheel, joined in a marvellous sweep your uncovered shoulders; your young breast, the colour of marble yet burning hot, fluttering from your quickening breath, while the phantoms of Paradise danced over your slumbering features—like spirits rising from the depths of still water to ruffle the glassy surface. You awoke and at once I thought I would forfeit everything, but no—I had regained everything, oh and more too! How I wished I could have taken up my brush and palette then and there, so the human form brought to life by its own sleep and by the impression left by my words would not escape me, so the youth with the shining brow would not dissolve in mist—a youth whose infancy was now being overtaken by manhood, by the violence of his first desire, by the weakness of his last moments of timidity, a youth already so strong, so proud, so greedy he was ready 'to kiss all women from north to south' on one set of lips,[49] or cut off with a single blow all the heads of the terrible hydra of this world, or gather all peoples to his heart like brothers in a single embrace, or drink a toast to all earthly pleasures from a single golden goblet—and to be famous, beautiful, happy, loved! Ah! And to love! Boundlessly, endlessly... That is indeed my Alcibiades, my Benjamin, the lover of my beautiful, my lovely Aspasia..."

Cyprian could not help abandoning himself in this way to his imagination; Cyprian was an artist. But I was still a child and I took real delight in… this happiness, not yet within myself—but in his words, in his Alcibiades—in the way he painted him in words. I felt something akin to rays or rings of burning heat spreading from my heart to fill my chest and from the back of my head to cover my forehead. I grabbed the canvas which Cyprian was holding and began in haste to rip off all the strings which had been wound around it. But at that moment the door was pushed ajar and my mother, anxious about her son, entered on tiptoe. Cyprian knocked the half-opened package out of my hands and rushed towards the woman who had just come in. If any of you possess a tendency towards mysticism, just try to imagine how in that moment two opposing spirits battled over my future. The spirit of darkness cast down by my brother's hand, still clumsily wrapped in the rough packing material, writhed about on the floor like a filthy reptile unwilling to concede its ground; whilst the spirit of light, the woman, the mother, with her calm smile, her affectionate word, obliterated its power, wiped away moment by moment its sway over my life; and it was repulsed to a point far off—repulsed at least for the time being.

Our mother scolded Cyprian for getting up too soon but when she saw him truly improved in health and more cheerful, she led us both downstairs to the room where everyone was gathered together, just as we are today, around the warm fireplace. Julcia sang a little, the children made a lot of noise, and when we returned to our room that night Cyprian no longer wanted to unroll his canvas. Every day of the Christmas holiday passed in this way and I left home without seeing the picture. And Cyprian was in better health.

> Blessed be my days of youth!
> On bed of flowers, my golden dream!
> Ideals of faith, of virtue, love
> And freedom's radiant beam![50]

Oh to possess a young and still unblemished heart! Swept up like a shell on a faraway beach, its every wound a precious pearl! Its every unease an ideal. Fling a handful of mud at such a heart and after one hour of its dreaming you'll find the mud crystallized into precious diamonds. Blessed, blessed be the days of my youth!

Ah, if you only knew how I crystallized Cyprian's words! And how I lived with them a full six months, almost entirely alone with them amid mountains and forests! I fell in love with Aspasia. But it was not that dreamy kind of love without aim; my dreams and longings were not for a feeling as yet unknown, the fumbling of a heart roused for the first time by surges of hotter blood. No, I was distinctly in love with my brother's words and with the woman in his picture, who surely existed though I had never seen her. I had some notion of my feelings and an object to fit the notion; all that was lacking was a glimpse of it. Sometimes, in my impatience, I was ready to mount my horse and rush back to my parents' home, but more often than not I would think: what would I gain from such a glimpse?! I loved Aspasia, priestess of happiness, beauty and intellect. Happiness, beauty and intellect, they were my love. Until then I had lived by whatever life brought me of its own accord; now I spread my covetous arms and reached out on all sides for dreams, revelations, knowledge. Until then, if something were not an object of my love, I would pass it by without paying it any attention, without giving it a thought; until then my world had been a wonderful world indeed, but it had been a small and limited world, a world where anything that did not concern me had simply fallen away into non-existence. Now, nothing was indifferent, nothing was empty. Now I had to take something from everything, extract a moment of pleasure, interest, learning—and if I was not able to do so, then I would let fly in indignation, distinguishing myself by my disgust, anger, scorn. And anything that was not full of life meant nothing to me. I had discovered a new world, a different other world, a complete world. And hence it was true, wasn't it? That I loved Aspasia? Now it seems to me that it was then that I loved her the most, the most truly, for then and only then did I unfurl all the powers of my spirit, like a bird unfurls its feathers to the wings of flight; only then did I let loose all the elements of my being, like a ship lets loose its sails to the wind, as I flew away, rushing headlong into infinity… into infinity! Oh, it was then that I loved Aspasia the most!

❦ IV ❦

O NE DAY IN JULY, a day rapidly sinking towards evening, it grew very sultry, without sun or storm, and so heavy—as when the sky cannot shed its tears of rain and must bear down ever lower upon the earth, with ever darker and more swollen clouds. If on such a day I had tried to sit quietly with my arms crossed, my breast would simply have burst. Honest Bazyl, my oldest friend from childhood, now more companion than servant, understood this only too well. On fine days he never inquired of me, but when the weather was inclement he always groomed my horse and prepared it for saddling, since once I had completed my day's work it was my unfailing habit to mount my steed and ride off into the mountains, into the forests. But on that day my journey had another purpose. For the past two weeks I'd been expecting with great impatience a letter from home, yet in vain! It had to be waiting for me at the post-house in the neighbouring village. My black steed Falcon, as if he knew all about it, leaped from an ambling stride into a regular gallop, while I was so tossed from side to side the reins flew from my hands. We sped through the forest. The denseness of the trees absorbed what remained of the impure light; all around, as often happens, there loomed only that other, visible kind of darkness. Then, all of a sudden, we were startled by a rustling as the branches of a tree snapped; something snorted, hissed; then the pupils of a wildcat flashed by like two blood-red sparks in the darkness and a body crashed to the ground right in front of my horse. Before I could make out what it was, Falcon whinnied in terror, flung himself to one side and bore me away like one possessed.

I was struck in the face by longer boughs of trees hanging over the road, struck in the eyes—I could easily have smashed my head on a tree-trunk. But what could I do, ladies and gentlemen? Oh, if you had only known how I whistled to Falcon with all my might, urging him to make greater haste. Then I buried my face in his soft mane like a child nestling into a pillow and thought: "Ha! Let my Falcon fly wherever he wishes and for as long as he wishes!" And so Falcon flew—while many different images, pictures, fancies, memories flew through my mind, until Cyprian's words heard on that memorable night likewise descended upon me. In truth it seemed to me I was racing against space—not figuratively, but in reality, visibly and in person. It was a strangely agreeable feeling: space receding behind me in a stream of black earth, slipping away beneath the horse's hooves; space rushing past alongside me in two lines of gigantic dark outlandish shapes; space outstripping me overhead in a vast cloud of outstretched wings that I could never have caught up with, that I always saw before me like the spirit of some fabulous bird. Ah, I tell you, it was marvellous! I whistled once more. But Falcon was no longer running, no longer flying—it was as though he drew into himself the whole fabulous remoteness of the place with his powerful accelerated breathing; for the giant figures suddenly vanished, the cloud of birds fled, and nothing remained except an immense open space—boundless, barren, void. But it was an open space vocal with the sound of the wind whistling in my ears and the horse's shoes striking the stony ground—an infinity lit up from below by a glaring hail of sparks, creating from time to time what seemed like the breaking of a great wave of fire, as they merged in their flight into beams of light; yet on both sides it was so dark, so dark as though the world no longer existed. Then, suddenly, an enormous black mass loomed ahead of us—the shape of a mountain, but far off. And on the mountain a beacon worthy of that landscape cast its glow. Perhaps it was a volcano erupting?... And then we were nearer... no, it was not a volcano. It was a large edifice as though engulfed in flame, its thick walls like black brimstone and solid iron grilles standing out against the blinding light streaming from all the windows. Was the edifice on fire?... No, some kind of banquet was surely in full swing for I seemed to catch the sound of music, the hum of human voices. But Falcon, uttering that awesome whinny of pain and foreboding they call the horse's squeal, stifled it all. I could feel his skin trembling; damp patches of froth covered my hands and forehead; I could tell he was summoning new reserves of strength. I tried to restrain him. I wanted to spare my black steed, but how could I restrain him? We struggled for a moment. I had scarcely made known my desire to turn back, when he twisted to one side and again flew forward like an arrow. But it was more my fault than his. I confess I loved that wild insubordination of his and never cured him of a thousand bad habits, for I somehow revelled in the wild self-willed creature; it gave me more pleasure to put myself to the test or, as on that day, to let myself go with his free, unyielding nature, than to have a tool in my hands always obedient to my will. Besides, I could be sure of three things: Falcon's legs—that they would not stumble; the saddle-girth—that it would not burst; and myself—that I would not fall off and that, if need be, I could jump to the ground unscathed no matter how fast I was travelling.

During the course of the day the swollen clouds had been gathering ever thicker across the sky. A long drawn-out clap of thunder reverberated and died away in a mournful protracted echo. From time to time a flash of lightning lit up the horizon and went out. A heavy stifling heat filled the air, but no breath of wind, no drop of rain relieved the clouds of their burden or refreshed the soil. I looked around me. It was as though everything—the mountain, castle, lights—had suddenly been swallowed by the earth and vanished without a trace. There was no way of discerning, or guessing even, where the road led. Then the tense harsh breath of another horse suddenly struck my ear. I turned to my right and made out in the general blackness a deeper patch of black, like my own shadow almost—because it too was the shape of a human being sitting on horseback.

"Out of my way, out of my way!" shouted a voice, imperious and sure of itself, yet soft as if it issued from the breast of an immature youth.

"Out of whose way? And where to, my invisible comrade?" I replied cheerfully. "I'd be grateful if you'd tell me, as I seem to be lost."

Instead of an answer I heard the powerful swish of a riding-crop and the lash landing on Falcon's head, then clipped defiant laughter and what sounded like the rustle of a long cloak brushing against my side even as it passed.

I sprung up in the stirrups so I might see for myself and myself be seen.

"Ha! If that's the way it is," I cried, "then out of *my* way! Begone!"

And in that moment I took charge of Falcon, his nostrils flaring, back arched, and tried to bend him to my will like a child, like my own hand, my own mind. I did not stop to think what I wanted to achieve, what I was going to do—all I felt was an instinctive need to thrust myself headlong at that madman, even though we might smash all our bones in the encounter. My black steed guessed my intention; enflamed by the insult to himself, he now fell in entirely with my wishes. Exerting all the power in his muscles he reared on his hind legs as though about to jump the highest fence, when suddenly... the sky was split asunder by a long snake of fire—a thunderbolt, a roaring crash, a blinding flash of light! It all happened in the twinkling of an eye. Can you understand how it happened so fast, so unexpectedly? And yet it lasted so long...

It was then I saw her for the first time.

That's how it was: the first time I saw her was in a single flash of lightning. And at first I saw only her face gleaming at me, pale and wondrously beautiful. I could not see the rest of her. I remember pulling up my horse with a jerk; he then did the same to me—by some strange miracle we managed to keep a hold of each other. So how did it come about? Somehow, soon afterwards, I had caught up with her and was riding alongside her, forcing my horse to keep pace with hers. I still can't explain it to myself even today.

For a long time we rode side by side in the most profound silence. A strong wind was rising. From time to time heavy drops of rain fell on my face and hands, and from time to time the riding-crop swished through the air urging ever greater momentum—but did not land again on my horse. On the contrary, it was clear that the dark figure of the woman wanted to prove she could beat me by winning a simple race. But Falcon was having none of it; my Falcon stretched out his body like a taut wire close to the ground and would not be overtaken by a single step. And so we raced on and on. And I could tell only from the style of motion or the sounds I heard that we were crossing stones, sand, ploughed fields or meadows awash with water. At last the road began to climb uphill and our horses' gallop slowed to a canter. My companion hissed a few times with great impatience—and I seemed to hear the pounding of other hooves behind us.

"No, no! They're not going to catch me either!" repeated the bold yet melodious voice, the voice which had seemed at first to be that of a young man; and I can't say whether it was with the aid of that voice or the spurs that her dark form moved out in front of me the length of a horse's neck. By now the rain was streaming down. The flashes of lightning had ceased. Round about me, I could see absolutely nothing. Amid the black images of that black night the only thing that glowed and imprinted itself upon my memory, as though conjured by some black art, was the face of that woman— disembodied, without the limbs of her body, without even the full rounded form of her whole head: a face carved as though from the silver disk of the moon against the backdrop of a colourless sky.[51]

Had I really wished to pursue her? It was my Falcon who had pursued her after all; and when we came to a halt at the top of the hill, it was his hooves that resounded on the cobblestones. I could make out the twists and turns of solid walls. From the echo of the horses' hooves, I guessed we were passing through one and then another vaulted hallway until at last I heard a chain rattle somewhere. Then the great looming mass burst open before us. I tell you in all honesty: it blew apart—and a fiery brilliance erupted without warning from within the gaping chasm. I could only assume that this was the blazing castle I had approached from a different angle, but I could not be entirely sure at first since I was instantly blinded by the light. Once the my eyes had grown accustomed to it I saw before me a delightful Arabian mare, a little like our own Zitta but of a much more handsome pedigree, held by two men and adorned with a crimson harness. The woman who had been riding her a moment ago had already dismounted and disappeared. Beside me stood a Moor in sumptuous yellow livery and waiting, it would seem, for the sole purpose of taking the reins from me.

If only I had asked someone then—no matter whom—to tell me the way back, if only my horse had wheeled round, returned home!... Ha! True, nothing could have helped by then. Nor did such thoughts enter my head. I leaped to the ground. The Moor took my horse while a doorman, who had been standing by the entrance to the vestibule holding a silver cane and dressed in yellow and black, bowed to me in silence and motioned to the doors on the left. I turned to the left. Led on by mute signals from the servants, I passed through an entire suite of drawing rooms furnished in oriental luxury until at last I entered a small room to one side, where two boys stood to attention ready to serve me.

"Your orders, Sir?"

"What costume do you require?"

It was high time for a human voice to deliver me from the stupor into which I had fallen since my arrival. The boys' questions convinced me that my dream was a reality and I had to deal with real, living people.

"I have no orders and want no costume," I replied after a while. "A most peculiar accident has brought me to these parts—I know no one here but am keen to make their acquaintance so I might explain and justify my presence."

The boys looked at each other in amazement.

"Before whom do you wish to explain yourself?" one of them began at last.

"Before your master or mistress."

"We don't have a master," replied the elder of the two with a certain pride, a bonny young fellow with dark brown hair, in Scottish national dress and a black velvet cap with an eagle's feather.

"The mistress is mistress of this castle, but she is not our mistress," added the other. He was younger than his companion, with lighter hair, lighter eyes, but otherwise so like the other that he seemed but a smaller paler reflection of the same image.

"Then be so good as to tell me whether I might see the mistress of this castle?"

They glanced at the clock and answered almost simultaneously: "The ball does not start for another two hours."

"But as I shan't be at the ball, will one of you go and secure me an audience beforehand?"

I had barely uttered these words when the door opened and a tall lean man entered the room, dressed entirely in black and wearing a gold chain that hung over his outer garments from shoulder to chest. "My mistress," he announced in a tone so monotonous it was as if a mechanism inside him merely repeated the words, "my mistress greets you as a guest in her house. She invites you to share in tonight's banquet and accept whatever attire you like, so you can change out of your clothes soaked by the rain."

"Please convey my thanks for her hospitality"—once again I was overcome by sleep though I answered with utmost gravity— "and inform her I shall obey her commands."

"And so you will be at the ball and will dress up?" inquired the younger boy once the tall gentleman had left.

"I shall attend the ball and I shall dress up," I said as if merely reciting words I'd already learned by heart.

"Oh that's good! Good!" cried the boys. And then one after another they listed the different costumes.

"Dress up as a Turk! Such a lavish costume, so many diamonds on it," suggested the elder boy.

"Dress up as a minstrel!" decided the younger one. "It's incomparably beautiful."

"Or as a mediaeval knight—the armour we have is light steel, studded with gold."

"Or an Albanian! Better as an Albanian!"

"Or better still as the king from Belshazzar's feast."

"What nonsense you talk! Our guest is a young man—is he supposed to dress up as an ageing king? I have it! I know what he'll choose: definitely the Levite's robe; you know the one, brother— the robe which Samuel wore when he was growing up in the temple: white, woven from the finest cashmere. He'll look wonderful in it."

"I confess I'd prefer him as one of Mithra's initiates."[52]

Their rapid exchange went on for a long time as they listed the splendours and costly apparel awaiting my command. But I could gather neither my thoughts nor the will to make a choice.

"Do you have any costumes worn by the Ancient Greeks? Garments of the Athenians?" I blurted out without meaning to.

"Oh, yes! They're marvellous," both boys exclaimed and clapped their hands.

"There are the costumes of Harmodius and Aristogeiton,[53] festive clothes and daggers hidden in myrtle wreathes."

"Then there is the costume of the philosopher Plato."

"And the costumes of the poets, of the victors of the Olympic games."

"And the costume of Alcibiades…"

The latter struck me as though my own thoughts had leaped from my mind and wanted now to return by means of someone else's voice—the impression was compelling, but it also rallied my mental powers suspended till then in a trance.

"No, no," I replied somewhat hastily. "I don't wish to greet the mistress of this place with borrowed luxury and a false identity. Give me some modest garb such as they wear in our native uplands, or I shall go to her dressed in my own clothes."

The elder boy winced. The younger reflected for a moment but soon smiled merrily enough.

"Well, I tell you," he said to his brother under his breath, "he'll be just as beautiful like that." And they returned soon after carrying the costume of a Tatra highlander, most faithfully copied but—how elegant!

I put it on. It was as though it had been made just for me: the white shirt of impenetrable thickness and the dark round cloak, the belt, hat, and even the bast shoes made from silky inner bark.[54] The elder boy stretched out his arm several times to touch my hair, my hair which had never fallen so gently onto to my shoulders in such rich lustrous ringlets. The younger one tightened the tie and my foot never felt freer or lighter. From time to time they looked me in the eye, nodded their heads in agreement and smiled.

At last a clock struck one in the morning, the second hour of my visit. Again the doors opened, and again I was shown the way by wave of hand. Again I passed from door to door, from silent signal to silent signal, through rooms and chambers, upstairs and downstairs, across what seemed like vast hallways, along endless galleries, whilst muffled music filtered through from somewhere— through walls, ceilings, tiled floors—and swarms of human forms floated about or flashed past in the many hues of their garments, each greeting others with a smile, a movement of the head, a glance, whilst I walked on alone—unknown to them and knowing none—yet proud and resolute. A final set of double doors were flung open before me by an African of Herculean proportions with glistening black skin and a sharp look in his eye—it was as though he had been positioned there deliberately as a contrast to the sight to be revealed behind him. For what a sight it was, ladies and gentlemen! What dazzling brightness shone from the candles, crystal lamps, costumes of men and women. From the slightest movement of head, arm, gossamer gown, there burst a glint of diamonds, a glitter of rubies, and how many heads there were, how many arms, how many gowns swirling around! And how many sounds too—the invisible music, the buzz of whispered conversation, the rustle of soft silk, and how many fragrant scents—of the rarest flowers, most costly incense. And how the whole scene was encompassed on three sides by three huge mirrors of staggering dimensions! While the fourth reached out into the infinity of a dark shrubbery which thrust itself amongst the revellers with its white orange blossom and fresh acacia leaves. And how everything was miraculously enclosed overhead by a glass cupola: you felt you wanted to kneel down and pray, for the storm had died away and the clearest of skies could be seen above, while God himself looked down through the stars to see if it were true that people on His earth could be so happy.

I flung myself on the first cushion I came across and took off my hat, as it was now too tight for my temples pulsating with hot blood. I clasped my hands to my chest and suspended my whole soul in my ears, my eyes.

Several people addressed themselves to me; I glanced at them, said nothing in reply, and they went away with a smile on their faces. No doubt they could not comprehend such speechless excitement, what it meant to be a new arrival like me: for they had been born and raised among such splendours. But was it so surprising that things went a little dark before my eyes, that my head began to spin a little when I, the youngest child of a poor family, I, a poor mining engineer, first sensed the fulfilment—beyond all expectation—of those fantasies sown in my mind by Cyprian and now blossoming wantonly into unbound dreams and desires? Even at that late stage, however, I still had it in me to resist—in my indestructible reserves of young strength, despite my great tendency to dissolve, shall we say, into soporific delusion, despite my extreme childlike vulnerability—I still had it in me to recover the complete equilibrium of my mental faculties, which to date had grown stronger with every moment of every more violent ordeal; it had usually been the case that whatever seemed predestined to ruin the weakened fibres of my cold judgment and resolute will, was the very thing that summoned me back from those external influences—the very thing that restored my judgment and my will, my stony will.

And so it was on that night I became intoxicated with the sounds, fragrances, lights, as though they were doses of some oriental drug contrived for just that purpose. But then the sound of her voice rang out right beside me, the scent of her gown spread round about me, the radiance of her wondrous face shone forth—I ought to have lost my reason then and there, gone mad... but in fact, for a brief moment, I came to my senses, to a commonsensical state of mind. Common sense is a slice of that daily bread which your mothers taught you to pray for in your prayers; common sense is the most average, most mediocre product of the human brain, the old rag which all the poor in spirit can afford, the paste which seals the bond between philosophers and simpletons when they lack a higher, religious rule, when they lack love. The French have a better expression than we do for this common sense of which I speak: *le sens commun*.[55] And indeed it is a kind of common, universal sense, with whose aid one can somehow acquire or become initiated into ways of thinking so general and universal that whatever one looks upon presents itself as it would to others; and it is only when I perceive something extra, something harmful or something entirely different that I can begin to call it my personal possession, my own creature. But I have always tried, come what may, to gather to my eye all the rays of sunlight under which my human brothers gaze upon God's world; I do indeed possess a universal sense—a *sens commun*—which, if you will, you can baptize as "ordinary" or "vulgar"—but which always unites me with the mass, the crowd, and always prevents me from lapsing into eccentricity or incomprehensibility. For I ask you, tell me in all honesty: what use is incomprehensibility? What use have I been?—

Agh! It's true. And God too is incomprehensible—the God who is necessity, the God who is our destiny. But He has time, eternity and as yet un-revealed truth, and what do human beings have? What do I have? Madness...

At that time I still had my common sense. And so you see, oh my good listeners! If it hadn't been for that tiny remnant of common sense, I wouldn't be in a fit state today to tell you what kind of woman took my life away. For how I saw her later... Oh, you wouldn't understand a thing, even if I were to begin to tell you! Whether words actually exist to express it, I have no idea—I have never sought them. But how she may have appeared to others, I shall tell you. Listen.

She was tall, fair-haired. She had dark green eyes and black eyelashes. What seemed like the hint of a fading blush hovered over her face, the creamy yellow whiteness of marble over her sloping shoulders and prominent breasts. Well, and what else? As though you saw her standing before you now? Oh, it's true she was very tall, but not tall like other people—tall only in stature and body— but tall in her person, in her figure, gait, way she moved. She was tall in the gaze of those who beheld her, for their gaze would surely crumble to dust, pinned steadfast to the ground before ascending to meet her countenance—and the distance from the ground to her countenance was as far as from the earth to the sky; and so people measured it according to the impressions they received: she was tall. And was she really fair-haired? Believe me, ladies and gentlemen, since I never received from her a "lock wound with pink ribbon or blue floss-silk,"[56] I have no knowledge or recollection of the true colour of her hair. In the first instance I would have called her fair, but that may only be because the coils of gold ringlets formed such a brilliant aureole around her face, shimmering with all the shades of amber, all the shimmering lights of topaz. As for her eyes, I spoke the truth: they were dark green, but green like malachite, not like emerald—lit up only in their surface reflection, without their own radiance, without that transparent film that lets you peer into the depths of someone's heart. It was as if her eyes were not her eyes; as if they had been lifeless for a long time, borrowed from a corpse. The most beautiful eyes, but eyes only for looking, only for her use, not to bring happiness. What a strange contrast to her lofty brow, where every word of her every thought was clearly etched! What a strange contrast to her pale countenance, which still seemed to burn with the blood that had just flowed from it, or the tide of blood that was about to sweep into it with the first beat of her heart! What a contrast, what an amazing contrast to her lips in particular! Delicate yet protruding lips! Lips fresh as sweet innocence, as the caresses of passion! Such eyes and such lips! Death and life! Such as you might see together only once! Oh! I have seen them. I have also lived and died. I was alive then. Now I am dead. You are alive now and you will die sometime, before very long. And that is the sum total of the difference that exists between us. You should listen to me out of curiosity at least. I will tell you everything about how you can die while still alive. But not just yet, for I am only seventeen and leaning against a gilded headboard in the grand salon of an enchanted castle. She stood beside me. The heavy moiré of her sapphire dress crackled as she moved. A weightless cloud of white gauze wafted before my eyes. A narrow band no thicker than a quarter-inch, but studded with diamonds of the exact same size and breadth, sparkled in her shining hair. And I recognized her: I recognized the face I had seen for the first time in the flash of lightning.

"And who was it who caught up with me? Who was it who drew level with me?" she inquired. "You have asked and sought in vain. It was he." And her fan nudged my arm, its priceless feathers swaying back and forth. I raised my head and eyes but did not rise from my place. Surely you understand: none of you would have been capable of leaping from your chair or couch, of bowing according to the normal rules of social behaviour, if some female saint or a vision of an angel had suddenly appeared before you! I sat and stared. Her stony eyes pinned me to my seat. But her lips began to spread slowly into a smile, slowly, very slowly until her dainty little teeth shone like a row of pearls.

"So admit it: is there anyone better deserving?" she went on still resting her fan on my arm.

A large group had gathered round in response to her first words; now more women and men drew closer.

"Oh, it's true! Oh, how handsome he is! Oh, how beautiful!" they were saying all around me, and I did not feel even the slightest embarrassment, which would have been natural at my age and in such a situation. I gazed at her and whether she spoke or remained silent, I heard only her voice.

"Tell me, highland child, how old might you be?" she inquired in that voice of hers, with those lips.

How fortunate it was—as I mentioned before—that in those days any desperate situation called forth some new strength from within me! I was able to answer her lucidly enough.

"And can you tell me, how many years make up the days of our dreams or one hour of their coming true?"

"So that's how it is, is it?" she said in that same slightly scornful tone which I had first heard in the dead of night. "So that's how it is, my poor highland boy? The days of our dreams and the hour of their coming true? Oho! I would say upward of a hundred years..."

"Then I am upward of a hundred years old," I replied calmly.

"Ha! ha! ha! worthy old man!" laughed another woman. "So now tell us your date of birth according to the calendar."

"All right, if I am to receive the same confidence in return."

"Just look what a little reptile we have among us!" Her voice rang out again, the affected severity of the words softened by its gay abandon. "Or does it seem to you in the world where you live—in your world, that miscreant time must always be in conflict with charm and happiness after only a short spell of harmony? Take a look around you. Are any of us here afraid of time or able to resist it? Do any of us lack beauty, strength, pleasures? Simpleton! And do you know how old we are? So look! Every one of us has lived just as long as their costume. The one who was talking to you is the great high priestess Isis,[57] and she was laughing with Napoleon who, when he stood by her tomb, blabbered something to his soldier ants about forty centuries.[58] I myself..."

"You, lady," I interrupted her keenly. "Do not tell me anything about yourself, I already know everything..."

"How strange he is! He already knows everything! But tell me anyway, let me discover whether that 'everything' resembles any small part of what I surmise. For I dare not say what I know..."

"You were born in an Olympiad year,"[59] I announced without smiling, without stumbling at all, in a firm and steady voice as though I were reciting an official document. "I'm sorry I cannot be more precise, but my erudition is insufficient to specify the exact dates in that period known in your homeland as the century of Pericles."[60] I stopped. The smile on her lips had disappeared. A deep furrow had appeared on her forehead between the two dark arches of her brows, as though she were straining hard in search of a lost memory. In the pupil of her eye her gaze had completely frozen.

"Well, go on, go on, soothsayer."

"I am no soothsayer. I cannot foresee one moment of your future or your designs. I see only the past—like an old man, an historian. In this past, your name was: Aspasia."

If her eyes had been able to look and see, not just stare, then I would have surely felt their long penetrating search into the very depths of my heart. But she, though she held her gaze enquiringly upon me, struck only the surface; she was unable to penetrate to the core. Other features of her face reflected a slight, transitory amazement and then regained their—I would not say innate, but rather affected—air of frivolous abandon.

"You have spoken the truth," she declared after a while. "I am Aspasia. But who are you?"

"My parents named me Benjamin."

"So you are Benjamin! Oho! Benjamin, that means beloved child, cherished child, happy child—also: loving child."

"Yes, you are right. It means all those things."

"Listen! Listen!" cried Aspasia. "He is loved and knows how to love." Then she sat down so close beside me I could feel her gown touching me whenever she moved. "And how do you love, Benjamin?" she added with a half-smile so provocative, so seductively enchanting that hotter blood began to course through my veins.

"And how do you love, how do you love, Aspasia?"

"Hey, little maids! Bring me my lyre! I love like I sing. And I know that I love only when I sing."

There was a stir among the group of young girls standing at a distance like a bed of spring flowers. And then one of them, faster than my eye could detect, handed her the lyre.

Was it a real lyre? The shape was similar, but it was made of crystal and had strings of gold and silver.

"How do I love?" she said again as though bemused, as though deliberating. Her hand struck all the strings at once—a hand so strong and muscular that despite its most perfect roundedness, despite the delicate purity of its curves, the strings almost ruptured under its blow and instead of uttering a pleasant sound they wailed; and with their wail, the whole room fell silent.

Everyone awaited her song in hollow silence.

"Oh! *This* is how I love!" shrieked Aspasia, and quite unexpectedly, in a terrifying howl of pain, the strings suddenly ruptured beneath her fingers and the spurned instrument struck the marble tiles in a lament of shattering glass.

Aspasia swept her eyes round about her and began to laugh proudly.

"Do you understand what this means? It means that I love as God loves—through destruction and mystery."

"No, lady, that is how Satan hates."

"What do you know, highland boy? What do you know, Benjamin?—Satan and God, hate and love: are they not the two faces of the same infinity?" And turning her back on me, she said to the others:

"I love as God loves. Is not God's love the most exceptional exception, the most total destruction, the most inaccessible mystery? That which lasts, that which exists, is what God has rejected of Himself and is of the world, of humans. Only the past, which no one remembers, is with God; the future, which no one can divine, is in God. Life which expires returns to God; the dying person is united with God; the maiden who rattles off her religious vows surrenders herself to God. God loves eternally because He possesses eternally; He possesses eternally because he destroys eternally. What do you imagine? That He has only heaven and earth? The sun and the stars? Thunder and lightning? You're mad! These are the things you have! But He has what your gaze will never desecrate, your hand never reach, your thought never defile: He has mystery and destruction. The alpha and the omega—the birth of the world and its demise. Do you not know, according to the words of Holy Writ: if you were to touch His property, His special quality, then He would cease to be God and you would become gods? So He must love that quality which makes Him God, and not the paltry alms He has loaned to you and over which you rejoice. You're mad! Mad! I tell you once more that I love with the love of God. I love what is mine; and mine is what belongs to me, just as the past belongs to God, the nun to her vows, forgetfulness to the mystery. Mine is that shattered lyre; mine the song I never sang; mine the pearl of great price, which—like Cleopatra[61]—I shall swallow dissolved in my glass; mine the man who chooses the grave. Look how the poor child has turned pale! Oh you must love in quite another way, I'm sure, Benjamin. Come play to him, sing to this infant your false songs!"

Uttering these mocking words, Aspasia stood up, while two boys approached and took her place. They were the same boys who had helped dress me for the ball. A gay and waggish smile lit up their childish faces. They sat down one on either side of me, leaned over me and peered into my eyes inquisitively and maliciously like a couple of students about to spring a surprise prank, like knaves blowing away the pious words from the pages of a young girl's open prayer-book.

"Well, if the lady Aspasia so desires, I shall sing to you, highland dweller," said the elder one at last. "But it's a shame you won't understand my song, because I sing only from inspiration and only in Italian—the language of my nature, my native and most beloved language."[62]

"Don't let such a small obstacle inhibit you, dear brother," said the younger one. "I shall interpret faithfully—in thought and in spirit—every stanza of your improvisation."

"And will our listener agree to that?"

"Our listener will agree to anything. Do you observe how he looks around him with a glazed and bemused eye? People inclined to musing never object to anyone; so sing, sing boldly, with fire and inspiration!"

"All right, brother! I shall render you the same service and translate your song, though it'll be a far greater sacrifice on my part, far harder work. It's often impossible to understand you."

"Oh, ignoble boy!... Brother Cain!"

"Slow down, slow down, gentle Abel. All I mean is that your tongue is less familiar, not so accessible to people. Let Benjamin judge for himself." And turning to me he said, "My brother always improvises in the language of the ancient Celts, yet to transpose that legendary dead tongue into words comprehensible to listeners today, to a highlander's ear, requires a hundred times more effort than explaining a living dialect."

"We'll see, we'll see; I am just warning you, son of Jacob,[63] to be on your guard when my brother starts to sing. For though he is the best, the most innocent and purest of all the children who have died before completing their fifteenth year, he is somewhat prone to the falsehood of luxury, debauchery, drunkenness and murder. Aspasia, who chooses our fate according to our talents, has promised him a magnificent career... in the worse case, the throne of the Great Mogul.[64] So be wary, be wary when he starts to sing!"

"And I tell you, beware of my brother before he stops singing, for although he is wittier, cleverer, more serious than all the rats who have ever grown fat on the diplomatic papers of Japanese and Chinese mandarins, he is at the same time just a little bit good-natured, sluggish and flirtatious; his nerves are on edge, his brain befuddled by opium, intellectual powers already deadened, bodily powers not yet aroused—I am telling you, in a word, that Aspasia, who chooses our fate according to our talents, has not yet found anything for him. She advises him nonetheless to stake all his money on one card and go to Germany; perhaps only there could my brother succeed in becoming a decent human being, take up a chair of philosophy or drink himself to death on Bavarian beer."

The words of their quarrel, of those empty jokes, crisscrossed in front of me for a good while longer firing away like Congreve rockets[65]; they spoke so fast I had no time to ask them even: Who are you? What do you want with me? At last the younger boy sat up straight while the elder adjusted his velvet and fur cap, wiped his forehead several times with his hand, and immersed himself for a moment in the muffled music that still echoed delightfully all around us. Then, striking his chest, he exclaimed, "I am a songster of the truth!"

"And this is my unfaithful interpreter," he added pointing to his brother. And at last he began his improvisation. But, despite the warning he had given me, he sang it in Polish, in a pure clear voice with perfect timing:

"Wretched was my lonely heart
In my poor breast, as echoless
It swelled with blood and
Pulsed with unimagined wants.

Then everywhere in this wide world,
In this wide world so frenzied, wild,
Damnably cast in gilded robe,
Thy hand strikes gold each time
It grasps the swaths of fire,
Its share of water, blood or mire;
In this wide world of ours so fair,
This one and only, loved and dear,
Cheating others, itself deceived,
Ridiculed, dissolved in tears,
Kissing still and fighting on,
Dissipating, moaning, groaning...
Canst thou trust me when I say:
I was bored in this wide world?

From out my books and paper notes,
The fresh fields' fragrant flowers,
The balding pates of my professors,
The azure's silver clouds,
Even from my glass or plate,
My mare's bright rippling mane—
Everywhere before mine eye
It loomed in ghastliness,
Yellow, hideous, pallid, foul,
Yawning, gaping, foolish, sour,
That malady—that incubus:
Boredom is its name.

And no desire I felt to eat,
No wish to mount my horse,
No wish to laugh at persons droll,
No wish to quench my thirst.

No desire to be alive:
I wanted but to sleep.

O sleep, o slumber without cease
From eventide to early morn,
From early morn to dead of night,
And if it were in human power
I would lock my eyelids tight
For years on end, for centuries—
For when I locked them—Ah! what wonders
I beheld and fancied, dreamed!
Will I succeed to sing of them?
Of what I was and where I roamed?

Ah! what wonders!—But in waking,
Though it lasted but a while,
Though I sensed my cheeks aglowing,
My lips, my breast, my loins afire
From kisses sweet, from fond caress—
Though the silken coils of hair,
The soft small palm so fair
Lay warm upon my trembling heart,
I felt I still was truly touched
In waking tight embrace...
And yet... and yet...: O imprecation!
O scornful sight, O tortured night!
To dream delight, such happy bliss—
And be nought but a foolish child!

I know not how to name the thing
That frenzied fanned my sails;
While tears coursed down my burning face
I chewed my fingernails.
Against a wall I smashed my brain
And frantic spread my hands
That she, that figure not yet seen,
Not grasped, not given name,

Might, ah! be clothed in flesh
And rush towards my arms;
That this mad swarm of fleeting dreams
Might fall at last, drop visible
And truly live, real and fully formed
In my too hot embrace!

Now I have lived through quite enough
Long nights of restless turning,
Long days of endless yearning—
Now well I know what they do call
Each heartbeat's rapid pounding,
My every bitter tear.
Now well I know what they do call
My fancy's drowsy phantoms,
The futile waste of my young years—
The longing outstretched palms,
The sighs that cause the breast to ache,
The burning lips, the pulsing blood—
Miraculous song of life...

O, I do know it, know it, sing it,
Now I shout, invoke her name:
Woman! Woman! Woman!
Come to me, fair woman, mine!
Long imagined, long awaited,
Come to me, to me, to me,
Desired and ever conjured!

I do love thee, woman, love thee!
Love thy dark mysterious eye,
Love the lustre of thy tresses
And thy noble lofty brow!—
I love the dulcet of thy voice
Thy footprint's tiny trace;
Love thy hand's cool snowy whiteness
And the breathing of thy mouth.—

Love the silk that wove thy gown,
The studded clasp that sparkles bright
   Upon the sash about thy waist;
      Love the pearls around thy neck;
The diamonds on thy temple,
The fan thy hand rocks to and fro,
   Billowing gauzes on thy breast,
      I love thy form's dark shadow.
My beautiful! My dearest one!
To me, O woman, come and come:
   I am thy poet and thy lover,
      Come to me, to me again!
Give me thy hand, my darling one!
Throughout the world let's fly! May it
   Marvel at thy beauty, at our youth and
      Happiness! Throughout the world
Let's fly! And may it also envy me
Thy sweet caresses and thy love
   And this my song to thee.
But, ah! beware. O save me, God!
May I not envy it! Be jealous
   In my love of thee, my only dearest one!
For when I do remind myself
Another man might take from me
   Thy glance, thy smile, thy sigh—
Then something flares up in mine eye
And makes my hand clasp tight the hasp—
   Like fire—like sword.—
At once I feel my face grow pale,
At once I see the corpse collapse,
   And though I know not whose it be
I sense my heart grow cold,
As though that corpse or murderer
   Possessed my own true heart.
Such dread, such awful dark I feel
As if beside me gaped my tomb
   And thou wert there no more.

O, I care not for such awesome thoughts
Nor want such sufferings,
   My head is reeling sick.
Be gone, be gone to Satan's lair!
Thou dost love me, thou art loved;
   So clear the way, the way for us!

Thou art mine and I am happy—
Hey bring music, dancing, songs,
Hey bring goblets, cups and bowls!
Champagne, port-wine, old Hungarian,
May they flow and may they gush!
Let's drink to pleasure, drink to wine,
For time runs on and death pursues;
And if there be but ought beyond it
Just ask the ancient monks!
Today we can but grasp at life,
Today yet feast and revel,
Today yet fondle, pet and kiss—
And he who squanders but a moment
Will never kiss his fill:
Never roll out all the barrels,
He who shuts his eyes forever
When a drop remains undrunk
Still yet within the bottle, or—
Through his own fault—one girl's last
Embrace, one yearning still in his cold
Heart… Shame upon him! Such a man
As he, upon him fall the thunderbolt,
The fireball's deadly blow!
   Five devils snatch away!!!"

A burst of raucous laughter concluded, as though with a final flourish, that infernal waste of wit and talent. Again I wanted to say something but was forestalled by the younger boy who had been sitting until then on my right, motionless like a porcelain figurine.

"And now, my dear listener," he said to me, "be so good as to hear it all again in simpler speech from a humble interpreter."

"The singer is still a raw youth, or so it would seem, but possesses a full-blooded temperament. He relates how everything had begun to bore him—he couldn't even laugh at the balding pates of his teachers, which means that at one time he must have cracked unseemly jokes at their expense quite often. And so he was like a vicious wasp, like a snake overexcited at the breast and so on.

"The singer had lost his appetite and no longer enjoyed a drink—which he considers to be the greatest of his misfortunes and which therefore proves that he was greedy and immoderate, with a propensity for the deadly sin of gluttony.

"The singer then tells of his dreams and daydreams, which support to the view that: ignorance is not at all the same as innocence.

"Finally, the singer declares that he has now completely lost that ignorance.—Today he is in love with a woman who has dark eyes, white hands and little feet, and who must be rather rich as she dresses befittingly in pearls, silks, fine gauze and diamonds.

"The singer wants everyone else to be jealous of him, but does not wish to be jealous of anyone himself on her account, for—as far as I could understand from his rather cryptic threat—he has a somewhat Turkish attitude in this regard: he terrorizes with fire and sword, even alludes light-heartedly to his lover's tomb—yet he does not say for certain whether he will slay her, or himself or someone else. But it seems to me he leaves us in the gravest doubt as to his own person.

"Next the singer brushes off these black thoughts like so many irksome flies from his nose. He advises us to drink wine, kiss young girls while we still have some life left in us, and concludes with the very emphatic declaration that anyone who behaves otherwise should be struck down by a thunderbolt and sent to hell—by five devils. Why five? I don't know. Maybe because the rhythm fits, or because it's some cabalistic number, or because it corresponds to the number of our senses?

"His brief stanzas are embellished with sweeping arpeggios, grace-notes, ornaments and thousands of other excesses, from which one can extract nothing except that the song is an expression of feverish excitement and its singer a complete scoundrel.

"And now may you be so kind as to lend me your ears! So be

attentive, interpreter!" And in this moment the roles were reversed. My neighbour to the left, who had been making his indignation quite clear throughout his brother's commentary through nervous movements of dissatisfaction, suddenly fell silent and sat motionless as his brother commenced his own song in his charming, seductive voice.

"I do apologize, ladies and gentlemen. I have to take my time—I have forgotten this song; wait a moment, please. Ah! now I have it. Yes, here it is…

"I once was told that here on earth
White angels walked with wings of snow
Who, when they took the human heart
In their most sacred hands, and carried it
Through all the byways of the world,
O'er muddied fields and precipices,
They bore it pure and undefiled,
Lit by the ray of God's clear thought,
Warmed by His breath of love.
　　And I would ask where angels dwelt,
　　And then my mother stood by me,
　　Parted my hair and kissed my brow
　　And uttered thus: There, little son,
　　Where dwells the woman that loveth thee.
The truth, the truth my mother spoke:
Angels dwell where life is peace,
Hearts serene and thoughts in heaven,
Where dwells the woman that loveth thee.
　　A woman's love is holy virtue,
　　Joyful strength, inspired and wise;
　　A woman's love the child's first greeting,
　　Its first caress on this poor earth!—
Life's first drop of nourishment
The infant's hungry mouth doth seize.
Thy mother's song as she kneels crooning
By thy cradle thyself to sleep;
A woman's love is God's own blessing,
Support and counsel all bestowing

Along the slippery paths of fortune
On thy voyage to lands unknown.
A woman's love—the common dreams
Thy sister shares in long debate
Upon thy future grand designs
And hopes of any youthful heart.
It prophesies fine deeds and fame
In which she so believes and trusts;
And when perchance thou beginst to doubt,
Her faith in thee remains devout.
A woman's love—the hand extended
When Satan tempts with evil thought;
The wild desires and craving thirsts
Plucked from the chasms of your heart.
Treacherous are the seeds of passion,
But e'er they multiply in poison,
Defile the temple of thy being,
Possess thy spirit's unsoiled ray,
The earlier feeling blessed in chrism,
On virtue graft, will bloom in joy.
A woman's love is thy reward
In hardened toil of man's career,
The priestess of domestic bliss
And family days beside the hearth;
The voice that hails thee in the door
When thou returnst from foreign tour;
The snow-white arm around thy neck
Held tight in sweet embrace, as
Worn by life thy faith grows cool
That in this world hearts linger still
To answer thee with vital beat
When thy hand knocks upon their door,
When brother, friend, thy will doth call—
'Tis then that her lips speak to thee:
'Forgive and love, for thou art loved.'
It is the one kind stroke of fate
That bides with thee and always leans

Towards thee when the world slings mud
Or thy own conscience raises hell,
Extends its arms to draw thee in
And swathes thee 'gainst the world's ill-will
In snow-white lace, its purest gown,
And shields thee from affliction cruel
With tears and anguish of its own.
From crime it shelters thee with pleas
And holiness divine, toward it
Bends thy step; deserting evil ways
It leads thee back to heaven.
A woman's love! Of all God's gifts
I ask this one the most, this one—
I shall be great and holy, good—
Deny all selfish wants and trials
To gain my own advantage, pleasure,
And seek instead the strength of heart
To sacrifice them for my neighbour,
Cause him good and bear much evil
Murmurless; the men that curse me
I shall bless, and clasp the hand that strikes.
Each tear I'll wipe away or weep
Myself with those that seek no other
Solace; support and love, forgive,
Forget myself.—But may the sacred one
Remember: my loving, holy woman…"

"Ta-ta ta-ta ta-ta ta-ta! That's enough of that, little brother!" He was suddenly interrupted by his interpreter. "Enough! Because otherwise I shall forget it and Benjamin will walk away without even knowing what was droning in his ear for so long. In its truest sense, this is what by brother was saying:

"My mawkish little brother heard from his Mama that a woman who loves him is an angel; he recollects those fine words and it occurs to him that it is indeed so, because it is very convenient to have first a wet-nurse, then a nanny, then a sister who believes in his boasting words, then a wife who always complies, kisses him on the cheek, doubtless cooks for him and knits his socks. And so a woman is an angel and his lordship even promises that he'll be well behaved, should he acquire such an angel. And so taken altogether, my most respected listener, taken altogether—it's not worth a pinch of snuff! It's a miserable insincere parody of what I was saying more directly: I was saying 'I want a woman!' He's also saying: 'I want a woman!' I was saying: 'I want a woman to bring me happiness.' He also says: 'I want a woman to bring me happiness.' He intones his mother's prayer, always harping on the same old theme. I feel sorry for you, having to listen for so long on your first visit to such rambling drivel. As recompense, I shall give you a brief summary. I shall tell you what human destiny is: It's a charade that I have learned from truly wise men—but my dear, I beseech you not to betray me to lawyers, authors, reformers, hypocrites, idiots and honest people. Here it is: the first clue is life, the second, death—and taken together they make: Enjoy! Enjoy! Enjoy!"

As he uttered these last words, both boys began chuckling loudly.

"So you're laughing too," I said to the younger one, taking him by the hand.

"Oh, I most of all." He squeezed my hand merrily and, bowing hastily, ran off with his brother. A terrible sadness came over me. I felt the tears well up inside me and lowered my eyes, because I did not want to make my tears the laughing-stock of those heartless people. In stark contrast to all that surrounded me, our poor family homestead rose before me in my mind's eye, and the figures of my loved ones passed before me. I felt sorry for that proud beautiful woman whom a moment earlier I might have idolized and adored above my saintly mother, above all my sisters. I felt sorry for her because I had already been feeling: how could I not love her? And if I did not love her—then who could? I was moved with great pity. I raised my eyes and searched for her amongst the throng until at last I caught sight of her sitting in the distance. She was not looking at me, another man was speaking to her; she was listening to him, toying nonchalantly with coils of white gauze that spilled like a transparent cloud from the band of diamonds on her head, covering her shoulders and enveloping her whole figure. She was so beautiful, so serene, so attentive to what that man, dressed as a Roman patrician, said to her. It was as if it had not been she who had uttered those blasphemous words only a moment ago, not been she who had provoked me with the songs of her young pages. Oblivion covered her face like a mask of innocence.

I could not contain my disgust at this sight. I stood up and went over to her. I stood right in front of her:

"Farewell!" I announced. But she frowned at me impatiently and signalled to me to be silent.

Well then, I thought to myself, remain here among your luxuries, without my greeting or farewell! Forgetting will come between me and you forever and ever, Amen. And I wanted to leave then and there, but she, as though guessing my intention, took me by the hand—without turning round, without even looking at me—as the young patrician expounded in scholarly terms his architectural plans for raising the ruins of the Eternal City and adapting them for practical or ornamental use, while she offered new ideas, praised or corrected him like an expert mistress of the art, and I was astonished by the accuracy of her judgment and the thoroughness of her knowledge.

"What was it you wanted, my child?" She asked me at last, quite unexpectedly, when it seemed she was no longer thinking about me and had not let go of my hand only because she had forgotten it.

"I have come to bid you farewell," I replied, but in a less decisive tone and without trace of resentment.

"What do you mean? Farewell? Is the morning sun already too bright, do my lamps burn too dimly?"

"Oh no, lady, the sun is not yet risen, and the perfumed oil of your lamps burns with a pure light. But I have come to say farewell because I don't feel right here, because I feel bitter, sad, stifled."

"Admit my little devils have stung you with their teasing!"

"It's true, they teased me horribly, horribly!"

"Well, and what of it? Or are you weaker than they? Why did you not take your revenge? You could have driven them away, banished them from your side or sung them your own moral song. I too would have listened, because I already know their songs but I am curious to hear yours."

"No, I would never sing any song of mine here, never utter a word of my own sacred words or feelings."

"And why not? From shyness, pride, faintheartedness, contempt, mistrust?"

"From fear of God alone, so the sad relics of my heart do not drive those who know how to sneer and blaspheme to commit new sins."

"So I see things between us have indeed gone from jest to anger. Calm down. I will summon my master of ceremonies and order him to give the elder little Lucifer a good flogging, because he must surely have put you in a bad mood. He has such sharp teeth, and when he begins to bite he can pierce to the quick... Heigh! Master Severius!..."

"Oh for pity's sake, don't jest so!"

"But I am not jesting. I am totally, sincerely and truly playing the game."

"Then don't play with me." And I tried to withdraw my hand, but her dainty fingers clutched me harder still.

"Listen, Benjamin," she said with that bewitching half-smile. "You are an admirable horseman and a beautiful monument to days gone by—when nature had not yet grown impoverished, when there must have been less people in the world and each man was an assembly of those fine qualities of strength, grace and happiness that his puny successors later had to divide among them, like a corpse is shared amongst the vermin that issue from it. You are beautiful, I grant you that, but—don't be angry with me—but... you are also very tiresome."

"I am not angry and I am not surprised. Only you may be angry or surprised, for you have no idea whom you allowed to cross your threshold. This costume, which no doubt seems to you a momentary plaything of our fancy, is in truth the only costume in which I could stand before you without deceiving you. I'm a simple man of the mountains, a poor, impecunious highland lad. I do not feel right among you, and it cannot feel right for you to have a guest who neither understands nor acknowledges this saturnalia of emotions, senses, riches—these excesses which squander both nature and our humanity. Adieu, adieu forever! I have seen piled beside you the pomp and splendour of oriental tales; I have seen crowds of carefree people elegantly dressed; I have seen old men of fifteen who—for the sake of amusing and ridiculing your guests—dress themselves in the most hideous thoughts and abuse the most sacred of notions, as though these were trinkets destined to be spoiled, jewels tossed onto the scrapheap. I have seen you, lady, so lovely and entrancing that at first I was intoxicated by the radiance of your face and believed your name to be 'Aspasia.' But I have seen you only as a rich woman, enjoying the feast, clever, witty, mocking—and therefore I am taking my leave. And in leaving I charge you before your own conscience, for you could have been kinder to the poor simpleton you met on your way; you could have been the answer he begged for in his prayers; you could have made true the ideal promised to his hopes—if only for a moment. Fate gave you every opportunity, but you, lady, threw away your treasures of gold on noisy banquets, the treasures of your mind on idle chatter; and your beauty you displayed only as an object to be admired. And so this errant highlander will leave your castle without even the consolation of a fond memory; he will brush the dust from his shoes, and when he relates his night-time adventure to his brothers and sisters, or his comrades, he will call you: 'that foreign woman.'"

"You are wrong, Benjamin. You will always call me 'that beautiful woman.' And you will return, oh, you will return to me..."

Her voice was like birdsong, a kiss, a magic spell. And yet she released my hand—doubtless she wanted to test the power of her charms. I bowed before her in silence and walked away with a slow stride. Only once, when I reached the doorway, did I take a last glance back at her. She sat motionless, lost in thought, without smiling—but without looking sad. It was as though her eyes were following me but did not summon me back. A beautiful statue, a masterpiece of the sculptor's art. And so I let drop the sumptuous heavy curtain that covered the double doors, and felt sad only insofar as I had made my first error in life. I hastily changed my clothes. My horse was brought, I mounted and hurried homeward. Bathed in the early morning mist, my forehead was steadily refreshed of its nocturnal visions and impressions.—Shame on you, madman! I said to myself. Shame on you for loving Aspasia and then muddying her image with the first pretty woman who happens to cross your path! Does nothing play on your heart except your curiosity to know life? Does nothing speak to you except the restlessness of your imagination? Do you seek adventures and sensational coincidences? Are you collecting dramatic incidents to include in some novel? Does every unusual occurrence amuse and seduce you? And do you also cling in your heart to a wish you won't give up? A truth, to which you will not lie even though it has lied to you, towards which you'll go on walking even though it has fled from you almost beyond the grave? Oh no, proud, strange woman! I will not return to you, I will not be unfaithful to my hopes, to the bride of my destiny! You are beautiful, magnificent—you may be loved, but the bright light in your eye has faded, the blood in your womb congealed, the thought beneath your brow poisoned. Your voice is fond and enticing, the touch of your hands soft and thrilling—but the breath freezes in my breast at the sound of your words. In your presence my heart suffers anguish and my reason strays. You reveal no sign of God. You will bring me no heaven, you poor damned one! Oh no, no! I will forget you, banish your image from my brain like filthy scum! And I shall say to myself of this night, it never was. And I shall go on, on, on; and one day in the future I shall meet *her*—more beautiful because she is able to love, richer by far because she is happy. And my love will reside with this one; with this one will be the blessing of my mother, with this one will be heaven and God...

V

I T MUST HAVE BEEN A LONG WAY from the castle to
my lodgings.

Left to his own instincts, Falcon galloped in a straight line by
the fastest route. He leaped over ditches and fences, yet by the time
I found myself standing before my house the shadows of the trees
had shortened and begun to shift slightly onto the eastern side.

Bazyl came out to meet me grumbling a little that the horse
was so exhausted, that I would break my neck one day riding out
at night; yet despite this he smiled mysteriously and mentioned
something about a surprise, about some guests who had been there.

A hundred suppositions flashed through my mind in the space of
a minute. I ran indoors as fast as I could. At first glance I was struck
only by what seemed like a vast slab, its varnished surface glinting
in the light. But when I stepped forward and stood in a better place—
oh, then it seemed for a moment that some spell was at work and
that it was impossible, could not be. On the wall opposite my bed
hung a painting of a woman caressing the head of a young man as it
lay in her lap. It was her! Clearly her—the same facial features, the
same unruffled noble brow; the same passionate lips—though here
they were pure and innocent; the same radiance in her hair, same
roundness in her arms, same proud breasts, same hint of a blush on
her cheeks and of white on her bosom—the white that was neither
the cold whiteness of snow nor of lifeless alabaster, but whiteness
where you could feel the warm beam of the sun upon it and see the
young healthy blood coursing beneath it. Yes, it was her! But it was
also more than her, more than that woman who had been illuminated
for me in the flash of lightning or the blaze of fashionable oil-lamps;

this woman's form was filled with another spirit: she was like the woman she could have been if she had loved; she was happiness, revelation, love itself. And that young man resting on her knees—so cherished, entranced, loved—was me. And I could not resist the charm of the delusion. If she had looked upon me but once with her stony glittering dark eye, then perhaps I might have shaken off the powers that were gathering around me—but no, her eyelids were lowered; and my face alone was lit by the bright ray of her pupil, warmed by the reflection of inexpressible delight, keenest adoration, the most loving gratitude. I divined, sensed instinctively the meaning of that look. My heart wrenched towards it; half my life drained away from me and entered the breast of the young man in the picture. And I experienced such a moment that not one of you is ever likely to know—you have dreamed, loved, desired, received, enjoyed, with your one poor soul, with your one miserable body—but I had two souls, two bodies, two happinesses. In the picture I trembled under her caress, drank in the bright radiance of her eye; I was made proud by her joy, great by her love. Yet outside of the picture I was filled with an unwavering certainty, a judicious calm—for this woman was after all a living woman, and though she was lifeless, though she was other, there descended upon my breast such faith in the possibility of her every good, so many dreams and hopes, that I felt that I who loved so much could create love in her, that I could enter even hell and save even a devil. The picture promised me everything, and the picture would live up to its promise.

Then Bazyl entered the room, motioned to me with his head and rubbed his hands.

"Well?" he said. "Is my young master not aware that fine company came to us late yesterday evening? What? No questions?"

It was true I had not asked about anything. The picture already seemed to be the most essential thing in my life.

"There is also a letter," Bazyl added, a little impatient. "The letter and the package were brought by someone passing this way."

"A letter?" I repeated, my voice trembling. My heart began to pound violently while from out of my soul, suspended in the spell of happiness, there suddenly loomed—without any outward justification—so great a feeling of anxiety and panic it stemmed the breathe in my chest. I tried to recall what I might be afraid of? I made a great effort to wrest my memory away from the present and cast it back into the past, but my memory had preserved only a tiny trace of some unpleasant impression, some uncertain threat. All this lasted no longer than the time it took Bazyl to walk across the room, extract the letter, which he had concealed between the books, and hand it to me. I can still see his honest joyful smile in the moment when he flashed the familiar signature before my eyes. I seized and tore open the envelope as fast as I could, and then my memory returned to me and I remembered everything, for my eyes had lighted upon the words written in Ludwinka's hand:

"You had a brother, Cyprian."

What happened to me then I cannot for the life of me remember. Yet they are not a bad thing—these sudden, unexpected downfalls that topple us from the clouds and plunge us straight to the bottom of a well. Our natural organism cannot keep pace with them; it misses a beat while time goes on as it always has done, measured by the wristwatch or calendar.

By the time my heart had missed the value of a beat, and that fantastic virtuoso known as fate had lain its diabolical clawed fingers upon the keyboard of my memory, it was night-time again—in so far as I am able to see and recall it tonight. A lamp must have been standing somewhere on the floor, close to the head of my bed, as light was flickering about the room and I could not explain to myself where it was coming from. But soon I figured that a loose floorboard must have been rising and falling, and from underneath this floorboard a stream of air was blowing in, clear and bright and inundating every object in the room to a greater or lesser degree; I admit I marvelled at my own sharpness in discovering such a simple explanation. I then examined everything around me with ever greater precision, and saw sitting on a stool at my feet the figure of an old woman rocking to and fro as though she were in a boat, raising and lowering her head in perfect time with the rising and falling of the light; beside her was the motionless form of a beast, standing on its four spindly legs, its white head in the middle of its body. The beast was speaking constantly in a hushed voice: "yes, yes, yes." Opposite me, however, but not quite opposite—above me rather, above the woman and the beast—a piece of the wall had been hacked out, and it was in that direction that the bright stream flowed most strongly. And then I saw distinctly a magnificent room spread before me: sumptuous cushions scattered about, and sitting on the cushions was Aspasia herself dressed in a white Greek tunic held together at the shoulders by two cameo clasps. I was embarrassed, mortified to be lying so close to her without being properly dressed. I wanted to get up but the old woman began to shake her head dreadfully; I was terrified because I thought she was going to scream at me and had she screamed, then Aspasia, who until then had been otherwise occupied deep within her chamber, would have arisen and come to see what was going on, and would have seen me as I was—in my nightshirt, my nightcap on my head, beneath my flannel quilt. No, I could not bear such a thought. I was suddenly so overwhelmed by fear, felt myself so defiled, that I became bathed in sweat; thus I lay huddled, while the old crone slowly began to nod her head at me, and then the beast nodded back at her—and yet all the time I was trying to think of what I could do to deceive them, how I might dress myself and escape into that other room where Aspasia was sitting. I was in earnest as my clothes lay at some distance from me. Worse still they were my everyday garments—a short close-fitting spencer made of coarse cloth and trousers edged with leather. There was no way I could make my appearance in such an outfit. I too wanted a Greek tunic, a purple mantle to throw over my shoulder, and Greek buskins, for otherwise Aspasia would say to me: "Go away, you're too ugly." In my wishful thinking I measured those garments against myself until at last I put them on and lifted myself up a little to see whether I was handsome. I looked beautiful in them. I could see Aspasia embracing my neck in the wonderful fullness of her arms, gathering me into her lap and gazing into my eyes raised towards hers.

"So you see, Benjamin, you have returned," she would say. "Now I love you, now you are no longer tiresome, poor and ridiculous. You have slain the Wawel dragon in its den,[66] recovered the key to its treasures, read all the books on display at the Leipzig fair.[67] Oh! I love you very much, Benjamin: you'll have me made a hot-air balloon out of gossamer and my Moor will bear it to the highest peak in the Himalayas, and there we will take our seats together as if stepping into our carriage; my two little devils will blow ever so lightly and we will fly high, high in the sky, to search the Pole Star for Cyprian. Only make haste, my love, and bring some warmer clothes—for the snows lie deep on the summit of the rock!"

I hurried. I was feverish, for I knew that any moment the old crone might glance round and pack me off to bed again, and then what would I do, unhappy man? Then Aspasia would find out that I had not slain the dragon, not read a single book, that I had no tunic, mantle, buskins and was lying under a flannel quilt. I was tortured by this fear which was like a nightmare lodged in my stomach; every time I thrust it aside, it insisted on returning. Scarcely had I stepped through the breach in the wall and rested my head on Aspasia's knee, scarcely had she begun to address me than it transpired I had to get up again, walk and move about, for either she sent me to fetch Cyprian or she asked me to read her my poems, which lay at the bottom of a huge trunk, or instructed me to bring her fans, pencils, compasses, mouth organs, bags of precious pearls or printers' type, bundles of flowering fern[68] or lictors' rods,[69] sets of dragons' teeth complete with jaws. But I, wretched man, as soon as I moved a muscle, immediately saw myself prostrate on my bed with that hideous old crone at my feet rolling in her boat ever higher and deeper, shaking her head ever more threateningly. Eventually I sought to move her through humility and submission; I began to address her in a voice no louder than a thought, and begged her, pleaded with her to let me get up and simply hand me the clothes that hung waiting for me in that room beyond the gaping hole in the wall. But the old crone pulled a hellish face and replied to me in a voice which, thank God, was at least as soft as my own:

"You will never escape from me, I shall hold onto to you until your hair turns grey and you lose all your teeth. I shall cover you with a German eiderdown, put a white nightcap on your head and two enormous leeches at the end of your nose."[70]

Those leeches, that nightcap and that feather eiderdown were killing me. Yet at the same time, above the old crone's head, I could hear Aspasia speaking:

"Benjamin, order them to saddle your Falcon and we'll go riding together! Oh always together, my Benjamin! Our horses will have trappings of coral and be shod in gold. We'll descend from the Carpathian heights to the Ukrainian steppes, leap over the Dnieper and with one thrust of our spurs—we'll seize Cyprian and return him to his mother. Make ready to leave with all speed, Benjamin my own!"

At Aspasia's words I was overwhelmed by despair; I fixed my eyes on my aged warder and when I saw she was paying me no attention, I climbed out of bed as quietly as I could. I thought to myself that should she turn her head and begin to shout, then I would strangle her—but she did not turn her head! Monotonously she immersed herself in the light, then emerged from it, again and again. Overjoyed at her composure, I tiptoed across to the cupboard where I kept my belongings. I pulled out only my overcoat, covered myself with it and—making the dubious assumption that, although this garb was less than adequate, I could obtain some other garment en route—crept like a shadow towards the door. I grasped the door-handle and was away. I soon imagined I could hear loud shouting behind me: "Master Benjamin, Master Benjamin!" But I could see what awaited me back there: the feather eiderdown, the nightcap and the leeches on my nose. I therefore said nothing, running constantly. The night was black as ink and my every step as gentle as a sigh, since I ran with bare feet. I meant to skirt round the house and enter the room where Aspasia awaited me from the other side: but when it seemed I was close to achieving my goal, my feet were suddenly cut from under me by an intense cold—I lost my balance and fell, fell into water. The reality of the danger brought me back to my senses. I tried to cry for help but the water was streaming into my mouth. I made a few mechanical movements in a desperate attempt to swim, and again my strength failed me; I was kept afloat only by the folds of my overcoat. The current drove me in the direction of the bank and, feeling the bushes and undergrowth beneath my hand, I grabbed them with all the strength remaining to me.

What must be, will be—this is what the Turks believe, and I believe it too: you cannot escape your destiny. When I recovered my senses for the second time, my head was lying in a woman's lap; my eyes—as though still caught in the morbid imaginings of my fever—were staring up at her beautiful face, bent over mine. "Poor child," she was saying in a voice so sweet and tender it was like a mother's. "Poor child, what has become of you? Are you really so impoverished and unhappy?"

At these words my grasp on life returned to me in all its pain and all its joys: a most terrible sense of loss struck my reawakened heart at the same time as the most wonderful hope. I was unable to control my feelings, sobs welled in my chest. I covered my face with my hands and dissolved into floods of bitter tears like a woman.

"Why are you crying, young man?" she kept asking. "Are you still weak? Have you caught a chill? Or are you sorry you did not drown?"

"No, lady, only I have been very sick. I must have run out of the house in my delirium. I don't know how I got here. I've no idea where I am, how I came to be with you."

"But do you recognize me?"

"Oh, I do!"

"And so who am I?"

"You are…" I hesitated because I could not remember whether she'd ever told me her family name, and was seized with terror lest she took an imprecise answer for a new symptom of my illness. Eventually her own words came to mind, I smiled and said through my tears: "You are a beautiful woman."

"You have a good memory, Benjamin," she replied gaily. "In which case, step into my boat and we'll return together to the castle."

"My house is nearer than your castle," I remonstrated shyly. "In a few moments I'll be strong enough to walk back myself."

"I don't think so, Benjamin. You are still very weak. Better to come with me, we'll get into the boat together. Lean on me, I'll guide you."

"Oh no, no! Don't get up yet, it's best for me as I am just now!" And indeed, that was how it was best for me. Waves of warmth, radiance and life broke over my breast, as though it were swelling with them, gently but unceasingly. The very mention of any change to my position gripped me with unimaginable alarm. Castle and boat: the very words almost stemmed the advancing tide of my returning energies with an odd nervous excitement. Ah! If she had suggested instead my own little house! If only she had come with me, as I later went with her! Who knows? May be this was the decisive moment? The moment in which our fates were weighed up, in which I could have drawn her to me and encircled her within the bounds of my own spirit, cast a spell over our future together with my own love and affection! Things turned out differently. I was ashamed of my poverty—no, that's not what I mean: I merely regretted to see my beauty cross my humble threshold, behold my unadorned walls. I did not dare demand that she follow my path, and when it seemed to me that she did not want to abandon me out of pity, could not abandon me—I promised at last to follow hers.

"But let's stay here, let's stay here a little longer," I begged like a child, winding her white arm around my neck.

"Aren't you strong enough to stand up now for just a moment?" she inquired gently.

"Oh, it's not a question of strength!" I replied. "I want to make the most of Cyprian's gift. With his death he bought me your appearance. You had to come. You had to fold me like this in your resurrecting embrace, clasp me like this in your lap—for he commanded it, and died."

"Hush, calm down, your fever is returning, and I cannot abide malignant raving."

"Perhaps you mean to ridicule me and scoff at me as you did that night, do you remember? Oh I shan't be put off by anything now—I no longer believe in any evil, because you will love me. You can see for yourself how everything is falling into place according to Cyprian's idea. I was suffering, threatened by death, but you came down to me like an angel, took me by the hand, summoned back the life that was ebbing away. How much you must be about to love me, since we love with a great love those to whom we do good! Is that not true, my fair one? Even if you were to cast out your heart from your breast, deny every emotion, smother this whole world with scorn and hatred, then you would still, still have to love the one who in his extreme need would accept your support, receive life from you in his time of danger. Tell me that you would love him, if only to give him an impression of pleasure, one kind word,

one pleasant memory. Oh, tell me that you would love him!"
She smiled, but her cold look of indifference, a little surprised
even, fell on my forehead like lead.

"You're determined to persuade me that I've done a good deed,
Benjamin," she said almost cheerily. "But you won't succeed. I
am beautiful enough to make do without borrowed merits. The
fact that I am here and restored you to consciousness in the very
moment my hands touched your head, is solely a matter of chance.
Judge for yourself! I was weary of the banquet, the beginning
of which you saw yourself—it went on for three days and three
nights. Travellers crossed themselves as they passed by my castle,
fear descended on the district, fantastic rumours spread across the
countryside. But it is quite true I was celebrating a great, great
feast..." And with these words she fell silent for a minute... and
became thoughtful.

"What feast?" I asked her.

"Oh, imagine a feast like one of your feasts!—I was returning
to life and at first believed I was recapturing everything as it had
once been. But early this morning, towards daybreak, I noticed that
something was lacking. I began to search, to search—but could
neither remember nor find what I was looking for. I was overcome
by emptiness and ennui, so I slipped away from my guests, flung
myself into this boat and let myself drift with the current. Ah! How
good it felt! Perhaps an hour later the sun began to come up—I do so
love the sun, and the water! How lovely the water was in the river!
Spilling over the oar with a pure metallic lustre, like blood. And
how the hazy mist spread in swathes of silver across the meadows!
Like vast seas, lakes, ponds. And the roofs of houses floated upon
them like little islands. Trees loomed like the spirits of giants. I
could not absorb enough of it when, quite unexpectedly, I glimpsed
a human form lying by the bank. I recognized you very quickly, for
I have keen eyesight and a faithful memory. But I did not cry out
because you appealed to me thus in your slumber. You looked so
beautiful, young god of the river's glassy currents, as though you
had laid yourself down by her side, of your own free will, to eternal
rest. Fresh branches of willow had wound themselves into garlands
and crowns above your head; your coat had arranged itself in folds

with a sculptor's precision; the water kissed your white feet like a lovesick nymph. I gazed at you for a long time in admiration. At last, when I saw the extreme pallor of your face, it occurred to me that perhaps you were dead, then…"

"Oh! Then, you see, you felt sorry for me and brought help."

"No, Benjamin, I felt sorry only for your beauty, for my image of you; I wanted to shield you a little longer from the sweltering heat of the sun, from the beaks of greedy ravens. So I came ashore, spread the canopy of branches you see above you; and when I decided to move your head into still deeper shade, I took it my hands. And it was then that you heaved a sigh and came back to life…"

"So that's all there was to it?"

"Yes, my child. But how come there are new tears in your eyes?"

"From sickness and grief. Don't ask me…"

"On the contrary, I want to know everything—everything and always. So confess, young man! Perhaps you have fallen wildly in love with me since that evening and, seeing that you were not loved, you tried to take your life?... I won't hold it against you."

"Oh, God, God! What terrible speculations, what stony composure… No, no, Cyprian must have been lying."

"Who is this Cyprian whom you mention for the second time?"

"Cyprian is the one who told me, who showed me, that you would love me…"

"Strange, I don't know him at all—and yet, wait a moment… love... love you… Oh! Wasn't that precisely what I was looking for?... Who knows? Why should I not love you?"

"Woman, don't utter such words! They're killing me, killing me!"

"And why should I not utter them, Benjamin, if they are to be the truth?" Suddenly, sunbeams began to dance on the glassy surface of her dark-green eyes. "If they are to be the truth, if I am to love you, I will be restored entirely—to new life and perhaps to my old life as well. If I say to you: I have exhausted all luxuries and extravagancies, turned the pages of all the wisest books, possess and know everything, but have lacked the world—and yet have been reminded of another world, of another happiness—so then I want love. Beni, my Beni,[71] love me, and I will love you…"

For a moment I could not utter a word.

"Listen, Aspasia!" I said at last with some difficulty. "Aspasia! For Aspasia is your name, isn't it?"

"They must have told you so at the castle."

"No, no, it wasn't at the castle, it was before that, far away. Listen, Aspasia, listen! For this is the one moment, and perhaps the last, when I shall have enough strength to muster what remains of my thoughts and utter these words. If you feel that what you declared just now is nothing but the free plaything of your imagination; if you know only how to amuse yourself with beautiful sounds and arrange them so as to make a vivid impression on your listeners; if you know that things can never be as you promise; if you do not want to, or are not able to love me, then Aspasia, Aspasia!—Oh, for pity's sake, I will not condemn you—only speak, speak the truth! Perhaps you desire homage, worship, love? Perhaps you are proud and wish me to grovel in the dust before you? Speak, and my heart will be satisfied! I don't intend to fight with you over who should have power. I shall content myself with your picture. I shall never profane you by choosing another woman. But tell me that your words were but in jest, that the hope you aroused was but madness! Tell me and leave me here alone, and even though I may not have the strength to drag myself indoors, even though I might perish here forsaken and wretched, I shall bless you still in my dying, and say before God in heaven: 'Oh, she was a noble woman!'—Aspasia, have pity on me! If you are unable to love yourself, you'll never understand how much of my happiness, how much of my spirit, became mingled with your voice when you uttered those words.

"If such joy were ever to seep into my life's blood, if I were to admit such a state even for a day and then had to part with it, if I had to wrench my heart away in pieces from the delusion—then, Aspasia, I would receive in that moment a revelation from hell telling me I would be unable to bear it. Aspasia, spare me this agony… Abandon me, forget me, now while there is still time… Now, when the only thing you can bear away with you is my happiness."

And I told her everything: who I was, what Cyprian had said to me, how he had told me to avoid unhappiness and how news of his death had reached me together with his painting.

"Look, Aspasia, my brother was right," I added at last. "I should never suffer. Look how I have been broken by my first bad adventure. You found me by your wayside an orphan, a beggar, wretched, sick, almost dead. Why should you tease such a feeble being? And why should you throw my whole future into uncertainty? Aspasia, if you are unable to love, be merciful! Be honourable, honest—even if it's completely mercenary! Have the courage of human kindness. Go away from here. Leave me, leave me alone!"

And I put my hands together and prayed. Her cheeks flared in a burning flush. She leaned over me, touched my lips with her lips, and I heard her saying:

"Don't be afraid, don't be afraid, my Beni. I shan't desert you. My Beni, I love you!"

The sky shone with the sunny day; the river flowed as though with the molten sun; the little boat glided on the river swiftly and lightly, and in the boat sat Aspasia. Again and again her white arms struck the surface of the sparkling water, powerfully, gracefully, with the decorative oar, its ebony handle strangely at odds with the white hands that gripped it. And at Aspasia's feet, on a tiger-skin rug, I lay, still weak, still dazed by the remnants of my fever and by the bright light of the day, and by my happiness.

"Who are you, Aspasia?..." I asked.

"Who am I?" she replied. "Does my child want a bed-time story to lull him to sleep? Does my lover not know me?" She laughed and began to relate thousands of wondrous tales of enchanted princesses, of salamanders, of the women of Ancient Greece, of slave-women who resided in the sultan's seraglio—and when she reached the most interesting places, she would stop and ask me: And do you like that woman? And when I smiled back at her, she would say: So that's who I am. And so we rowed upstream together and I forgot about everything, forgot about Cyprian's death. Aspasia relieved my soul of grief for the dead man.

From that moment on I remained at her side. I abandoned my profession, did not return home.

But… but… my dear friends, I promised to tell you one of the fairytales my sister Terenia used to tell me when I was a child; I have just remembered one, so listen before I forget it again:

"Once upon a time above a very deep sea, on a very high rock, there stood a very high castle, and on a very low shore there stood a very lowly cottage. In the cottage there lived a fisherman, young and handsome, and in the castle there lived a princess, young and beautiful. The fisherman fell in love with the princess; and the princess promised to love the fisherman. One night, the fisherman fell asleep in his cottage, and the princess died in her grand castle. The fisherman wept all day and all night while the princess was mourned by old monks with long beards and old crones with sunken eyes. On the following day and throughout the following night the fisherman prayed constantly while the princess was dressed in golden robes and encased in a crystal coffin. The coffin was laid to rest in a tomb held down by a heavy stone slab, and the stone slab was sealed with the royal seal. Throughout the third day the fisherman sat by the seashore with his arms folded; he did not cast his nets or repair his boat. And the princess lay in her cold dark tomb beneath the enormous stone slab—beneath the royal seal. On the third night the fisherman lay in his cottage but could not sleep. At midnight the doors of the cottage were pushed ajar and the princess entered in her golden gown, trembling and very pale. The fisherman stretched out his arms towards her:

'Did you love me, fisherman?'

'How could I not love you?' answered the fisherman. 'Now that you have died and I am not afraid of your corpse?'

'I thank you, fisherman,' the princess replied. Bending over him, she swept back the hair from one side of his head and kissed him on the temple.

And so it was the next night and the night after that, and every night for three years.

And during this time the fisherman's face grew paler and paler, his hands weaker and weaker. He never stepped beyond the threshold of his house, never sat by the seashore, never rose from his bed. A priest came to him and said:

'Make your confession, poor fellow, for death is nigh.'

But the fisherman gave the priest a strange smile, placed his hands over his heart said:

'No, not yet. I still have another six nights. Come again on the seventh night.'

And on the seventh night the priest came again. And behind him came a small boy carrying a lit candle and the sacramental oils, holy water and aspergillum.

The priest and the boy saw a figure in a golden gown standing over the fisherman's bed wringing its hands, and the fisherman already lying ashen and lifeless.

The priest crossed himself. The figure vanished but the fisherman did not rise. His body was white as chalk. Only above the right temple his hair had been drawn back, and here there was a tiny mark, no bigger than a pinprick.

The terrified priest hastened to the castle. He summoned the chaplain and everyone present, and they went together to the chapel vaults. There they found the huge stone slab that had covered the princess's tomb split asunder and the royal seal severed. They rolled aside the stone and in the crystal coffin they saw the beautiful princess, fresh and lovely as though she had merely fallen into a voluptuous sleep. Only on her lips, like a seed of coral, a small drop of blood still glistened."

I see, ladies and gentlemen, that this tale makes little impression on you. Perhaps you are displeased I inserted it so unnecessarily, yet you won't believe what a strange influence it exerted in my childhood years. I remember how whenever we reached the place where the princess sweeps back the fisherman's hair and kisses him on the temple, a cold shudder ran down my spine, because I knew that she was drinking in a drop of his blood with that kiss, and I grew uneasy as though I could feel the touch of those deadly, murderous lips.

Albert, you once had proof—did you not?—that intuition really exists?

Oh! I too…

First of all I surrendered to her the memory of my dead brother. She drew it into herself with a kiss, and then despoiled it with her words.

Then I relinquished all the things I liked. I stopped loving flowers. They began to appeal to her: she wore them in her hair, at her side, arranged them in Etruscan vases. Everywhere was filled with flowers, and I was intoxicated with joy that having relinquished my own, I had brought her at least one pleasure in life.

One day I went to great pains to bring her a fuchsia-tree, a beautiful shrub that sheds its little bells like tears of blood. Aspasia broke off the branches with the most blooms. She fondled them, consoled them as one would a grieving heart. Then they withered in her hand and she threw them out of the window. Then on the third day, the rest of the fuchsia withered in its pot and again she ordered it to be thrown out. And when I asked, distressed and saddened, why it was no longer alive, all she could say was: "I've forgotten."

Then one evening, as we sat beneath the balmy sky of some southern land, I lifted my eyes and stared at the stars—with the old gaze of my childhood.

"What are you brooding over?" Aspasia inquired. I pointed upwards with my finger and said:

"Look, my love, do you see all that? Take it! It's beautiful, magnificent; it completes our moments of happiness because it promises eternity."

Aspasia looked in the direction my hand was pointing and repeated, "Ah! It's beautiful, beautiful. Why had I forgotten to look at it? Thank you, my Beni, for reminding me once more. Ah! Beautiful, and yet so immense, immeasurable that it seems to cry out: 'Remember thou art dust, a mere instant. Spare thy thoughts, thy hand! Squander not thy strength on the knowledge of good and evil—for the only truth in our infinity is our being, any fulfilment of that being is mere chance, while the forms things take, events, tears, smiles, are matters of pure indifference.' Ah! How I love these stars. They tell me that I am young, that I alone am the almighty mistress of my destiny, that no other laws weigh upon me, only the laws of my own will—and those of time, and these are written out in clear bright syllables: 'Everything has been—You are—Everything will always be.'"

From that moment on Aspasia gazed at the sky more often and I stopped loving the stars.

Then… I no longer remember where it was—I see only soft carpets spread before me, walls hung with coils of dark fabric woven with gold, windows encased in gold and marble and flung open onto a dense grove of fragrant, spreading trees. Aspasia, half lying, half propped on one elbow, was staring nonchalantly at the pages of a book that rested before her against the head of an ebony sphinx. I was seated at a distance and cannot now recall why I was feeling downcast. Then from among the dark trees, through the open window, a pure melodious voice drifted towards us. It was humming a love-song—simple, unadorned, yet so mournful, so moving I remembered my former self and my sister Julcia and the bench where she used to sit and all the old ballads I loved to hear as I sat at her feet.

"Come to me, come to me, my Beni," called Aspasia's voice. I threw off my memories and went over to her and she put her arms round my neck. "Do you hear?" she said to me. "Do you hear how that song kisses the lover's ringlets of hair, kisses the beloved eyes, forehead and lips?" And with her every question Aspasia caressed me in accord with the words of the song. And from that moment on the sound of someone singing was beautiful to me only because of the impression it made on her—and I stopped loving songs.

Then I received many letters from home, all at once.

My brother Adam wrote: "Benjamin! I have said farewell to my wife and children. Come back to us!"

My brother Józef wrote: "Benjamin! Fire has destroyed my farm. Gales blow through the empty stables. There are no hands to take up the plough and harrow. Come back to us!"

My brother Karol wrote: "Benjamin! Everything will turn out for the best, but come back to us."

My father wrote: "Benjamin! At the time of your birth I praised God that another child had been born unto the world, that there was one more heart made to love, two more hands to do useful work. Today we need that heart and those hands, come back to us!"

My mother wrote: "Benjamin! I bore you in my womb, suckled you with the milk of my breast. You will return when your mother cries out in sorrow and in need: My son, my son, come back to us!"[72]

But Aspasia said: "Where your heart is, there will your treasure be also"[73]—where your loving is, there will be your power to act; where your free will is, there will your duty be also. Father, mother, family were given you by chance, but me—you chose, took me for yourself from the whole wide world and so your whole world is only with me. Or are you a mere plant which has set its heart on one place, one soil? From pole to pole the earth is ours for the taking: where the wind wafts more fragrantly, where the nightingale's voice is more caressing, where the blood flows more keenly in the veins, where hearts beat more passionately, where the irksome moans of others' pain cannot reach us—there let us pitch our white tents. And there may we live and love, for there will be the promised land of Canaan, there our chosen Jerusalem…"

So I did not return… From then on I ceased to love my parents, my sisters, my brothers—anything, everything that I had loved before. I loved only Aspasia. And I was not at all afraid of such moral bankruptcy. In her I discovered myself, whilst she lent me new powers and talents.

She wanted riches, so I threw myself into reckless commercial enterprises. Ships sailed to the coasts of Europe from all corners of the world bringing me profits and gold; millions flowed through my hands.

She wanted great deeds, honours and distinctions. Before long I was wearing round my neck the crosses of all the saints in the calendar and images of every animal under the sun, from elephants to lambs—and once I was even awarded a garter to tie round my leg…[74] Oh! I forget now what roads I trod inspired by the wild schemes of restless imagination. The black gondolas of Venice, the smokes of Vesuvius, the English Parliament, Viennese waltzes, Parisian *salons*, the Escurial, the pyramids of Egypt, German bookstores—everything is so confused now in my mind like the many-coloured glass nuggets of a kaleidoscope. I remember, as though through a haze, that I was addressed as count, baron, lord, *eccelenze*; that a doctoral cap was conferred on my head[75;] and that once, when I was speaking, a gathering of solemn men in mortarboards and long black gowns bared their rotting teeth at me and applauded with their fat, lean or bony hands… Yet none of these curtain calls added much to my treasury of memories, nothing entered permanently into the history of my life. Because they were not me. They were the fleeting desires, fantasies, fancies of Aspasia. I existed only in her smile, in her mirth, in her word of praise. And so, in this manner, several years of my life went by.

During this time Aspasia squandered all the glorious things we shared in common: zeal, inspiration, love of beauty—the power to enjoy, to constantly conceive and create ever new dreams and make them come true, the power to be happy. She took all my love and frittered it away. Agh! And then came the awful tomorrow. The void in my soul became filled with other elements. I began to suffer—to be resentful and anxious, to be jealous and to hate. It is hard to describe to you how the corruption gradually spread in my breast, how the moral gangrene slowly took hold of me.

The hand which Aspasia no longer pressed in return, the indifferent look in her eyes as they lost their lustre and hardened to their former stoniness, the clipped strident tone of her voice, the long hours of distraction, inattention and gloom—it would be very tedious if I were to describe it all to you, and for me too it would be unspeakably pointless and tiresome. I will mention only the final incident. By then I had gone beyond that stage in pain and moral disintegration when a man is more ashamed of unhappiness than he is of catching leprosy, and grinds his unhappiness into a kind of powder, which he then scatters over everything that surrounds him—objects, circumstances, events; when he pits his strength against every visible shard of the invisible whole, seizes on extreme methods, and is then amazed he has managed to survive such battles, overturn such mountains—and yet the hydra grows ever new heads; his foot stumbles on ever new heaps of rubble. A kind of blind fury takes possession of him. Instinctively he lashes out at everything around him with his fists; and if he smashes what is dearest to him, strikes his own head or breaks the law, then he no longer cares so long as he can relieve his pain for just one gasp of breath, stop suffering for just one stroke of the pendulum... And so, in the moment I am about to describe I was suffering, as I said, from this very disease of unhappiness. We were sitting down to a magnificent banquet. The table sagged under the weight of silver, gold, cut glass. Little blue flames of smouldering punch flickered here and there like the souls of the damned, whilst a dazzlingly reddish brightness streamed from the black spouts of the iron lamps cast in patterns from Herculaneum. There were only three of us: Aspasia, myself and another man. She took the man's hand and clinked his cup with her goblet. Then the man leaned forward and touched the rim of that goblet with his lips in the very place where she had touched it first!

I stared at the man. He shuddered and signalled to Aspasia, whispering quietly: "Benjamin will kill me."

Aspasia burst into laughter.

"No, he won't kill you," she said merrily. "I do so love the fiery gaze in your black eyes. I feel so happy when you speak in that strong voice of command, seductive as temptation. But Beni loves me so sincerely. Beni lives only through my life. Beni feels only through my pleasure, so much so he would never be able to kill you. Isn't that so, Beni? Your love is of the highest, the truest, the most complete. Your love feeds only on my happiness. Your love does not desire me but only loves me. Isn't that so, Beni?"

Poor Aspasia was wrong in her timing.

What she said had been true earlier on, but by then it was a lie… Her former unshaken faith in my heart, certainty that I would make any sacrifice for her, had kept me chained to the slightest movement of her hand. Yet earlier on there was still much good left in me; earlier on I had loved her. But by then I could feel only hatred towards all the people with whom she shared—as though at my funeral wake— the crumbs of the loving I had once bestowed upon her.

When the banquet was over, the stranger left. I went after him and followed him for a long time through the twists and turns of the dark alleyways. One of the streets led into a wide empty square. The entire space was lit only by two tiny points of light that came from two streetlamps flickering in the damp misty air. I drew near to the man and said:

"Today you guessed my fate. I am going to kill you."

The man was armed. He had a sword at his side and a dagger in his belt. He defended himself bravely, desperately, but I killed him. I returned by the same route. And instead of the streetlamps, I saw gleaming before me the whites of two ghastly gaping eyes.

I returned to Aspasia and told her everything. Aspasia listened without resentment, without revulsion, yet she pondered deeply. After a long silence she coldly passed sentence:

"I do not love you. You do not love me. Let us go our separate ways, Benjamin."

When I heard these words, my eyes clouded over and my tongue grew stiff and numb. I stared at the woman for a moment, and her posture became impressed on my brain with the same exactitude as the posture of the wolf that once leapt at Zitta's breast. Not a single knot in the finely wrought pearled net she wore in her hair, not a single fold of her bright-green cashmere dress, escaped my attention. I remember every shade of light reflected in the two magnificent opals she wore on her bare arms, adorned with bracelets; I remember how she held those arms in front of her resting them on her elbows, leaning on a dark-coloured table inlaid with a mosaic of fantastic arabesques; I remember how she rested her chin on her interlocked hands and how her neck arched backwards, how her whole head was thrown back and how this gave her an air of arrogance and insolence, and how she looked me in the eye with those eyes of hers, grown black now from the black blood of her heart. Then, oh, then! Contempt sprang from my breast to my lips. My tongue grew hot and excited as I spat out every insult I could think of, all my torments, every possible curse and obscenity. Aspasia listened with the same calm composure as when I told her that because of her and for her, I had killed a man. That composure provoked in me a savage, frantic desire for revenge. It occurred to me that if were I to kill her, then at least her facial features might twitch and mouth groan in pain beneath the thrust of my dagger... This desire brought me to my senses so forcibly that I suddenly saw the deed as though accomplished and, terrified of my own self, rushed from the room... It's an odd thing, but you'll never guess what I regretted most when I calmed down after my first transport of fury; it's an odd thing, but I regretted that I had not killed Aspasia before, a long time ago—Oh! Long ago, when I still loved her. I was overwhelmed by despair—not for the woman, but for my love. Not to have love, to lose so fundamental a condition of one's existence, to gaze thus upon the funeral pyre of one's soul, because one had gazed upon the hideous villainy of one's chosen object—is terrible! Would it not have been better, a hundred times better, if I had killed Aspasia when we were gazing at the stars together? When she was kissing my hair and eyes as we listened to the song wafting from afar? Would it not have been better? I would have wrapped the dead woman in my memories and buried her at the bottom of my heart without soiling her image, without a slur on her person as she was laid in her tomb, and I would have loved her forever. And then I recalled almost the first words she had said to me: "God loves through destruction and mystery." Now I understood them. Tears welled in my eyes. Aspasia vanished from my memory and there remained only unutterable grief, a desperate nostalgia for the past, the wrenching of all my spiritual powers towards what was passed and gone!... If only I still had what was passed, if only through destruction and mystery, then at least I would still have it. At the time my mind could not aspire to a higher logic.

To still have the past! To have it! Those were the words into which my every thought was now transposed while I, poor wretch, no longer had anything. I cast off my rich attire, removed my shoes, flung over my shoulder nothing but my overcoat, and strode out of our palace just as I had been when Aspasia had first encountered me on her way. Just as I had been? Oh no! Not just as I had been at all! As I passed through the drawing rooms, vast and empty yet always ablaze with light, and as I caught glimpses of my dark emaciated figure reflected in the Venetian mirrors on all sides, broken and leaning on my traveller's stick, I was moved by a great pity for myself. Why had I not remained a child in my parents' home? Why had I been sent so far away from my brothers and sisters? Why had an evil spirit goaded my horse in the direction of her castle? Why had she rowed down the river to the place where I might have given up the ghost—in my first happiness and my first grief? Given up the ghost—innocent, serene, white as a lily before the dust and torrid heat of day beat down upon it? Why did she not go away when I had a premonition of what was to come and begged her to leave me alone? I could have died, or could still be sitting throughout the long evenings beside Cyprian's painting, my day's work done. And I would have dreamed, loved or perhaps... And then I remembered the letters from my brothers, father, mother. I hung my head in shame, did not wipe away the streaming tears and continued on my arduous road. And I journeyed long and far—through thick forests, over steep mountains, across rivers and lakes. Meanwhile the European newspapers were translating into every language an important, extraordinary and unexpected piece of news:

"Count Benjamin," one of them reported, "Commander of Crosses, Companion of Orders... member of numerous learned societies, disappeared suddenly on the night of 1st to 2nd November following a duel with Duke... whom he killed. The next day a great ball was held at the palace... Countess Aspasia received the cream of high society with her characteristic charm and we could not sufficiently admire the calm cheerfulness with which she no doubt wished to deflect all speculation and suspicion. Everywhere our sources say that Count Benjamin—a young man of uncommon abilities, brilliant author of the renowned scholarly work *On the Antiquities of Ethiopia* and of the delightful little book of short verse *Sorceries*, as well as one of our most distinguished diplomats—had been on intimate terms with the lady for a long time. A mystery, yet a mystery full of fascination and fine taste, such as is tolerated by even the severest judges amongst the high aristocracy, and before which even the sumptuous rooms of the Margravine of ***—a pillar of morality by today's standards—were thrown open; just such a mystery, we say, veils the lives of these two beings, entirely worthy of one another. It is with pleasure, however, that we can inform our readers that any shameful speculations surrounding the birth of Count Benjamin are slander of the most sordid kind. His noble features bear ample testimony against those who would accuse him of Israelite origins. And now a reliable witness from among his trusty friends has revealed to us the full story of his background, but at the same time imposed on us the difficult obligation to preserve the mystery. We feel we betray nothing of the mystery, however, in saying that this extraordinary child, destined to go so far and vanish so suddenly, most likely took his first steps somewhere beyond the Beskidy mountains,[76] in the delightful seclusion of a princely garden, upon oriental carpets and marble tiles."

With a bitter smile I read this entire passage on a scrap of newspaper thrown from a window. Count Benjamin, man of genius, allegedly a Serb or Wallachian princeling, sat in the meantime beneath the wall of a wayside inn. Snow and wind lashed his face in turn and his blood froze and congealed on the coarse rags with which he had bound his feet. He still had a long way to go to the end of his journey. Oh, a very long way!

VI

IT WAS NOT UNTIL CHRISTMAS EVE that I saw the black outline of the tiny hamlet emerging ahead against the white canvas of snow. A wayside cross loomed before me at the parting of the roads. Behind the farm buildings four poplar trees pointed upwards into the sky like the fingers of some gigantic hand. And in the middle of the yard the leafless skeleton of the lime-tree rose up, motionless and solitary. I did not even give way to my tears; I just found it more and more difficult to wrench my feet from the ground and take the steps which were to bring me closer. Even in my own eyes I was a dead man, a mere shadow, returned as no more than a ghost to the place whence I had once taken the forms and time of my life. As I walked into the yard the dogs first began to bark horribly and then to howl, and yet none drew near or tried to bite me: "They sense a corpse," I thought to myself, and stepped into the hallway. I could not take hold of the latch; I dared not. I was overcome by a great feeling of panic and alarm, a kind of childish, effeminate embarrassment. I felt like burying myself in the ground, but in the parlour they must have heard me enter. Suddenly the door creaked ajar and a tiny head appeared in the strip of light.

"Aunty, it's a poor man!" said the silvery high-pitched voice of a little girl.

"Take this to him," answered another voice, one I knew well—that voice of penetrating mournfulness, unfathomable sadness.

After a while the door opened again and a little girl stood before me holding a large piece of bread and a coin.

I took the bread, took the coin. Then I kissed her dainty hand and followed her inside.

"What do you want now, old man?" she inquired.

"I wish to thank those who have given me succour," I replied standing in the threshold.

The hay had been spread on the table and the places lain. In one corner of the room sat a pale-faced woman with silvery white hair, dressed in a black gown and black cap. On either side of her sat the young wives, their husbands, also still young, and their growing lads and lasses as well as the smaller children including my little helper. And the wafers had already been broken... And everything was just as it was years ago...

"Mother," I cried. "My mother!"

The woman in the black gown leaped to her feet but strength failed her and she fell back into her chair. A commotion arose among the others. I know someone shouted, "Benjamin, what have you done? Mother, calm yourself!" But I no longer remember it, remembrance returns to me only from the moment when I nestled sobbing and distracted against the knees of the woman dressed in black, and when I felt her burning hot tear touch my forehead along with her kiss. It was my mother's tear!... I still had a mother!

"And where is father?" I stammered timidly, hiding my face in her lap.

"Where Józef is and where Karol is," she answered quietly but in a voice that seared my heart with its unspoken grief and anguish.

I raised my head and looked around—it was true, none of them were there.

"They died a Christian death," my mother added.

"But it was not over their deaths that we shed our bitterest tears," declared Bronisława. And that was the first and only accusation that greeted me.

I said nothing and no one cross-examined me. Ludwinka embraced me with the full solicitude of her heart. That evening, that one evening, was surely intended as the culmination of my sufferings and atonement. To find yourself so much a stranger among those whom you had once held most dear, so condemned among the pure angels, so mourned in pity and compassion by those who had looked upon your first footsteps with such pride and consolation, those who had prophesied virtue to your heart, glory to your talents, happiness to your fate, those who had repeated with such joy and delight the first words uttered by your childish lips, taken such pleasure in the first ideas of your young mind—to find yourself in such a position and to still go on living! Oh what iron strength is required for that!

My mother was much altered and very weak. In her sunken lustreless eyes, in her hollow and deeply furrowed cheeks, I could read every word of my damnation, every word of the curse which her lips never uttered and her mind surely never imagined—but which pierced my heart no less with appalling affliction and infernal suffering.

One of the grandchildren announced she was going to midnight mass.

"I'll go with you," said my mother. "There are days when I have to pray more, for on such days I have been happier than usual or I have suffered more."

"How many years is it since Cyprian came back like this on Christmas Eve?" I asked Terenia who was sitting quietly beside me.

"Six years, Beniaminek."

Oh, dear ladies and gentlemen! At that simple reply the tears began to stream down my cheeks. Six years! Six years, and throughout those six years no one had ever said to me "Beniaminek" in the way Terenia said it at that moment. I sprung to my feet and ran out into the other, unlit room. I threw myself upon the bench, that very same bench where I used to listen to Julcia's songs, and felt better once left to weep. They, good people, understood me then. No one came after me. Only when they had parted company and gone to bed did my mother come to me, take me by the hand and lead me to her room.

"Do you remember," she said, "how long you slept in your cradle and then in that little red bed? From the day of your birth till the first time you mounted a horse. And your father said with a smile: 'He's a grown man now! Let him fend for himself among men!' And that was when your bed was moved upstairs to your brothers' room. And then there were your studies, your employment that bore you still further from your mother's side, carried you so far away I thought I'd lost my sweet baby, my youngest child, forever. But now you've come back I feel as if I've given birth to you a second time, as if—just as then—you won't survive without my efforts, without my constant care. So look, Beniaminek, I have made up a bed for you in the very place where your cradle used to stand twenty-four years ago. Sleep tight—as if your eyes were to open to the light tomorrow morning for the first time! Forsake evil, Beniaminek! Cast out the past from your heart, only don't cast out the love you had for us in former times. With the help of that love we shall begin another beautiful life. We are not short of time, are we? Oh! Though I am old, you will see how I shall nourish and tend your newborn youth. A mother's heart knows many miraculous secrets about how to bring eternal renewal to every moment of her child's past. You'll see, Beniaminek, things will be all right with us..."

And with a trembling hand she made the sign of the cross in the air above my head.

Oh, how I believed in those promises! I felt I could be resurrected by the warmth of her heart. I slumped to the floor at her feet and laid before her all my crimes and iniquities, all the misfortunes I had brought upon her.

My mother listened to me with deep sadness. She absolved me with a pity that was saintly, divine. But when the bells pealed in the night summoning the people to mass, my mother could not get up. And she never got up again.

For several weeks I never left her bedside. I administered the medicines, carried her in my own arms. My sisters, in a manifestation of Christ-like kindness, did not try to rob me of my right to the one consolation I could still enjoy. Sometimes when I gazed at my mother's face, pale and motionless in its torpid slumber, a terrible voice would cry out to me: "You're killing her, killing her!"

But when my mother opened her eyes again, when she looked at me, when her smile of peace and forgiveness illuminated all her facial features, then my heart experienced once more a sensation of bliss and relief, as though a silent angel had descended and said: "You have done well to return. Your mother will not die with her last thought one of fear and distress."

One evening she felt better. She demanded to be placed in the big armchair and moved close to the fire. My sisters and their children seated themselves around her. Terenia's little daughter, the same who had brought me alms that first night, came and rested her head on her grandmother's knee, but when Terenia tried to draw her away, her grandmother held her tight and began to stroke her with her trembling hand. But as she gazed at the luxurious abundance of those bright ringlets spilling over her lap in a torrent of gold, she said: "I remember our Beniaminek had this same hair." And she signalled to me with her eyes that I should go over to her. I went over and kneeled beside her. My mother ordered me to lean forward; she was surely comparing the two heads resting on her knees, for her fingers touched mine and that of the little girl in turn. At last she spoke, as if concluding some train of thought:

"I always told him he would return..." But then a feverish red flush suddenly appeared on her forehead and cheeks; it was clear she was mustering her strength so as to utter a few final words. "Benjamin," she said eventually in a broken voice. "Don't forget to visit your father's grave... There beside him rests Cyprian... Józef and Karol are somewhere else... but they have their crosses... don't forget, I shall be there..." She sighed, her hand slipped from my head onto her lap... and I no longer had a mother!

My sisters and brothers did not want to take me with them to the funeral; my despair seemed too violent to them alongside their silent grief. It seems I even fell ill, but I don't really remember—it was not a benevolent kind of sickness that simply suspends life and memory for a time but a sickness of nought but appalling impotence. Sleep was not granted me, not even for a moment. I saw and experienced every suffering separately, yet was capable neither of becoming so distraught that all my sufferings taken together might have killed me at once, nor of consoling myself sufficiently to slip into a state of numbness. All strength of mind, strength of will, completely deserted me. I allowed myself to be ordered about like a little child whilst I suffered, suffered...

After a time they all departed and went their separate ways, only Ludwinka remained with me in the forsaken house. My brothers and sisters had so arranged our affairs that when I was restored to health I should take over the running of the farm and village and live there with my most beloved of sisters. I did not reject, but neither did I accept this arrangement. I lacked judgment or ability to reflect upon the most insignificant detail of everyday life. The unity of my being had become unhitched—in every separate part I could feel a separate pain. I was unable to weep, yet my face would sometimes grow so livid, the veins on my forehead stand out with such terrible clarity, my eyes become so bloodshot, the joints of my hands crack with such a hollow crunch, that Ludwinka was afraid to come near me. And then I would remind her of Cyprian's words: "Even Ludwinka will turn away from you in disgust." And I would torment her poor heart with the harshness of my reproaches, as though she had no cares of her own—probably of longer standing than mine—to clothe in new mourning and exacerbate with fresh tears. But Ludwinka possessed a strange virtue, to me incomprehensible: she knew how to be unhappy. Her sufferings never poisoned her heart, never disrupted the order of her daily life. With unwavering patience Ludwinka bore my eccentricities; she treated me like a sick child and sometimes… sometimes her kindness reminded me of my mother.

"We have to stifle that voice of pain piercing our hearts, Beniaminek, with constant movement and constant activity," she said to me on one occasion. "We have to escape from our own breasts, tear ourselves away from our own selves and turn to face the outside world, think about another person, some employment, other things. We need to observe the objects surrounding us, the work of our hands, and never look too deep into our own souls, never drown our thoughts in the hidden world of our own feelings; this is the only way we can march straight ahead. Though it may not console us or ease the pain, it at least diverts it and divides it up. Today you bring all your powers to bear on one central point, and that point is your torture. Heed my advice: if you try to wrench away just one of those powers—if you succeed in detaching just your attention and directing it elsewhere, Beniaminek, you'll make your life more bearable, you'll see."

"More bearable, Ludwinka?" I quizzed her suspiciously. "Are you telling me it will be more bearable? In a tomb such as mine with the lid already closed, with such foul putrefaction lying at the bottom? It's not possible; it would be like living a twofold death."

"I assure you it will be more bearable." Her voice was gentle in its supplication. And she pressed my hand with conviction and faith.

"Ha! I understand you," I said. "It'll be just like holding a bottle of vodka to my lips the whole time and drinking myself stupid..."

"Such a comparison never entered my head," replied Ludwinka sadly. "But if it's like that, then at least our stupefaction doesn't offend God or shock other people."

"What are you saying, Ludwinka, it doesn't offend God? Then your God must be some indifferent figure floating in the sky, dressed in a red robe and blue cloak just as he's usually depicted in the paintings above our altars, because if He is as Bronisia described Him to me—if He is beauty, love, happiness—then admit yourself, the thing that should offend Him most must be the sight of a suffering man resigned to his suffering!..."

Ludwinka stared me in the eye for a long time.

"A man not resigned to suffering," she said at last, "still lives in hope he can cast it from his life. Do you live in hope, Beniaminek?"

I remained silent. To that one question I had no answer.

The next day I threw myself nevertheless into unaccustomed activity. I browsed through the books lying on the shelves, arranged just as they had been when my father was alive. I opened the old Bible and that *in quarto* volume with the busts of the Polish kings as well as the book which had fallen from my father's hands before my first reading lesson. And I found on the dust jackets of some of the books various sketches by Cyprian, and between the pages a number of pictures he had painted at our request. In one volume I discovered eight of them, arranged according to the age of their owners and signed by my father's hand—no doubt he had kept them as a memento of our childish games.

For Adam there was a drawing of a mirror, positioned in such a way that the outline of a lovely girl was reflected in it though she had had not yet entered the room.

For Julcia there was a likeness of old Paraska who had taught her the old ballads and country dances[77] she knew. For Józef there were the farm buildings of some wealthy holding—or so it would seem—for the roofs of the stable and barns were on a level with the treetops while large ricks and haystacks could be seen in the distance. In front of the manor was the harvest home, and on it stood Józef, dressed as a farmhand and about to dance with the leading girl.

For Ludwinka there was only a small aspen branch.

For Bronislawa—a woman leaning on a lion.

For Karol—the apotheosis of the huntsman: Karol himself leaping from cloud to cloud on his Zitta, Moloch sitting to heel before the moon while a tiny shooting star fell to earth like snipe shot down by Karol's "mistress."

For Terenia there was a handsome boy half hanging out of the cup of some miraculous flower, its leaves as though composed of the most fantastic objects: one was a witch unfurling on a shovel, a second a tongue bursting into flame; another was shaped like a dragon, another like a maiden wearing a crown, yet another looked like a ten of hearts set in rubies against a background that changed colour like the eyes on a peacock's feather.

For me there was a picture of the young Tobias on his way to meet Raguel's daughter, resting with his as yet unidentified companion[78]; a city of some sort could be seen in the distance, beyond the city the sun was rising while Tobias looked towards the city and towards the sun with his hand held to his brow.

I could not explain to myself why in the first instance I was not saddened by the sight of this picture, as I had been saddened by every other memory of my early years. I took it and kept it by me.

Then I inspected every corner of the house. I even went down to the cellar where often in summer, as tiny children, we used to compete over which of us would stir the butter in the churns. I dug my way through the snow as far as the stream that divided our garden from the meadows. I went everywhere, except I did not have the courage to enter the little room upstairs where Cyprian had stolen my youth, my beauty, my happiness—my soul's innocence—and worked them into the idea for his painting. But as evening approached, as I was reviewing the course of my day, I observed that Ludwinka had been right: that such constant activity even when it had no purpose, that such change simply in the objects of one's pain, was a great relief. I wanted to exhaust its possibilities. I lit a candle and made my way upstairs. The key to the room was rusted and slow to open the lock; I realized that no one had been up there for a very long time. I had to force the bolts—the door opened and... well, you can never escape your destiny!

Once again she sat before me, sat just as I had always desired her, such as I had awaited her in the happiest... no, I'm expressing myself badly—in the most impassioned, ecstatic moments of my love. I grew dreadfully pale, something flew at my throat as if some unknown hand, some fist of iron had clasped it. I took a step forward, but in that same moment a light gust of wind passed through the room, drawn no doubt through the door which I had left open behind me. I felt its cold breath on my face like the gentle puff of a quiet sigh. The candle went out and though I was surrounded by darkness I kept my eyes closed, because I was afraid... But in vain: it was as though I had taken her into my very gaze, underneath my eyelids; her face rose before me, her expression resembling in part the face in Cyprian's painting, in part the face that had once flashed before my eyes in a dazzling burst of lightning. I ran downstairs. The face went before me. I summoned Ludwinka, questioned her about numerous unimportant trifles and listened to the answers she gave me. The face hovered constantly in front of my eyes; wherever I turned, it turned too; whenever I stood still, it stood still. I ordered a fire to be kindled. I stared into its flame; the face burned in the flame but was not consumed, like Moses's burning bush.

"Ludwinka," I said suddenly to my sister. "What would you do with me if I went out of my mind?"

Ludwinka stared at me in alarm. She took the pulse in my arm and anxiously counted the beats.

"Well?" I said. "Is it the pulse of a madman?"

"Don't speak in that way, Beniaminek!" my sister retorted. "You have a slight fever. Perhaps you overstretched yourself today. Once you've had a sleep, you'll feel better."

"And what if I don't fall asleep?"

"Why should you not fall asleep? Sometimes it's possible to make yourself sleep, and sleep is so welcome, as welcome as death..."

"And you know all about it, Ludwinka?"

"Oh! I know, Beniaminek."

"And do you also know, have you ever experienced what it's like when a certain word or idea, for instance, gets fixed in your mind? Or a name you can't shake off, though you've tried a thousand times to drive it away? Or when a particular face stands before your eyes, and whenever you look at it, it always leaves its imprint like those green and red rings that always pursue you when you stare too long at the sun?"

"I know that too, little brother."

"So what do you do then?"

"Then I listen and watch…"

"But if you don't want to hear and don't want to see…?"

"I, little brother, know no word or face I would disown, even if it proved to be an illusion."

"Oh! Then you must still be very happy! Tell me, have you seen that picture upstairs?"

"I have seen it… yes, I have seen it twice."

"And you never wanted to look at it more than that?"

"No, because it reminds me of terrible moments: I saw it for the first time the day before Cyprian died, and then I saw it again when Bazyl brought home your things. And where were you? He could find no words to tell us. Since then I have recoiled in horror from that painting, for such is my strange disposition! I, who so like to amuse myself with sadness as a distraction, flee from any genuine source of pain."

"But it's still a beautiful picture, Ludwinka?"

"Too beautiful to be true!…"

"Why too beautiful to be true, Ludwinka? Women like that do exist. Cyprian used to say so, and I have known such a woman myself."

"Perhaps you have, Benjamin. I wished only to say that not such a woman, but such a moment in life is too beautiful to be true."

"Blasphemy! Blasphemy!" I cried, consoled by the worthless consolation of broken weak people who believe they can ward off their own thoughts and fears by confronting them in others. "Such a moment is an absolute necessity because it is both happiness and perfection."

"But it occurs to me, brother, that a man might forget the world in such a moment and forget God. Therefore a good God never grants him such moments."

"Here we go again! High-minded stoicism, self-denial, renunciation: those are your virtues, Ludwinka. And it no doubt seems to you that I sank so low because I didn't possess them. Well, I ask you! That really is exquisite! A man can only be one of the best when he possesses nothing—happiness is a sin: think about it, Ludwinka! If I had met and had all my life a woman like that, would I have done evil to other people as a result? Would I have not been happy? And don't I deserve happiness? Happiness!... Ludwinka, Ludwinka! If she were to come here to me now, if we were both to recognize our mistake and begin to live another kind of life, calm like this poor home of ours, filled with good works like a day in the life of our own dear mother; if her heart were to exude love roundabout and her word enchant this enclosed little world and turn it into a place of beauty… what then? Do you imagine I would be as evil as I am?—so stubborn and jealous that even when I recall how terribly the eyes of the murdered man stared at me, I am not afraid of them and only repeat in my fury: 'she will no longer say: "I do so love the fiery gaze of your black eyes"'? Would it not be so, Ludwinka? If she had loved me as she loves me in the picture, I would have been good, useful to others—I would never have come back to menace you…"

Ludwinka wept silent tears.

"Why should you not be loved?" she said at last. "You are young, still handsome. And after all, you would have loved like that, wouldn't you?"

I became lost in thought. In my reverie I kept rolling and unrolling the *quarto* paper on which Cyprian had drawn my Tobias in coloured chalks. After a long silence Ludwinka came over to me wishing perhaps to change the subject.

"What are you holding in your hand?" she asked.

I glanced down because I'd even forgotten I was holding something in my hands.

"Ah! A picture I found this morning in one of the books."

"Careful or you'll spoil it! Look, the city is already torn. And yet that picture is a good omen for you, Beniaminek. Sarah had seven bridegrooms. Seven were taken by death. But the one who came to claim her was the one who loved her with a pure love, the love of God."

"You speak the truth, Ludwinka—to simply love and never doubt..."

That night I wrote a letter to Aspasia...

"My mother has died," I told her. "I suffer terribly, but before she died my mother forgave me. And I must forgive you—no, not forgive you, Aspasia, but tell you that I am now a better man; my anger dissolved into tears under the breath of my mother's lips, my curses were struck dumb by her blessings, the hatred in my soul yielded to her love. When I left you, Aspasia, I was unable to mention your name for a very long time without the final moment of our parting returning to me in all its horror—then I would relive every detail of that ordeal, imagine that if I should see you again I would be forced to kill you—though I had not killed you before—and then once more I would be assailed by madness and overwhelmed by insane fury. It's a strange thing! We spent almost five years together yet I could not salvage any other memory except that most terrible one. Today this is no longer the case; today I saw your picture. You do remember it, don't you? The picture that was our first go-between, heralding your coming. And so, when I saw it, I experienced a violent thrill, a thousand conflicting sensations— but believe me, Aspasia, I swear on my mother's memory, not one of these sensations was one of hatred. Aspasia! As I stood before the picture nothing but our beautiful days arose in my mind and I felt a great gratitude for all the good things I had received from you—for the study and learning you made so much easier for me, for the moments of inspiration you gave me, for the hours I spent harkening to your voice and gazing at you in adoration. Gratitude for everything, Aspasia—for the fact that I can decipher the words on mouldering old manuscripts; that the pointed arches of gothic churches or pilasters of Greek temples must relinquish the secrets of their beauty to me at a glance, at once and in minute detail; that not a single brush-stroke of the wonderful paintings of the great masters is lost on me; that the treasures of so many languages were opened up to me; that I know so much, have experienced so much—I owe it all to you. Before I considered it all as nothing—and what is more:

resentment is such a scheming calculator, I even numbered these gains of mine among your mortal sins against me. I had come to see them as empty ridicule, because they did not restore my happiness, could not heal my wounds. Today, Aspasia, I am fairer, more just. I recognize your acts of kindness. I also remember your love— your caresses, your transports of passion, your unwavering faith that I loved you above everything else, just as you were, with all the heaven and hell contained in your soul. Today I remember our whole past and acknowledge the whole of it, so much so I wish to reject from it neither murder nor crime. And do you know why, Aspasia? Because I am convinced that I love you again. My crime may testify against the way we behaved, against what happened and against the circumstances; but my love testifies to the truth of the feeling that unites us. If I had not had love, then everything that took place would be an irredeemable evil worthy of eternal damnation; if I had not had love, then I would see myself as an abject scoundrel and you as so defiled that life would no longer be worth living. If I had not had love, I would have to call six years of my life debauchery, harlotry; if I had not had love, I would never have been restored to my old haunts, my familial places, not experienced the death of my mother, not touched her grave with my unworthy foot. But I love you, Aspasia. It's true, we went astray, failed to stretch our happiness into infinity, went from one moment of pleasure to another just like the one before—instead of aiming to know a higher one. From the world around us we spun a web of delight for ourselves alone; from ourselves we spun nothing for the world. In our shared breast all the bright rays of illumination converged, but they never stepped outside of our breast, never warmed, never shed light on anything. And then we broke apart, collapsed under the weight of our own excesses. Good which does not give rise to new good is the worst kind of evil. Stupidity does not bring about so much harm, hatred so much ruin, as intelligence when it expends itself in fruitless works, as love when it squanders itself on selfish feeling; this is why we suffered, why I was jealous and you were cruel. But I love you, Aspasia. I trust we will make good our mistake with happiness and perfection, just as we have atoned for it in pain and tears. If at this moment I speak to you only in a letter,

Aspasia, rather than with my living voice, don't imagine, oh my dearest, that I fear your scorn! That I do not trust your heart, that I wish to conceal the remnants of my injured pride with some false ploy. No, my only pride is that I extend my arms to you first, that I have discovered a new shared happiness for us both. For me, my love is the guarantee of your love. Today I know that whoever has loved once loves forever, even though misfortune may have sown discord in his mind and sin so corrupted his heart he once cried out in distraction: 'I hate!'; he will go on loving because loving is humanity's only immortality. Look, Aspasia! I have cursed and abused you with my words, I have survived an appalling sickness of frenzy and spite—and yet in my first moment of calm, in my first glance at your picture, in the first word of hope that my sister cast my way, I feel again that I love you as I loved you before—better than before, Aspasia! When I arrived back here, all the people who had been forgotten for six years, saddened and aggrieved for six years, embraced me with joy; no one even mentioned forgiveness, for each gave it speedily and absolutely. And if no one here has ceased to love me, why should I fear that you have ceased to love me? Is it even likely? No, Aspasia, if it seems that way to you, if—moved by bad memories, or a fit of that unhappy state of mind that blights your smile with gall and your words with venom, if you reject me, condemn me to orphancy, despair and indifference—then do not believe yourself, my one and only! God cannot say to the past: you were not; so a human being cannot say to a heart that once loved: you love no more. In this impossibility lies the whole sanctity of God's truth, the whole sacramental value of human life: you loved me, Aspasia—therefore you will love me again. Cyprian's picture will come true. You will love me as you love me in the picture, as spur, reward and partaker in noble deeds. For you can see it all in the picture, see that some beautiful perfect moment will be born out of the embrace of those two beautiful perfect creatures, that for them their caress is an infusion of new strength, not the release of strength already mustered, that Aspasia will take up her lyre, that Alcibiades will wind his inspired ideas in words around the scytale lying beside him.[79] Is it not true that our future will become as Cyprian's ideal? As you read these words, do you not believe me? And believe yourself, and think of the moment when you will come to me? For I, Aspasia, will not come to you. There where you are, there is only death and corruption; you and I would defile each other afresh and suffer for it. But here, where I am, all is pure, sacred, God-fearing— as it usually is among loving hearts, among graves where tears are shed yet no one despairs. So I shall remain here, Aspasia. I shall improve myself, make myself worthy, and wait for you here: I shall wash away your misdemeanours, and mine!..."

For a whole month I lived in feverish expectation vacillating between total certainty and total despondency, for let any man who wishes flatter himself to the contrary: he who has stopped believing will never truly believe again, and once he has begun to suffer, moments of hope are as cantharides[80] sprinkled on his open wounds. Every evening I experienced something akin to a fit that lasted several minutes, I cannot say whether it was more like happiness or a paroxysm of fever. I would be sitting in the little room upstairs, someone would come and light the fire for me and I would gaze at the picture for a whole hour—that is until the wood laid in the fireplace had been consumed—and never once did a sad though enter my head. Whenever I tried to put this to the test at any other time of day, the experiment was never successful. Only at twilight, by the light of the fire in the hearth, did a blissful somnolence, benevolent and invigorating, descend upon me without fail, as though someone were casting a spell. Then, in my imagination, I would read the most affectionate words of her reply; sometimes I even supposed Aspasia was already driving up to the door, entering the room, throwing her arms around my neck and saying: "Let us be good! Let us be happy!" Most often, however, I would lose any sense of my own reality, while the canvas came to life and the figures seated upon it acquired life-like movement: now Alcibiades's cloak would slip aside, then Aspasia's hand would twitch, now the bright wisps of their hair would blend together, then their soft words would somehow emerge. Say what you will, but I wouldn't have exchanged that hour for anything… wouldn't have exchanged it even if someone had offered me some happiness guaranteed in the real world, as yet concealed from me; of course, had they told me such happiness was the living Aspasia then I would not have hesitated, but had they thrown me once more into the uncertainty of conjecture, then I assure you I would have spared them—and myself—the pain. I was so happy with my one hour, my one hour a day without suffering!...

I have already mentioned that this went on for a whole month, for thirty days; I remember exactly, because I was urgently counting the days. On the thirty-first day I was sitting upstairs when the boy came as usual to light the fire. Before he stoked the fire, he handed me a letter. As soon as I touched the paper my head began to reel, my ears throb and reverberate and my heart pound so violently I was unable to break the fragile seal. I stood there for so long clasping the slight, minutely folded paper in my hand that the boy had finished fanning the coals and departed, taking the candle with him, before I succeeded in opening the envelope. I could have taken fright then, because it was now too dark to do anything—the boy was too far away to call him back, whilst the coals, as if to spite me, smouldered lazily, and the logs—again to spite me—would not catch fire. At last they suddenly burst into flame all at once; I had even kneeled in front of the fireplace to hasten the moment. And thus, without rising to my feet, I was to unfold the paper and to regret my vain and violent emotions: I did not recognize the script at all, written as it was in some masculine hand. I began to read calmly enough.

"Piety, my son, is a sacred virtue! And remorse for one's sins leads directly to heaven! But I tell you in all honesty that if a beautiful woman were to laugh at my letter as Aspasia laughed at your prayers, then I would truly renounce both sacredness and heaven, and blow out my brains. Let me inform you, first of all, that it does not hurt, and then, my son, that it is the only cure for your melancholy, your pangs of conscience, as well as for the laughter of the woman who does not want you, and who is looking over my shoulder at this very moment and saying: 'You'll see, he'll even be prepared to carry out that act of stupidity!' I bid you farewell, my son, because I must inquire of Aspasia why she described suicide as an act of stupidity when some of the most respectable citizens

of Athens, Rome and London put an end to intelligent lives in that
very same way.

N.B. I advise you first to drain a bottle of dry wine into your
stomach. It'll clear your last thoughts—and you'll look better for
it in the next world! I hope you'll appreciate the high esteem with
which I am, my son, your spiritual father,

your first teacher, *vel* Satan, *vel* a page, *vel* Cain."[81]

When I read those words... If any of you have suffered in your
life, suffered so terribly, so frantically that your soul hurled itself with
all its strength into one single bid to cancel the pain, if there is such a
person among you, God forbid, then he or she will not be surprised,
will not laugh, when I tell you what I did when I read those words.
I grabbed the burning coals and held them in my clenched fists until
they were extinguished; the physical pain was an instinctive need, it
helped me collect my runaway thoughts. The first of these was the
thought expressed in the letter: "You have to kill yourself." I sprang
to my feet accordingly and ran to the door. But before I reached it,
my glance fell upon the picture. I stood riveted to the floor—only
after while did I wring my scorched hands and scream at the top of
my voice: "You liar! You liar!" And then a second thought occurred
to me: one of pity and posthumous compassion. Ha! At least now you
won't be able to lie to others! And as I spoke I took down the picture
and carried it to the fireplace. With the precision of a sleepwalker I
carefully lodged it in the hearth and covered it with burning logs.
Then I sat down opposite to watch how it burned, as the wind
whistled outside and rapped against the window-panes in every tone
imaginable. I had barely glanced at the fire when I felt myself under
the influence of an incomprehensible power; it was as though my own
being was divided against itself: the will had stepped out of me, the
pain had deserted my breast and merged with the picture, while my
body was withering away, paralysed and unable to move, like the flesh
of a corpse; and then I knew that I wanted to rescue Cyprian's picture
at all costs, and that touching the fire would roast my limbs before
my very eyes—but I could not stand up, could not walk. The flames
gradually advanced, yet the picture—either due to some miracle or
because it had absorbed damp from the wall—did not catch alight

immediately, even though it had been painted in oils; it was as if the flame were absorbed in contemplating its act of destruction. I could feel the flame lodge itself in my breast, gnaw at my heart, gouge out my eyes, and then how it enveloped Aspasia's hands and then her lap, kissed her white lap with its kiss of death—how it touched her lips, then her noble brow, and then... how only a few tiny sparks chased one another along the outer rim of the background, and then how nothing remained: we had both died.

That's right, ladies and gentlemen, both of us: for from that moment on a perfect numbness overcame me. I no longer even wanted to kill myself. I went to bed calm and collected, and that night I did not dream. People say that I am alive. True, my organism has preserved itself in a remarkably enviable condition. I have not lost my memory; neither have I gone mad or grown fixated. When I talk about something, it would seem I understand and feel every word. I am not a criminal; nor am I a misanthrope or an egoist. I am not even indifferent: given the choice between good and evil, I would always choose the good. Only I am not sure how it happened—but the power to be joyful and or sad has been entirely blunted in me.

I went with Ludwinka to our parents' grave. I cried, but felt my tears were no more than artefacts wrought by my fraught nerves, that nothing actually caused me pain. Later I visited Adam; his children dragged me into their games, I romped and ran around with them, laughed—and yet none of it made me happy. I met Józef's widow, heard all the details of her husband's death—yet none of it made me sad. I saved a drowning man, yet my heart didn't even flicker with gladness. I was even with Terenia in the moment she lost her daughter—the very same little girl who had opened the door on the evening of my return and stood together with me before my dying mother; I looked upon my sister's despair, at the terrible agony endured by the poor child, and yet in my soul's depths I remained placid and detached. Nothing had the power to draw me from this state. Occasionally, desires of one kind or another would still flit through my mind like so many flies in an open room. I imagined I'd even like to suffer a little, just for a change—if the moment when Cyprian fainted could return, for example, or when my mother died or when I burned the picture? If only I could strike my paralysed soul with something so it might stand up and walk—but all my efforts were in vain! I reflect upon myself now as upon a curious medical phenomenon and am more and more convinced that any endeavour in this direction is futile. At first I was often misled: every time the wind whistled, whenever I sat watching a blazing fire, a shivery clamminess would creep over my skin and I'd lapse automatically into deep silence. I tried to persuade myself that this was caused by the anguish of reawakened memory. But far from it, ladies and gentlemen! I perceived that it was merely the result of the physical scalding and hence a new property of my skin: a similar sensation of cold strikes me when I'm thinking of something completely different; it even struck me once when I was standing near a fireplace shielded by a screen and did not know at the time that a fire was burning there; the condition is thus an entirely pathological one. You too, listening to me now, might imagine I was touched to the quick, affected in the very depths of my soul—what generosity on your part! But if that had been the case, I would never have dared to touch upon these painful memories, never uttered a single word. I have simply told you my life-story as if it were a tale I'd learned by heart. I now do everything by heart: politeness, sympathy, outrage, goodwill—always reminding myself of what best suits the moment. But don't call me a hypocrite! Had I been able to dress up the truth by playing some sham role, you'd see me now kneeling in the middle of the room with my hands raised to heaven, my head sprinkled in ashes. And besides, my actions never contradict the signs you see on the surface! Just as I squeeze your hands, so too I shall not retreat from any sacrifice. You want me to work? I shall work. You want me to suffer myself to be nailed to the cross? With pleasure! And I shall carry the tree to make that cross, and I shall spread my arms wide upon it and let my hands, my legs, to be pierced. And I shall give up the ghost. Only... Oh, my brothers! ... Only I shall not save you, though I shall give up the ghost ... I shall not save you, because I do not love you...

"**A**ND YOU NEVER HEARD any more of Aspasia?" Tekla said after a long silence.

"I'm sorry, two weeks ago a letter which had been lying neglected on my desk for nearly two years fell into my hand," replied Benjamin. "Satan alias Cain informed me that on 23rd March, in the company of her serving women who had been dressing her for a ball, Aspasia was struck by the most terrible convulsions and in the course of fifteen minutes ended her life: at the same time her body became black as coal. Satan *vel* Cain suspected me of poisoning her, but I could only burst out laughing because Cain may have been right! According to the date and estimated hour, Aspasia must have died at the very time I was burning her picture…"

"Awful! Truly awful!"[82] cried Anna. "So that woman really was…"

"I thought I had already told you, ladies and gentlemen… No? How so?... I must have forgotten to say that… that woman was a Heathen."

With this final word a hollow silence descended on whole room. It was only after a pause of several minutes that Leon the Methodist shook off the impression it had made, and passed judgment in his own mind that here was a most suitable set of circumstances with which to offer us a salutary dose of "moral good sense." I can still remember how he began with those formal, conventional words which everyone surely knows by heart because they've heard them repeated as many times as they've borne some loss, been threatened by some danger, not been clever enough to avoid suffering or chanced to leave their door open to misfortune:

"And so you see! Did I not tell you so? You see, I was right all along!" (The subsequent part of Leon's moral dictum was gleaned more from his own character and personal feelings than from Benjamin's story). "Here we have a talented man, honest, 'well born' in the most sacred meaning of the term, amid the most propitious astrological projections; he brought with him into the world a heart of gold, a crystal imagination—he could have become a poet or a prophet—a Tyrtaeus[83] or an Esdras,[84] but he became instead... the lover of a beautiful woman. And observe, my dear friends, observe and remember forever how broken he is today! How impotent, lifeless, useless! Woe to a love that flings itself upon an individual in that way and squanders..."

"But what if it had not squandered its opportunities?" Edmund ventured. "If that woman had not been a heathen but been reborn in the Christian spirit? Had accepted the treasure thrown to her along with the responsibility attached to possessing it?... And, having accepted it, had invested it so well that every thousand talents, every single jewel might have yielded both interest to God and profit to humankind? If..."

"It's not right to place so many 'ifs' beside the 'immediate case,'" interrupted Seweryna, pointing her finger at Benjamin.

"I too shall forget the 'ifs' and answer you with the 'immediate cases'!" declared Henryk indignantly. "Ha! Master Methodist! You show me Benjamin as a broken man, useless and impotent. But I invite you to come with me beyond the threshold of this room—we shall walk from house to house and I shall show you in exchange whole museums, galleries, mansions, tenements, crammed from cellar to attic with heroes who have never loved, never squandered their feeling as Benjamin has squandered his: fat swindlers, emaciated Harpagons,[85] courtiers clad in garments embroidered with gold, fools rotting in debauchery. I shall set whole legions of them before your eyes, I shall present every one by name and swear before the crucifix—on behalf of all of them together—that none has ever fallen in love with a woman. If you wish, we can also make a brief tour of the prisons. Ask criminals, murderers, fraudsters! No, they too have never succumbed to such abject weakness. And what about your neighbour, Leon? What a great man he is! Married half a million without love. And your friend, the judge?... What a wise head! How wittily he scoffed when among poor Jan's papers a few letters were discovered from his betrothed! Only Benjamin is a criminal. He dared to love a ravishing woman with all his soul, with all the powers of his intellect... And when the godless woman betrayed him, he dares to suffer, has the courage to throw up his arms in despair... Well, aren't we fortunate to have the Methodist among us, to dish out moral justice...?"

"Hey! Henryk, Henryk! You'd argue the case better if you didn't leap to such extremes and wield your sword with such sarcasm," Anna upbraided the impetuous Zealot in her gentle, motherly voice. "We can pose Leon a simple question, calmly and categorically: what kind of people, in his opinion, constitutes the nobler subspecies of our tribe? Those who love to excess? Or those who are incapable of loving, even to satisfy their own need for happiness?"

"The noblest are those who fulfil all the obligations of their humanity," answered Leon, now under attack.

"Oho! Leon is already trying to save himself by dodging the question," observed Augusta maliciously. "Instead of answering the question directly, he palms us off with generalizations. It's obvious the case is already lost in his conscience."

"Why lost? From beginning to end I stand by the same premise, demand one and the same thing. I want people to live to the glory of God and to the benefit of their neighbours. I would like to see their every day, their every hour even, filled with work, study, good deeds, noble love for the whole of humankind. But what does individual love have to do with these demands of mine? It concerns me very little. I have already seen how it stands in the way of the very best. Henryk has reminded me that without it the very worst are even worse. So be it. The romance, the love-affair, I recognize as a pedagogical tool for the very young and mediocre. But, forgive me, lovely Augusta, as for the giants, the Prometheuses—I would never make a halo, a holy thing, out of a love-affair."

"And it is precisely in this," proposed Jadwiga, "precisely in this, in my opinion, that your mistaken argument gets tied up in knots. Among the throng of ordinary mortals, it's hard to imagine such emotional hygiene serving anyone; to one person it may be a help, to another an obstacle. But as for the giants and Prometheuses, the already redeemed and hallowed—their hallmark, Leon, is that they always have virtue in their hearts and a halo above their temples. And I advise you that until someone gives you proof, until they pass the test in their own lives, you don't them a giant or a Prometheus."

"You know, Jadwiga," said Albert the Philosopher, "there is one notion in what you say that throws much light on the whole matter for me: 'until they pass the test in their own lives.' For indeed, love is a test of a human being's genuine worth—a symptom of the activity going in the organism, the pulse by which we can monitor its state of health or disease; love is not a value in itself, nor is it an organism, nor is it health or disease. According to ancient logic, it's our witness, and should testify only to what is good in us, to what is praiseworthy. Further argument concerning its salutary or damning effects seems childish to me; such effects always depend on the inclinations of the person who experiences them. We must recognize in principle that love unfurls the most beautiful flower of human life, rightly desired as a source of happiness, justly valued as a noble feeling—but only in principle. The practical applications present a multitude of exceptions: there are those who abuse happiness, others who cannot endure even in their noblest feelings, still others who must sacrifice them in certain circumstances for the sake of a higher truth—for in the chaos of our world, it takes all sorts. On the surface, it seems sufficient to topple evil to ascend towards the good, but in reality evil has already dug such deep pits beneath our feet that even if we uproot its ancient trunk, it's not enough to just level the ground—and we sometimes have to cast down the merely pretty for the sake of the beautiful, what we are merely attached to for the sake of what we need, a woman we fancy for one we cherish and honour. Ha! Too bad! Don't scowl at me, Henryk! The practice of real life has departed fatally from God's habitual plan. God's plan gave us space, materials and skilled architects. When the porticos are raised, when the pointed arches of Gothic churches and vaulted ceilings of grand basilicas soar towards heaven, we glorify the splendour of the city, applaud the Brunelleschis and Michelangelos[86]—and yet there are moments in history when we glorify the splendour of the city glowing red as its buildings burn, when we applaud the people who march sure-footed over the smouldering ruins of our ancestral palaces, *impavidum ferient ruinae.*[87] The value of every fact should be judged in the light of circumstance, cause, intent and effect. A base and abject man will never know love, but an upright one often has to forgo it." "Forgo it? Oh no, that's madness!" protested Henryk, "Because then he'd have something to surrender when the moment of sacrifice comes... because he would stand apart from those whose are prepared to do anything because they have nothing to lose..." "Now, now! That's enough, enough!" cried Emilia. "Shame on you, my dears, arguing like mediaeval scholastics over the subtle choice of words! And yet here among us sits a man who is suffering, weary of life. Here a human soul is dying—and it hasn't occurred to any of you yet that above all, first and foremost, we should be saving the soul and the man. You can spin out your long disputations *ad nausiam* later—about whether love is like this or like that—but can Benjamin be restored to life in your midst? Do you have any efficacious word in your hearts to cure his debility? Oh, someone ought to have been attending to *that*, a long time ago."

Benjamin, who until then had been sitting in silence, holding his head in his hands, raised his eyes towards Emilia. There was a kind of indifferent curiosity in his gaze... but no sign of grateful sympathy. After a while even curiosity was extinguished and a cold lifelessness crept into his pupils; his eyelids turned towards the ground again, and again he remained motionless, as though he were a stranger, absent from the place where he sat.

"You are right, Emilia. Your counsel is saintly," Tekla seconded her. "We should be thinking about Benjamin, not about moral systems. Let's find him some useful work, that's the best solace, the least deceptive remedy."

"Useful work?" Felicja joined in. "And what might you call useful work? If you mean a certain type of employment, then tell him to chop down trees or publish a description of his travels. If by useful work, however, you mean work that yields moral fruit for his neighbours, work that affords them light and warmth, the wisdom and strength to be virtuous, then don't give him any orders! You could make a very beautiful caryatid of him.[88] Train an expert correspondent for a career in journalism. But the youthful Alcibiades, young and full of talent, will not rise from the dead. The beautiful Hellene has gone to pieces, yet Christ's warrior has not risen to his task. Oho! Useful work!... There is no useful work other than Christian work, self-sacrificing work. Self-sacrificing, but not necessarily through suffering as many envisage it today, as some interpret and teach it—self-sacrificing not through a cross that makes our arms wilt, but through a cross that makes us resolute and redeems us from evil; self-sacrificing from richness of soul, not from the soul's deprivation, self-sacrificing through gifts of charity and through genuine selflessness that has visible results. Only those who give constantly of themselves, or of something they possess—money, feeling, clarity of thought, courage, resourcefulness—work usefully for their neighbours. What do you expect Benjamin to bring them today, this bankrupt, impoverished Benjamin, lost and unloving?"

"Let him give them his time," replied Tekla. "In the beginning I demand nothing more. But then let him give hour upon hour, day upon day, year upon year, and you'll see how his breast will gradually fill with life, his thoughts blaze with light, because work on behalf of our neighbours, Felicja, is not only expenditure, it also brings an enormous profit—perhaps our only real profit; it moulds and enriches not only our neighbours but chiefly ourselves—we receive and absorb more than we can possibly give. Therefore just try it! Put Benjamin to work, and though at first he'll stagger from side to side, prop him up on one side or the other! Soon you'll see for yourselves what a workman we'll make of him."

"It's too late! Too late!" Seweryna's voice rang out like a harsh sentence. "Useful work should not be regarded as an exercise or incentive. The Lord God keeps it only as a reward for his chosen ones. Look around you, ladies and gentlemen, and see how many people try to train their hearts and minds, how they toil, sweat, busy and bustle about! And yet how many of them are allowed to work usefully? A tiny handful—from thousands of willing people, an exclusive handful, a priestly caste… a handful, to which perhaps none of us sitting here may be able to add their name in future. Because other stigmata, new sacraments will be needed. And you imagine that this poor man, this man without a soul, would accept the stigmata on the empty void of his annihilated self and receive the sacrament? Your efforts are in vain! Better to leave him on the battered, deserted road he has chosen. Let him settle the debt he owes to society with the one benefit he can offer: may he threaten and forewarn by the terrible example of his own downfall."

"No, no!" Emilia hastened to contradict her. "There must be some means of redemption for him! It is not right to lose all hope of saving…"

"Ah! If only this Benjamin could pray!..." sighed Tekla.

Benjamin sighed too.

"Ah! If only this Benjamin could fall in love with me!..." whispered Augusta in her melodious voice.

"Phanariot!"[89] Benjamin whispered back, without even raising his eyes.

At this moment Henryk leaped to his feet and stretched both arms towards Benjamin as if to embrace and caress him:

"My brother! Brother! If only you had a mother!..." he exclaimed with a cry of such intense feeling, of such profound truth, that its echo resounded in every one of our hearts.

"If only I had a mother!" Benjamin repeated and also rose from his chair. His lips were trembling, a tear glistened in his eye. "If only I had a mother! Oh, for sure, only our mother can save us from eternal damnation…"

"So listen, Benjamin, I shall tell you… You do believe in the immortality of the soul, don't you?..."

But Benjamin was no longer listening. He walked slowly towards the door and stepped outside "without being bid farewell and without bidding farewell." And what became of him subsequently? There's no point in asking. Since that evening the balding Humboldt never took his place at our little fireside gatherings.

For some time to come any reference to him always sparked lengthy debates about the need for exclusive love or about its dangers. Once, when fresh doubt arose in this respect, I promised to supply new facts for our deliberation and informed my beloved friends that I would read them a manuscript which had fallen into my hands by accident and which might be able to clarify many an obscure point. They all consented to this willingly and I began my first reading from *A Book of Memories*[90]; the second followed on from the first without a break; the third was also not delayed for too long; but after that the intervals between one reading and the next grew longer and longer. Each of us had something more important, something altogether more selfish on his or her mind, and so the readings too proceeded extremely slowly, not many pages were turned at a time... until it came at last to that "In the end..."

But about this my "present" readers will learn only in the very end.

Notes

1. Emilia (affectionate form Emilka) = Anna Skimborowicz (c.1808–1875). Hipolit Skimborowicz was her second husband. The names of the fireside friends are explained in the Introduction.
2. Felicja = Bibianna Moraczewska (1811–1887).
3. Seweryna = Tekla Dobrzyńska (c.1815–c.1876).
4. Tekla = Wincenta Zabłocka (d.o.b. unknown–1875).
5. Jadwiga = Kazimiera Ziemięcka (1820–1874).
6. Augusta = Zofia Mielęcka-Węgierska (1822–1869).
7. River in Central Poland, tributary of the Vistula.
8. Other sources indicate that Węgierska was born in Górki Borze in Podlasie, not in Great Poland.
9. Anna = Stefania Dzwonkowska (dates unknown), sister of Władysław Dzwonkowski (1818–1880), according to Żmichowska's letter to Izabela Zbiegniewska (see Introduction) not, as Boy-Żeleński claims, Faustyna Morzycka (dates unknown), known to Żmichowska and other close friends as Fochna—not to be confused with a female activist of the same name (1864–1910). In her letter Żmichowska states that Stefania is no longer alive, so she must have died before March 1871.
10. Friedrich Moritz August Retzsch (1779–1857), painter and engraver.
11. Explorer, travel writer and naturalist Friedrich Wilhelm Heinrich Alexander Freiherr von Humboldt (1769–1859).
12. Albert = Jan Majorkiewicz (1820–1847).
13. Henryk = Edward Dembowski (1822–1846).
14. Dembowski, one of the leaders of the Kraków uprising against the Austrians, died in Podgórze in February 1846, aged only 24. ecause of the great contrast between his conservative aristocratic background and his utopian socialism, he was known as the "castellan's red son" (*czerwony kasztelanic*). He was secretary to the "dictator" of the uprising, Jan Tyssowski.
15. In her Letter to Izabela Zbigniewska of March 1871, Żmichowska explains that Leon is a character made up of several separate individuals.

16. According to Boy-Żeleński (drawing on Hipolit Skimborowicz), Edmund = Karol Baliński (1817–1864). However, in her letter to Zbiegniewska (1871) Żmichowska says this is another poet, Teofil Lenartowicz (1822–1893).

17. Pseudonym of Żmichowska, the overall narrator of the frame and of the novel, sometimes also spelled: Gabryella.

18. Hipolit Skimborowicz (1815–1880).

19. This seems to be a reference to the "True Self" (atman), the inner person or soul, of the Sanskrit *Vedas* and *Upanishads*. Brahma is the first god of the Hindu trimurti, the others being Vishnu and Shiva. It is possible that Żmichowska gained knowledge about Indian religions when she was in Paris (1838–1839), at that time the centre of western learning on the ancient texts thanks to the work of Eugène Burnouf, and this fed into her own quest for spiritual enlightenment beyond conventional Catholicism.

20. The Livonian Brothers of the Sword, founded in 1202. In 1237 they were incorporated into the Order of Teutonic Knights but continued to have a considerable degree of autonomy as the Livonian Order.

21. William Parry (1790–1855) and James Clark Ross (1800–1862), polar explorers.

22. The Order of Cistercians of the Strict Observance founded at La Trappe Abbey, Normandy, in 1664. Monks observe a rule of silence, speaking only when absolutely necessary.

23. See Introduction for an explanation of this form.

24. Genesis 35; verse 18. *Benoni,* the name given to her son by Rachel, means "son of my sorrow" (RSV and Jerusalem Bible) whereas Jacob changes it to *Benjamin,* meaning "son of the right hand" or "son of the south" (RSV); "son of the right hand = son of happy omen" (Jerusalem Bible). As with other forms of his name, "Benoni" anticipates an aspect of Benjamin's future. It is worth noting that a reduction of possibly both forms (Benoni and Benjamin) "Beni" is the affectionate form of address used by Aspasia (the only character who employs this form).

25. Benjamin Franklin (1706–1790), philosopher, scientist, hero of the War of Independence, President of the United States (1785–1788).

26. Diego Velázquez (1599–1660), Spanish artist. His *Cato* depicts the suicide of Cato of Utica or Cato the Younger: Marcus Porcius (95–46 BC), grandson of Cato the Censor. It is possible that Żmichowska viewed the picture when she was living in Paris in the late 1830s.

27. Józef Bohdan Zaleski (1802–1886), Polish poet of the so-called Ukrainian School.

28. Moloch: Canaanite god to whom children were sacrificed (Leviticus 18:21); appears in other biblical texts and in literary works, including John Milton's *Paradise Lost.*

29. Or Lemberg; present-day L'viv in western Ukraine.

30. Marshal François Joseph Lefebvre (1755–1820); following the siege of Danzig (1807) he was given the title Duc de Danzig.

31. The Zaporozhian Cossacks: the Cossack Hetmanate was an independent military state from 1654 to 1775, based at Sich on the Dnieper River, "beyond the rapids" ("za porohami").

32. Region of south-eastern Poland and western Ukraine that was absorbed into Austria as the Kingdom of Galicia and Lodomeria (1772–1918) following the first partition of the Polish-Lithuanian Commonwealth (1772).

33. Żmichowska's original has "augustówka," which may refer to the type of gun or to markings on the gun's barrel indicating date of manufacture, i.e. to the reigns of the Saxon kings August II (1697–1706 and 1709–1733) and August III (1734–1763).

34. This may well have been a specific published volume, listed in Karol Estreicher's bibliography and in library catalogues as *Ducum, Regumque Polonorum Series a Leko ad Augustum hodie foelcitur regnantem deducta.* Typis, ac sumptibus Dominici de Rubeis. Ioan. Iacobi Haeredis. Romae 1702; Estreicher also lists the same, possibly another edition, as: *Lectori humanissimo Comes Hier. Curtius Clementinus. Ducum Regumque Polonorum a Lecho ad Augustum effigies, cum epitome histor.* Aeri incidi curavit Domenicus de Rubeis Ioan Iacobi haeres. Romae 1702. Benedict. Fariat sculpait. Ant. Barbey scripait, "in quarto with 52 illustrations." (K. Estreicher, *Bibliografia polska*, Part 3, Vol. 26, ed. S. Estreicher. Kraków 1915, 439). Fariat's illustrations appear to be those described by Żmichowska; she also notes the size and age ("old *in quarto* album"). I am indebted to Grażyna Borkowska for identifying this book.

35. Daughter of Krakus, founder of Kraków, the legendary eighth-century Queen Wanda; according to one version of the story, she succeeded her father but committed suicide by jumping into the Vistula to avoid an unwanted marriage. She was the inspiration for many later works of art.

36. Jadwiga, Queen of Poland 1384–1399. Her marriage to Jogaiłło, Grand Duke of Lithuania in 1386, united the two jurisdictions under one throne. She is not usually depicted wearing a ruff.

37. The legendary Duke Popiel lived in the ninth century. A corrupt and cruel leader, he was deposed and imprisoned in a tower where he was allegedly eaten by mice (the so-called Mouse Tower in Kruszwica).

38. Michał Korybut Wiśniowiecki, King of Poland 1669–1674.

39. Kings Zygmunt I (the Old, 1506–1548) and Zymunt II Augustus (1548–1572), portrayed in portraits wearing golden chains.

40. Ellipsis appears in the original.

41. This descent into hell specifically refers to Satan's fall in Milton's *Paradise Lost*, but it may also have been inspired by a text closer in time

to Żmichowska: the fall of Ambrosio at the end of Matthew Lewis's *The Monk* (1796).

42. The so-called Congress Kingdom (*Kongresówka*) was created by the Congress of Vienna (1815) within the Russian partition but with a degree of local autonomy, which ceased following the November Uprising 1830–1831. In territorial terms, the Congress Kingdom was based on the lands of the Napoleonic Duchy of Warsaw; it thus contained the former capital Warsaw (Kraków was made a free city under joint protection of the Congress powers).

43. Creature from Greek mythology having the body, claws and wings of bird and a woman's head.

44. Possible reference here to the influential role played by the historical Aspasia of Miletus at the court of Pericles.

45. Greek mythological figure Medea is traditionally portrayed in a dual role—as witch and rejected lover of Jason, whom she helped to find the Golden Fleece; in revenge for his desertion she murdered their children.

46. The historical Alcibiades was an Athenian but defected for a time to Sparta; the mention anticipates Cyprian's casting of Benjamin as Alcibiades in his picture, which he seems to be describing here to Benjamin in its ideal form.

47. The Sabians were an ancient Middle Eastern religious group, popularly thought to worship the stars, or angels dwelling in the stars. The Guebres were Zoroastrians, fire-worshippers. The choice of references is clear from the next sentence: "worshippers of all that glitters."

48. The best-known ancient personalities with these names were Aspasia of Miletus and the Alcibiades of Plato's *Symposium* and Thucydides's *History of the Peloponnesian War*, but Żmichowska could also have been alluding to lesser characters also bearing these names or to no particular character. Boy-Żeleński implies in a note to the 1930 edition of *The Heathen* (2nd ed. 1950) that these two were lovers in real life, not just in art. Aspasia of Miletus, however, was the lover of Pericles of Athens. In the frame of *The Heathen,* Alcibiades is associated with Henryk the Zealot (Edward Dembowski), whose personality seems to have more in common with the historical Alcibiades than does Benjamin's.

49. Quotation unidentified; it may have been from a text known at the time known to the group of fireside friends.

50. Opening lines of the poem *Water Nymphs* (*Rusałki,* 1828) by Józef Bohdan Zaleski (1802–1886).

51. Boy-Żeleński believes the inspiration for this race on horseback to have been a picture Żmichowska saw in the studio of artist January Suchodolski (1797–1875) famous for his paintings of soldiers, horses and battle scenes. In a letter to Bibianna Moraczewska (September 1845) she describes how the picture depicts a battle on horseback between a Scythian

and the Queen of the Amazons. She notes its violence and the determined vengeful expression of the woman, comparing her face to that of Paulina Zbyszewska (the model in Boy's interpretation for Aspasia). It seems the picture has vanished without trace as it is not recorded by art historians.

52. The Polish "Mitra" here could be a reference to a deity in Sanskrit texts, or Mithra, a Zoroastrian divinity.

53. Harmodius and Aristogeiton led a conspiracy to assassinate the tyrants Hippias and Hipparchus (514 BCE).

54. The traditional costume of a "highlander" (Polish: góral) of the Tatra Mountains region, to whom Benjamin is compared in the course of the novel.

55. The Polish equivalent used in this passage is *rozsądek.*

56. Quotation unidentified.

57. Egyptian goddess, usually known by this Greek form of her name.

58. Reference to Napoleon Bonaparte's campaign in Egypt. His army defeated the Mamluks at the Battle of the Pyramids on 21 July 1798. In a speech to his soldiers before the battle he declared that forty centuries looked down upon them from the heights of the pyramids. The reference to "Isis's tomb" is most likely to Napoleon's visit inside the Great Pyramid and to the Queen's as well as King's Chamber.

59. Held every four years, the Olympiad was used in Ancient Greece as a calendar division.

60. Pericles of Athens (c. 500–429 BCE). Aspasia of Miletus (c. 470–c. 400 BCE), a *hetaera* or courtesan of renowned intelligence and education, was his mistress and companion, and wielded considerable power in Athens. As with Alcibiades, Żmichowska's references to these figures should be regarded as inspirations rather than accurate historical portraits. Aspasia's exact dates are unknown.

61. It is generally thought that Cleopatra committed suicide by encouraging an asp to bite her, although there are some theories that she poisoned herself.

62. The two boys appear to be Italians.

63. Father of the biblical Benjamin.

64. Possibly a reference to Akbar the Great (1556–1605)—but probably not to any particular ruler of the Mogul Empire (1526–1857).

65. Reference to the military rockets invented by Sir William Congreve (1772–1828).

66. The Dragon's Den (Smocza Jama) is a famous cave at the foot of Wawel Castle Hill in Kraków, where the legendary dragon is alleged to have lived. Versions of the legend of the dragon which devoured young women date back to the twelfth-century chronicle by Wincenty Kadłubek.

67. The Leipzig Book Fair began in the early seventeenth century, overtaking the Frankfurt fair in 1632 in the number of books exhibited. In

the eighteenth and nineteenth centuries it was the most important fair for the European book trade.

68. Although ferns are not flowering plants, flowering ferns in Slavic mythological and folkloric tradition are supposed to have magical properties and bloom only at the time of the summer solstice, hence they are almost impossible to find.

69. The reference here is to the Roman fasces, i.e. an instrument of punishment, but also a symbol of power, authority and domination.

70. Here Benjamin possibly associates contemporary German culture with staid, conformist (but comfortable) bourgeois values. In this scene, Benjamin displays a similar disdain as the sick Cyprian for being nursed back to conventional notions of health.

71. Beni: Aspasia is the only character in the novel to use this form of Benjamin's name. It is the closest to Benoni ("born in pain"), the biblical Rachel's first choice of name for her youngest son.

72. These pleas from back home are a probable allusion to Polish conspiratorial resistance to the partition and occupation of the former Polish lands by Tsarist Russia, the suppression by the authorities of the 1830–1831 November Uprising and the imprisonment or forced exile of many Polish patriots. They may also be a hidden reference to conspiracies in the 1840s, also against the Austrians, in which Żmichowska was involved, although these did not explode until 1846–1848.

73. This seems to be a sarcastic inversion by Aspasia of a well-known biblical reference; from the Sermon on the Mount, Matthew 6, verse 21: "For where your treasure is, there will your heart be also," in Polish: "Bo gdzie jest twój skarb, tam będzie i serce twoje" (*Biblia Tysiąclecia*, 1980).

74. Benjamin refers here to his having been awarded a vast variety of eminent orders and medals. Żmichowska rather overstretches the reader's credulity: the lamb would appear to refer to the Order of the Golden Fleece, the garter to the Order of the Garter, accolades of knighthood which he would have been unlikely to have achieved.

75. Not only has Benjamin become a successful businessman and entrepreneur, been awarded high honours of state by various countries, and travelled the world; he has also made a name for himself as an academic. The use of the term *doktorski biret* (Italian "biretta" to denote a scholar's cap) suggests he gained this doctoral degree somewhere in Italy, even at a pontifical institution.

76. Beskidy or Beskids—part of the Carpathian range situated in the south of present-day Poland, also covering parts of the Czech Republic, Slovakia and Ukraine.

77. Ballad (here: "dumka") and "round" or "circle" dance

("kołomyjka"), like Paraska, the name of Julcia's nurse or servant, suggest Ukrainian origins. These, together with other references (Karol travelled to Lwów/Lemberg/L'viv; Benjamin's "highland" costume from the Carpathians) suggest that the family village was somewhere in the southeastern part of the territories of the former Polish-Lithuanian Commonwealth, then in Galicia (Austria), now part of modern Ukraine.

78. According to the *Book of Tobit*, one of the apocryphal books of the Bible, Tobias was the son of Tobit and was destined to marry Sarah, daughter of Raguel, a bride who had already seen seven husbands murdered by the demon Asmodeus before she had slept with them. Tobias's fellow traveller was the archangel Raphael.

79. Scytale: a device used in ancient Sparta for communicating secret messages. Words were written on a strip of parchment wrapped round a cylindrical wooden rod; the parchment could then only be read again by being wound round a similar cylinder of identical dimensions.

80. A vesicant or irritating powder or ointment made from the dried beetle *cantharis vesicatoria* (pl. *cantharides*), now rare, sometimes used as an aphrodisiac.

81. Here *vel* = *aka, alias.*

82. In Żmichowska's original this exclamation from Anna actually appears in English, but in somewhat strange English as "*Horror, most horror!*"

83. Tyrtaeus was a Greek poet who wrote in Sparta but who may have come originally from Athens. His dates are disputed, but he is thought to have lived in the seventh century BCE. His poetry urged his fellow countrymen (Spartans) to defend their state against foreign enemies, and he is said to have died in the process. He was an important symbol for Polish Romantic poets (Adam Mickiewicz and Juliusz Słowacki) as a poet prepared to sacrifice himself for his country.

84. Esdras or Ezra, prophet and scribe to whom the Book of Ezra in the Hebrew Bible is ascribed.

85. Harpagon is the main protagonist of Molière's satirical comedy *The Miser* (*L'Avare*, 1668).

86. Renaissance architect Filippo Brunelleschi (1377–1446); sculptor and painter Michelangelo Buonarroti (1475–1564).

87. "the ruins will cover the undaunted." Quotation is from Horace's *Odes*, Book III, 3: si fractus inlabatur orbis,/ impavidum ferient ruinae. In the Loeb translation: "were the vault of heaven to break and fall upon him, its ruins would smite him undismayed." Horace. *The Odes and Epodes*, with an English translation by C. E. Bennett. London: Heinemann, 1914; reprinted 1988 (The Loeb Classical Library, 33), 178–179.

88. Caryatid: a human figure, usually female, sculpted as a pillar to support the entablature of classical buildings.

89. Phanariots: residents of the Greek quarter of Constantinople/Istanbul known as Phanar. After the Ottoman conquest this group formed the official and administrative class of the Christian population. The term identifies Augusta as a representative of a privileged elite. Benjamin seems to use it as a term of disdain.

90. Żmichowska's next and unfinished novel *A Book of Memories* (*Książka pamiątek*) was published in 1847–1848, also in parts in *The Scientific Review*; its completion was interrupted by Żmichowska's arrest and imprisonment. Several extra chapters were added to the 1861 edition, which appeared like *The Heathen* in the 4-volume *Pisma Gabryelli*. Many of the themes of the novel develop those of *The Heathen*—such as the nature of the Romantic artist, the relationship of art to society, the loss or suppression of love, the consequences of the loss of the mother (literal and figurative), sibling relationships, female education and emancipation, questions of Christian ethics.